# Heir of Svartån

L. L. Nelson

Nelding & Michcomb Publishing

# Contents

When the capital of Lohikärra falls, Haldrek's world is thrown into disarray and he must scramble to keep the young woman from his visions safe.

Injured, weaponless, and with little support, will Haldrek be able to save the woman and change the visions he was given? Or will he, his homeland, and his loved ones fall to their enemies?

Get a free copy of the prequel
***Visions of Lohikärra*** here:

https://www.llnelsonauthor.com/newsletter/

# Dedication

To my husband - For always supporting me, even when I doubted myself.

To my kids - For inspiring me to be a better mom and showing me what it looks like to have limitless confidence in yourself.

To my dad - For always believing I was an amazing writer and being my cheerleader.

To my sisters - For inspiring me and just being plain awesome.

# Chapter One

Mattie and I faced the wall of video games inside *Gamer's Joy* at the mall. She smiled as her eyes locked on to one in particular: *Lohikärra: Heir of Svartån.* The latest game in a series we were both hardcore fans of. Next to us was a full advertising display, letting people know it was now available.

"Ina?"

I looked over at my best friend as her grin broadened, making me smile a little.

"They really outdid themselves this time, didn't they?"

Mattie had talked about the game for weeks, sharing various bits of trivia. Tidbits about the games, the world and her theories on what the different plot lines and quests might be.

I nodded. My stomach churned too much to say anything. If we got caught being here, my mother would be livid. With me, at least. Mattie had more freedom. Even so, we weren't supposed to be here. She had cajoled me into checking out the promotional materials after we picked up our paychecks from the Mexican fast-food joint where we both worked.

"Looks like they're almost sold out." She picked up the empty game case and inspected the cover art on it. "But what can I say, it's an epic series. My dad knew what he was doing."

"He definitely did." I glanced out to the main hall, trying to focus on Mattie's words while still making sure that Robert—my mother's live-in boyfriend—wasn't around. His primary job was as a mall cop, and he had a shift today. Without thinking, I pulled my long, blonde hair in front of me, as if it would keep me hidden.

"Anyway, I guess we should head home." Mattie put the case back on the wall and pulled a strand of dark brown hair behind her ear. "I downloaded the game to my console this morning, so it's ready to go. And the longer we stand here, the less time we'll get to play it before your mother or Robert gets home."

"Yeah... Hopefully Robert hasn't seen us yet." My fingers started tingling, and my throat tightened as I tried to suppress the anxiety inside me. My mind wandered toward a variety of worst-case scenarios.

Mattie grabbed my hand and squeezed it. The pressure comforted me. "Even if he does, we'll tell him we were here at the mall to get our paychecks. It's not a lie."

"Yeah. I guess." I peered over at the guy behind the register. As soon as I made eye contact, he looked elsewhere. I got the uncomfortable feeling he'd been watching us.

Turning back, I focused on Mattie's shoes as we walked away. When we reached the front of the store, a familiar, deep chuckling sound made me glance up. I froze as I saw Robert in his uniform. His face lit up with a smug grin.

"Well... what do we have here?" He stood in the open archway, arms crossed in front of him as I stepped back, wishing I could disappear.

Mattie took my hand again and positioned herself between him and me. "We were just heading home."

Robert shifted his stance, blocking our path. "Hey, I'm your friend, not your enemy. And Ina knows where she's supposed to be." He stared at me without blinking and I ducked my head. I hated confrontations with him. Either he'd snitch on me to my mother or get me to buy his silence somehow.

Mattie leaned into his line of sight. "We came to pick up our paychecks. And I wanted to check out the promo stuff for the new Lohikärra games. Ina's not doing anything she's not allowed to do. Just being a good friend."

He smirked at me and then turned to Mattie. "I dunno about that. And I still dunno why you're working at that food stall with Ina. Her mom told me about your inheritance from these Lohikärra games. If I had that kinda money coming to me, I'd never work another day in my life."

Mattie ignored the comment and pulled us between Robert and the door frame. He stood still instead of moving away, so I had to squeeze my body against his. His smirk lit up as I popped out of the tight space and into the main mall area. As soon as I was out of the store, he glanced back at the promo materials.

"Still dunno what you kids get outta these games. There's so much crap in them that isn't real."

Mattie stopped. I knew how much she loved those games. And Robert knew insulting them was one of the few things that got her angry. She turned back to him. "*What?* Name two things that are 'crap' and 'unrealistic' about the games. And not something like dragons. They're *fantasy* games. They're supposed to have fantastical things in them. But the stories and lore are amazing." Mattie's glare intensified as Robert smirked.

He closed in on us while staring Mattie down and held up two fingers. "A dark-skinned Ixafean whelp like you, Mattie, would never survive in Lohikärra. And there aren't any half-breeds, either. Or at least there shouldn't be. Lohikärrans don't mix with outsiders. Whether they're human, elven, or otherwise."

Mattie's eyes widened, and I gaped at him in stunned silence. After a moment, Mattie scowled. "You're an idiot, *Bob*. And so much more. Just saying *stuff* because you're jealous that you didn't come up with the idea. Because you're stuck being a mall cop for the rest of your life, never—"

A panicked shout to our left and then the sound of something colliding with a trash can and tumbling to the ground pulled Robert's attention away. I grabbed Mattie's hand this time, wanting to escape the situation as fast as possible. We hurried off and just as we got to the door, Robert spoke up in a tone that made me cringe:

"See you at home, Ina..."

Once we got home, I relaxed. The house was empty—for which I was grateful. My mother's shift at the local hospital ended late, so we could try to relax tonight. I didn't know when Robert would return, but I avoided the thought. For the time being, we had the basement to ourselves, including the room we had shared since her mom's death and Mattie's subsequent arrival in Fargo four years ago. After both her parents had died, Mattie had had the misfortune of my mother becoming her legal guardian, though neither of us fully understood why. Only that she had little in the way of a biological family outside of her parents.

As soon as the door was closed, I curled up on my mattress and watched Mattie turn on the old console. *Lohikärra: Heir of Svartån* was the newest title from Gunvald Gaming Studios—the company that Mattie's dad set up and ran until just before his death thirteen years ago. Now a big shot gaming company owned the series, but the games themselves still revolved around the original world and lore that Mattie's dad created. According to her, he made sure that was in the contract when he sold his company. Along with what royalties he or his heirs would receive. So, Mattie's inheritance—and the living stipend she received since her mother's death—got a healthy boost every time a new game came out. She turned back to me and beamed as the game's introduction started. As usual, your character began as a prisoner. This time it was in a cart, along with five other warriors. Mattie twisted her view on the screen around to a young man sitting next to her character. He surveyed the character up and down.

"So, you are the new thegn of Svartån?"

A narrator continued where the young man stopped. *War has ravaged Lohikärra for decades now. We have threats from both outside and within, and it is no longer the powerful nation it once was. With enemies combining to destroy Lohikärra for once and for all, as the heir of Svartån, you must rally your allies to protect your homeland and its dragons from ultimate destruction. Do you have what it takes, oh thegn?*

Mattie squealed as I pulled together a bittersweet grin. These games were my only escape from reality, and I loved them.

She sighed, glancing over at me. "Dad had such a knack for creating worlds. Do you want to play first?"

I shrugged. The excitement I felt earlier in the day had disappeared. "I... You can do it. It's your game."

"Ina... Don't let *Bob* get to you. Pretend you're in Lohikärra and everyone else is far, far away. At least for the afternoon." She offered me the controller. I knew she was trying to cheer me up.

"Sure." I grabbed the controller. Eighty-three days until I was on my own. The first thing my mother did each year, on my birthday, was to remind me that the moment I turned 18, I was no longer allowed in her house. It didn't matter if I had another place to live or not. Once I was an adult, I was out. Not that I minded the idea now, given my relationship with her and Robert. Mattie and I had been planning and preparing for months now. We'd found a place willing to rent to a couple of eighteen-year-olds without a massive upfront payment or a co-signer, and we'd figured out a rough budget with bills and other expenses. It was doable, and I'd be able to pay for my part through my meager savings and my part-time job. But...

It meant that I'd have little to no time for playing video games after my birthday.

The background music started up again as I put in the information for my character—a comforting, powerful chant that played in the intro of every game. Whenever I heard it, I relaxed. Felt safer. The song—called '*A Plea to Tenelth*' in the game lore—built up again to a guttural crescendo as I finished creating my character and a dragon's shadow darkened the screen for a split-second. The NPCs began reacting to it as I watched, admiring the graphics and enjoying how beautiful—how regal—the dragon looked. When it landed, the music boomed, and our room shook. We both screamed a little, startled by the loudness. Then another sound.

"*Ina!*"

My chest froze in panic at my mother's voice. I dropped the controller and scrambled to my feet. Why was she home? Mattie's eyes widened with fear, and she hurried to shut off the game.

"Ina! Where are you? Get upstairs now!"

"Com... coming." I forced myself to open the bedroom door as my palms began to sweat. My mouth dried up and nausea joined in as I walked to the stairs from the basement to the front hall. Mom shouldn't be home yet. She only came home in the middle of a shift if something important happened. Or if she was in a rage about something. I got the sinking impression that Robert had called her soon after we left, and now I had to deal with whatever fury she decided to unleash.

Mattie walked behind me, but that didn't bring much comfort as I went upstairs. My mother wasn't in the front hall, much to my surprise and dread. But I could hear her up on the main level. I braced for whatever mood she was in. She stood in front of the table, still in her scrubs, arms crossed and a scowl across her face.

Once I stopped, she glanced at the floor and her mouth formed into a tight line before her focus returned to me.

"What were you doing at the mall this afternoon? Don't you *dare* lie to me. Robert said he saw both you and Mattie there. *At the game store.*"

My mind blanked for a moment, searching for the right phrase to defuse this situation before it got worse. "We were there. Just looking. We grabbed our paychecks from work and... Mattie wanted to look. At the promotional stuff."

"And?" My mother's eyes widened, looking me over.

I stayed silent, knowing her question was leading to something, but I had no idea what that 'something' was. Had Robert lied to her and told her I stole something? Probably. But knowing my mother, it could be another thing entirely.

She focused on something behind me, her expression changing to a polite smile. "Mattie. You and Ina are close, I understand, but this is something I need to discuss with her alone. Understood?"

Mattie said nothing, but I heard the steps down to the basement creak and my heart fell.

"Where is it?"

My hand brushed my pocket, and I felt my pay stub. Maybe she was upset about that? Had my paycheck not gone through yet? Or was it less than she expected? Had she noticed that I'd pulled some out already? I scrambled to pull the stub out of my pocket and hand it to her. "The money is... it should be in the bank account already." I flinched as she slapped it out of my hand, her nails scratching my palm.

"Don't play stupid with me, Ina. Where is the game you stole?"

The game? Everything clicked inside my head. A little ball of anger lit up inside me and I tried to suppress it, keeping my voice calm. "I didn't steal anything. I didn't—"

My mother grabbed my shoulder, twisting the fabric of my shirt sleeve into her fist. "Of course, you did!" She shook me with every word. "Give. Me. The. Game! You think I'd let you keep it? You're lucky we haven't called the police on you." She paused, glancing past me, and released her grip. "That game is mine now. And you can say goodbye to the rest of your paychecks while you're in *my* house." She paused, and I stiffened. "And all the money you've been sneaking out of your paychecks." She smirked. "I noticed those little withdrawals. I *know* you're a petty thief. You keep secrets from me like your father. How on earth could anyone trust you with anything? Money, a job, *anything*, when you keep... When you keep acting like *him*."

My mother focused on me. "I know you two are planning on getting an apartment this summer, but I can't imagine why anyone would want *you* as a roommate, Ina. You are just like your father and mark my words, by the end of this year, you'll have disappeared on her, just like your father disappeared on *me*." She paused for a minute. "Now give me that game."

My chest tightened as I struggled to keep my growing anger from showing. Dad *hadn't* disappeared on her, and I didn't have any games, but if I challenged my mother, her retaliation would be swift and vicious.

"No." It was a terrifying word to say, but my anger propelled me forward. "I stole nothing. So, I don't *have* a game to give you."

I flinched as her hand landed across my cheek. The burn and sting from her nails followed in an instant.

"Don't you *dare* speak to me in that manner. Not after everything I've done for you, Maja *Ingmar* Svanunge." She twisted her face into an uglier scowl. "I hate your name, you know that? I hate that your father insisted his name be part of yours. It's an ugly name. And I despise that you insist on being called *Ina*. The day I gave birth to you was the worst day of my life. You have been nothing but trouble to me since then. *Nothing.* Yet I slave away to keep a roof over your head, and you repay me with this attitude and humiliation? You ungrateful—"

Mattie cleared her throat, and I turned in surprise, unaware that she had come back upstairs. "Mrs. Svanunge, Ina didn't steal anything." Her tone held a hard edge to it. One she almost never used with adults. "We were there because *I* wanted to see the promo materials that they'd created for my dad's game. So, *I* dragged her along after we got our paychecks."

My mother exhaled, and I glanced up to see her straighten back up with a smile. It was a fake smile. We both knew it, but if Mattie could convince her of the truth, that might defuse the situation.

"Mattie, you've been a good friend to Ina. Better, honestly, than she deserves." She paused. "You don't need to defend Ina. Robert told me what she did and how he tried to be discreet. But I know my daughter. And I *know* Robert wouldn't lie to me."

Mattie remained silent as I returned my focus to the ground. I knew what she was going to say, and how my mother would react.

"Robert did nothing discreetly. I was there. He came in, pushed himself up against Ina and then threatened both of us when I called him on it."

Another pause. I looked up to see my mother staring at me. "Is this what you wore at the mall?"

I was wearing my usual winter attire. A baggy, long-sleeved knit shirt and jeans, along with thermals underneath to keep me warm. "I... had my heavy jacket on too."

She rolled her eyes. "If you don't want men to touch you, Ina, don't dress like you want it." She gestured at my outfit. "Honestly, you're asking for that kind of attention with this kind of outfit, so it's obviously not *unwanted* attention."

My chest and throat tightened into two hard knots as I stood there, my anger rising faster than I could push it down. This wasn't the first time my mother had defended Robert when Mattie or I had called him out on his actions. "I have *never* asked for Robert's attention." The words popped out of my mouth before I could stop myself. "I've told you *plenty of times* and you never listen. My clothes aren't the problem. *Robert* is the problem. *You* are the problem. You believe him over me when I've done *nothing* to make you not trust me." My chest squeezed tight with guilt, anger, and fear once I stopped. I took it as a point of pride to never lose control. As soon as I did, my mother could twist anything I said back at me. And I had just lost control of my emotions. I had shown my anger.

"Are you done yet?"

I wasn't done. But it wasn't like my words would do anything to help me. "Yes."

She turned to the table and grabbed her purse. "My break is almost over, and I need to get back to the hospital. If you won't admit to stealing or being a slut, then I can't help you." She walked past us, slamming the front door.

I heard her car rev up and pull out of the driveway. As soon as she was gone, I exhaled and put my hands on my knees, my body beginning to shake violently as I mentally cursed my mother with every obscenity I could think of. Mattie wrapped her arms around me tight.

"I swear, your mother's the biggest *qumayo*... the nastiest *witch* I've ever met."

Hot tears rolled down my cheeks. "Eighty-three days, Mattie. I wish... I wish I could disappear today. I don't know if I can survive eighty-three days."

She gave me a tight hug. "You'll make it. In eighty-three days, we'll both be out of here. We'll have an apartment through the end of the summer at least. Then we can go wherever we want to go. We don't have to call Fargo home. We can go to Seattle. Or somewhere else. Where would you want to go?"

"I don't know. Anywhere. Lohikärra." A bitter laugh popped out of my mouth at the ridiculousness of it. "Lohikärra feels more like home than any place on earth."

Mattie laughed too. "I don't know about that. But Lohikärra is kinda like Sweden or Norway. We could get passports and move there. I think that's the closest to Lohikärra that we'll get here on earth." She paused for a moment. "But for tonight at least, you can be the new Thegn of Svartån, okay?"

I stood up and shook my head as we walked back to our room. "Not tonight. You can play and I'll just watch."

Mattie sighed. "Ina, you can't... Don't let people, especially not your mother, treat you like this. You need to learn to stand up for yourself. And let people know that they can't treat you this way."

My laugh came out bitter again as I wiped tears from my eyes and felt a flash of anger toward Mattie. She hadn't lived with my mother her entire life. She hadn't been told from a young age how worthless she was. A pang of guilt made my lungs and heart twist at the thought, and instead, I directed that anger inward. None of this was Mattie's fault. She was trying to help and... she was right. I couldn't let people treat me like this.

But... I had tried standing up for myself, and it didn't work. It never worked. "Did you see what just happened? She just blew it off like I'm some little kid having a temper tantrum." I exhaled. "I just... I wonder sometimes. What if my mother is right? What if I'm just destined to let everyone down? I mean... I still sometimes wonder why you've stuck around. You could've left two years ago. Declared yourself emancipated. Gotten away from my mother."

"Ina, I stayed because you're my best friend. I'm not going to ditch you just because it's 'easy'. Plus, you needed—need—someone to remind you that you aren't worthless. And that your mother's full of crap. She's a narcissist, and her behavior is abusive. You're *not* 'asking for attention' when you dress normally. She's a horrible mother and she should be protecting you from Robert. Not defending him."

Mattie got the game started up again as I picked up the shell-shaped trinket that my dad had given me before he left, from off of our shared bookcase. He'd called it a dragon stone and told me it was important. Luckily, it was an unassuming rock, so my mother had never given it a second glance. It was a relief, given that she had destroyed so many other items associated with my dad after he'd disappeared. It was oval shaped like a clamshell, but thicker and greenish-gray with tiny, horizontal ridges running across the top and a smooth dent on the bottom. Whenever I felt anxious, shaken, or jittery, I'd rub my thumbs in the curved indentation to calm myself.

I settled on my mattress, rubbing the stone and kneading it in my hands as if trying to bend it. Mattie paused before turning to me. "You sure you don't want to play?"

I shook my head. "You play. I can watch you be an epic mage and shoot fireballs and stuff at bad guys. Figure out how to not get myself killed within the first five seconds too." I gave her a weak grin, hoping that my joke would lighten the mood.

She hesitated and then started a new game for herself. The intro song started as I continued playing with the stone. Mattie created her character, and the dragon reappeared on the screen.

Wiping my tears away, I wished, as I had many times before, that Lohikärra was more than just a video game.

That night, I had another vivid dream about Lohikärra.

There was no actual logic or pattern to the dreams, but they popped up at least once a month, ever since I was a small child. The only connection between any of them was that I was always in Lohikärra. And this dream was no different. This time I was at the gates of the mighty city of Drattüjert, one of my favorite places to visit in any of the previous games. Only now, they were in shambles and there was chaos. Everywhere. Soldiers and warriors fought around me. I, too, wore armor and weapons of war—covered in heavy cloth and chainmail, while wielding a generic sword and shield from the games. The enemy soldiers swung at me as I blocked them and forced my way into the city.

The fighting made me feel as if I was in the game like usual, except... this time there was a sense of urgency in the dream I had never felt before. I had to get to the palace. My legs moved as if they were wading through mud, while blows from swords danced around me. Enough to feel like I was in the middle of a battle, but not so much that I was in danger.

I blinked as I had done so many times before in these dreams and in an instant; I was inside the palace. The main hall leading from the front doors to the throne room rang with swords clashing and the screams of people just outside of my field of vision.

"Ina!"

I turned to look behind me, surprised to hear my name. In my dreams, no one ever called out or acknowledged me. But as I did, I found myself in the throne room. Amidst more fighting. Turning around almost a full circle, I saw... my father?

No. Someone who looked like what I remembered of my father. It was as if my dream had combined my memories of him with the Lohikärran video game world. He wore Lohikärran clothing and fought several men with ease as I watched. Their armor identified them as Blodnar soldiers. The main 'enemy' in the most recent game, and one of Lohikärra's long-time foes. Next to him stood another younger man fighting, the original Gunvald Gaming Studios logo on his shield. My 'father' glanced over at me after pushing a couple of soldiers away from him, knocking one to the ground. He smiled for a moment before going back into the fight.

A guttural cry came from behind me, and I turned to see an older man with a crown and finely made armor crumple to his feet.

"Kalle!"

Intense dread washed over me as a Blodnar soldier pulled his sword out and plunged it in between the king's armor plates again. The young man, who had been fighting with my father, jumped to the king's side, cutting down the Blodnar soldier. But as soon as the king's eyes rolled back, a dragon's screech echoed through the building. I glanced up, half expecting to see the dragon from the game's intro appear.

"Retreat!"

The Blodnar soldiers fled from the throne room as another dragon's screech roared above the palace. The young man knelt next to the king in despair as a groan to my left made me look back. I glimpsed my father's lookalike. He laid on the steps leading up to the throne, his face contorted in pain as his left hand held his side, and his right held a pendant close to his chest. It glowed through his fingers and reminded me of the ones worn by the major characters in the Lohikärran games.

"Ingmar... stay with me."

The young man now knelt beside my father as he began mumbling some kind of chant, most of which I couldn't understand. He gazed at the young warrior. "Maja Ingmar Svanunge. My heir. Thegn of Svartån." His voice faded as I knelt next to him. From my new view, I saw that he had many more injuries across his body, including his face and neck. All of his injuries bled heavily. He moved his head ever so slightly, as if looking at me.

"My Inka. I'm sorry."

Horns bellowed in the distance as the pendant disappeared from his hand and his arm went limp against his chest. My throat tightened, and I closed my eyes as I tried not to cry. I told myself this was false; This was a dream, and that everything around me was only my imagination. And yet... kneeling over the dead body, the overwhelming sense of loss and heaviness was too real to just be a dream.

Whatever kind of dream I'd had the night before, had left me restless and with little sleep. When Mattie and I got home from school the next day, I was more exhausted than ever.

"You want to play this time?" Mattie asked as I settled down on our gaming rug and stuffed some crackers in my mouth, hoping food would help me wake up.

I nodded and waited until my mouth was empty. "I think playing will keep me awake for a few more hours. And I can eat while I'm playing."

"You should have had some of my fries today."

I shook my head. "I don't want to mooch off of you. The chocolate milk you got me helped, but..."

"Ina... Your mother mooches off of you more than you'd ever mooch off of me. It's not like she needs your paycheck. Or should. Either way, chocolate milk isn't exactly going to break the bank."

"I still feel bad."

Mattie shook her head and got the game started as I stood up to grab my stone from the night before. Even though I was still eating, it had become a habit to rub the stone a few times for comfort as soon as I got home.

"Sometimes I wish Lohikärra was an actual place we could visit..." I said, settling back down on the gaming rug.

Mattie offered the controller to me. "You know, I was thinking about what you said last night. About wishing Lohikärra was real. My mom always said she thought Lohikärra was an actual place, even though my dad would tease her about it."

I furrowed my brow as I took the controller from her. "What?"

Mattie fiddled with something in her backpack. "My dad would talk about it as if it was an actual place that he had grown up in, and sometimes he'd get nostalgic about it. But whenever my mom asked about it or pulled out an atlas to have him point out where Lohikärra or his hometown of Andrattür was, he'd tell her that no map of this world would have it. So, she always thought it was something from his childhood, some kind of imaginary version of where he lived growing up."

"Huh." The idea lingered in my head as I created my character again. The games were realistic enough. Mattie's dad had made the world as detailed and nuanced as our own. Even though each Lohikärra game centered on a different 'hero' and area of Lohikärra, there were a few places that popped up in every game—Drattüjert, the capital and the different thegn's estates in particular. Each place even had its own unique style and history. Svangendom, the thegn's estate in Svartån, was my favorite place to visit. Mattie's had always been Mirratoft, the thegn's estate in Andrattür—a 'province' named after her dad's hometown.

"I'll be honest," Mattie continued, "I'd love to find out once and for all if Lohikärra was all just my dad's imagination or if there was some truth to it. Like it could be based on the stories he grew up hearing as a kid. Or what his hometown was like ages ago. I mean, there's a Svartå in Sweden. That's pretty close to Svartån. Maybe Andrattür is an ancient name for some place nearby?" She nudged me. "We could go live in Sweden... or Norway..."

I grinned as I placed my stone on the edge of the desk holding the console and television screen. "Maybe."

Mattie left the room as I started the game up, imagining what I would do if I was in Lohikärra—not just the game as a character, but if that world was real. It was a tantalizing thought. As I led my character into the wintry hills away from where the game started, a shadow crossed over my character and I maneuvered the controller to look up. A dragon sailed over my head as fighting music started. A thrill coursed through my body. The dragons in Lohikärra never threatened the main character—unless I had my character attack one—so the fight music meant there were enemies ahead and I was about to stumble into a fight.

As I broke out from some snowy bushes, I found a group of Blodnar soldiers running around, their archers shooting at the dragon as it swooped down, knocking them to their backs. It sailed off and made a U-turn as the remaining soldiers scrambled to their feet. A yellow button icon popped up on my screen as the dragon opened its mouth. I slammed my thumb on the matching button, knowing what was about to happen. But I was a second too late and as the dragon screeched, the edges of the screen blazed red and then black and white as my character died and the buttons to respawn popped up.

"Pretending to be in Lohikärra again?"

I jumped at the sound of Robert's voice. He laughed as he walked up to me. "Your mother said you're supposed to be studying."

My body tensed up as I stared at the screen, trying to both respawn to a safer spot and avoid a conversation as much as possible.

"Just... holding it for Mattie." I put the controller beside me as soon as the character came back to life.

Robert laughed again. "You're a terrible liar." His attention turned back to the game and snorted. "Is *that* supposed to be Lohikärra?"

I knew better than to engage in conversation with him. It always ended badly. But his comments at the mall yesterday and given Mattie's and my conversation today... "You act like Lohikärra is an actual place." I tried to sound as if I thought the idea was stupid.

He snorted again and squatted next to me, rolling his eyes in derision. "Of *course*, it is. Most beautiful place in the world. And I'm trapped in this frozen wasteland."

I shifted away from him and against my better judgment, asked, "Where... is Lohikärra then? Compared to here?"

A condescending chuckle this time. He turned his attention from the game and poked me in the shoulder. "You honestly think Lohikärra is real? Even if it was, I don't think you'd survive there for a day."

My insides curled up, and I shook my head. I should have known this would make me sound like an idiot. Embarrassment at even the thought of Lohikärra being real bubbled up inside me. "Never mind."

He knelt down so that his mouth was next to my ear. "No matter how much you wish Lohikärra was real, you'll always just be stuck here in Fargo." Humiliated and angry, I shoved him away, scratching him for good measure.

"Go! Just get out of here!"

He shoved me to the floor and stood up. Glancing at the television screen, he slammed his arm into it. It crashed into the floor and the screen went black as it cracked.

"Hey! What are you doing? Get away from my stuff!" Mattie ran into the room and dropped whatever was in her hands.

He pushed her aside as soon as she reached him and stalked toward the door. "Whatever." Turning back to me, he growled, "Like I said, you wouldn't last a day in Lohikärra." He stormed off, slamming the bedroom door, and making the flimsy walls shake.

Mattie opened her mouth to say something as I saw my stone wobble on the edge of the desk.

"My stone!" I grabbed for it as it fell off.

Bright light hit my eyes as I heard it shatter on the floor like a ceramic plate. Mattie and I screamed as the light enveloped the room.

# Chapter Two

I woke up to my face in a warm, fleshy, horizontal groove and my arms stretched out above my head. My head throbbed and my wrists were bound together as I tried to pull them apart. Something rough was in my mouth and I gagged on it as I tried to move.

*What the hell was going on?*

"Shh. Hold on a minute. Uncle, will you help me?" A man's voice was quiet above me as I froze and got shifted around on his lap.

*I'm face down in someone's lap.* Why was I in someone's lap? And why was I tied up? The gag in my mouth loosened as the two men untied it. They pushed me into a sitting position where I could see what was going on. I whimpered as I surveyed my surroundings. Five men in bloodied armor stared at me wide-eyed as we sat facing each other on rough wooden boards inside a cold metal cage. A cold metal cage that was moving. A wagon. Outside the cage, two men sat with their backs to us, urging a couple of horses in front up the incline of the mountain that towered above us on one side and keeping them from slipping off the path and into the valley on the other side. In front of me, my hands were tied and instead of my normal winter gear, I wore a thick, but worn and faded jacket over my torso and arms. My jeans were stiff and cold, barely keeping the wind from chilling me further.

The young man, whose lap I'd been face down in, studied me for a moment and whispered, "What's your name?" His wrists were still bound, and I wondered how he'd been able to get my gag off.

He seemed familiar, but I couldn't remember from where. A strange sense of safety and trust emanated from him as he sat there. His gaze wasn't uncomfortable or leering, and I got the impression he was just as curious about me as I was about him. He was built burly, like a wrestler or football player—seemingly unfazed by the bitter cold weather around us—with long, brown hair tied in the back. He also had neatly trimmed facial hair where most guys I knew were clean shaven. Either way, it was a good look on him, and I bit the inside of my lip to keep from smiling. Now wasn't the time to go soft over an attractive stranger. Instead, I focused on my surroundings and on his question, both my curiosity and nervousness grew as I tried to figure out what had happened.

"Ina..." I leaned back, but that made me lean into another man to my right. He grumbled and glared at me out of the one eye that wasn't bruised and swollen shut. I stiffened up back into my sitting position, trying to suppress, or at least hide, the panic that swelled up inside of me. This scene was uncomfortably familiar, despite the young man in front of me, but I couldn't figure out why.

"Ina what?" the uncle of the young man also spoke in a soft tone, gesturing to the two cart drivers in front of us with his bound hands. "Is that your full name?"

"No." I kept my voice quiet as well. "I... It's just what I go by. Why do you want to know my full name?"

The younger man's uncle replied, "You look an awful lot like a dear friend of ours. He always talked about having a daughter, but most of us thought it was just a story. Then you show up."

I stared at the old man, trying to gauge his intentions. I hated giving out my full name. "Maja Ingmar Svanunge. It's... a weird name, I know."

The uncle grinned, revealing a mouth full of crooked teeth. "No. It's a fine name. And it means our friend wasn't a liar." He turned to the young man sitting next to me.

Following his gaze, I saw the young man grinning at me.

"So, you are the new thegn of Svartån?" he said.

*No.*

My heart stopped for a moment as I stared at him. This wasn't real. This had to be a dream. I was dreaming about Lohikärra again. That was it. I couldn't be inside a video game. I tried to remember what had brought me here. Nothing. My last memory was of being in my room with Mattie. Mattie. Where the hell was Mattie? Where the hell was I?

There was laughter behind me. I turned to see a dark-haired man with a thick, bushy beard smirking at me. Just like my mother. The sides of his head were shaven, but the top was braided or matted, with two bauble-decorated strands framing his bloodied and scarred face. *His* stare unnerved me. "I think you may have terrified her, Haldrek."

The young man whose lap I'd woken up in—Haldrek—glared at the man as I glanced between the two. "She'll be fine, Gustav."

Gustav's smirk turned into a scowl. "It won't matter. We're all dead, anyway. Or we will be soon."

I turned back to Haldrek in alarm. He shook his head. "We can still call on the dragons."

Looking back to see his reaction, it surprised me to see Gustav's expression darkened.

"There's only five of us here. And her," he growled and gestured to me. "And she's not even a real thegn. Not yet, anyway. If she is Ingmar's heir, that is."

Haldrek's uncle cleared his throat and leaned forward to stare unblinking at Gustav. "We don't need all the thegns to call for a dragon's aid. It is just easier that way. I'm surprised you don't clamor for rescue. Unless you are expecting something else?"

Gustav scowled, but said nothing, instead turning his attention to the road behind us.

The man behind me groaned again. "What are the chances we'll survive this, Haldrek? They slaughtered almost all of my men today. And if the High King is dead..."

Haldrek turned back to me. "Are you willing to help me?" He gestured to the rest of the group. "Us? Summon a dragon?"

"I... have no idea what to do." My voice came out sounding smaller than even I expected.

"You just have to get the soldiers' attention once we stop. How you do it, I don't care."

I didn't want to die. Not in my actual life or in this video game dream world. So, I nodded.

Haldrek focused on the others and took a deep breath. "You all still with me?"

Three of the men bowed their heads in agreement, and after a moment, Gustav huffed and bobbed his head as well.

The caged wagon bumped along a rocky road, making a bit of straw fall out. I crinkled my nose at the pungent smell around me, wondering if it came from the men or something else. The lands below us were snowy, barren, and rocky, while pine trees towered from the side of the mountain above us. Just like a real-life version of Lohikärra. I tried to find a familiar landmark from the games. No luck. Haldrek's conversation with me played out almost identical to the new game's introduction. I twisted around again to see a small valley beneath us. Smoke rose from it, but that wasn't necessarily a good sign. A village might be down there with people tending to their everyday lives or... it could be burning.

"The Blodnar won't make this easy on us, will they?"

I turned around to see Haldrek leaning toward me. He shifted so his pant leg and mine touched. Much to my surprise, he was still warm despite the weather.

"Am I really in Lohikärra?" I whispered. I still believed this was a dream. But... it felt different. I never felt cold or other physical sensations in my dreams.

"Your father told you of this place before he returned here?"

I shook my head. "No. My friend Mattie. Her father made—told—her stories about Lohikärra and its history. She'd... she'd share them with me. So, I'm not sure if this is a dream. Because this is the type of dream I would have."

Haldrek nodded. "I don't believe this is a dream. This world seems real to me."

It seemed real to me too. Almost too real. I had wished for Lohikärra to be real, but I hadn't expected to fall into the game scenario. I closed my eyes and tried to imagine the rope around my wrists disappearing. Then I pulled my wrists apart. Nothing.

"What are you trying to do?"

*I am an idiot...* "Sometimes... sometimes I can manipulate my dreams. I figured if this was a dream, I could make the ropes disappear."

Haldrek laughed. "I wish it was that easy."

I stared at the rope around my wrists. This *wasn't* a dream. The thought hit me hard and my throat tightened as I squeaked out, "Are we going to die?"

"Not if I can help it." He hesitated. "But they've already killed the High King and his family, including all the aethlings—his heirs. And..." He paused as he looked up at me from his hands. "If they execute us thegns, Lohikärra won't have anyone to protect it, save the dragons."

"Dragons..." I turned to him as the thought sunk in. "Like real, fire-breathing, screeching dragons?" I thought back to my dream and the games.

Haldrek frowned. "Do they not have dragons in..." He faced his uncle. "Keldan, where did my father and Ingmar go again? Someplace Fartogo? In the North?"

The uncle nodded. "That is what your father said. Before he left. A snowy flat place is what Ingmar reported when he came back. Though your father never went to Fartogo. Ingmar said he went west. To a Sea Castle."

I narrowed my eyes in confusion. "Fartogo?"

Haldrek's uncle continued, "It is a city in your land, I suppose. Your father, Ingmar, told us it was in the ancient land of the Dagoda. Skilled warriors—horsemen and archers. But foreigners wielding powerful weapons ran them out." He sighed, the wrinkles around his eyes making him look ancient. "Much like the Blodnar are doing here."

I gasped once I realized what they were talking about. "It's not Fartogo. It's Fargo. North Dakota. Where I was born and raised. But there aren't any sea castles near us. North Dakota is landlocked. The Dakota Sioux were fierce warriors, but, yeah, 'foreigners' took over." I didn't mention that the foreigners resembled people from Lohikärra more than not.

Haldrek sighed. "It's too bad you don't know where the Sea Castle is. If you did, I'd go there and see what the allure was. To make *my* father abandon his people and spend his last years there."

His uncle shook his head. "Don't dwell in the past, Haldrek. Your father was not happy here. Not after your mother's death. Even with the dragons at his side."

Haldrek leaned back against the bars of the wagon and exhaled. His breath materialized as soon as it hit the surrounding air. "I suppose you are right. Not that it matters now." He turned his head as a small camp came into view. The wind whipped the bright-colored flags atop the tents. I could make out the image of a garish, but familiar red and yellow sun on each one. A Blodnar war camp. The ruthless bad guys from the games were now real. My chest tightened and my stomach churned as I wondered whether they were as brutal as the game made them out to be.

"You ready?"

I hesitated to answer. I wasn't a warrior. But this was real. I wouldn't respawn or wake up if I died here.

"I... I guess."

Haldrek smiled grimly. "Just keep the soldiers' attention. Bite them, swear at them, whatever. We'll take care of the rest."

As soon as the cart stopped, my panic threatened to overwhelm me as my heart raced and I grew lightheaded, trying to think of what to do once they dragged me out of the cart. How would I cause a distraction? Was I going to make things worse? I struggled to push away the looming threat of death and failure as two of the soldiers chuckled at me crudely and others removed the men from the wagon. They weren't from my 'world', but the gestures were similar enough.

As I lurched off the cart, one soldier grabbed my arm and breast. It still ached from when Robert had last hit me a few days prior to all of this, and indignation rose inside my chest.

"Pardon me, pretty little *thayn*." The soldier chuckled and grabbed my chin, pulling my face too close for comfort. He sounded like Robert, and my insides curled up with anger. Without thinking, I pulled back and jabbed him in the throat with my elbow.

"Don't touch me like that!" My heart started racing as he tumbled backward. Everyone's attention focused on me as I struggled to pull away. I hated being the center of attention, but this was me causing a scene. Another soldier took me by the arm and squeezed my butt with his free hand, causing me to gasp in pain. "Touch you like what? All you Lohikärrans be whores. Spread'em high, spread'em wide." His friends laughed harder.

I twisted around and stepped back before swinging my hands at him. He dodged them and smirked, entertained by my antics. My fury at him and at the fact that I was in a very uncomfortable situation fueled me. "Shut up!" I kicked him in the stomach and wobbled back. I wasn't strong enough to knock him down, but he stumbled back a few paces, stumbling into a fellow soldier.

"You filthy wench!" He lunged at me, and I stepped aside, raising my arms again and clipping him on the chin. He dropped to his backside as someone else seized me and twisted me around to face him. Egged on by the adrenaline coursing through my body and my ability to hold my own against these soldiers, I spat on the next man without a second thought. As I stared at him, though, his attire gave away his position as a leader among the Blodnar soldiers, and I froze.

"Enough!" Spit dribbled down his nose and face as the man's grasp on my arm tightened until it was painful. "You can be the first to perish. I planned to give that honor to your friend, Dragon Breath, but I'll be taking all your heads to my king myself anyway, so you can die first." He kicked me with the flat of his boot and I stumbled to my knees next to a low square stone, stained dark with dried blood. A nearby soldier yanked me around, arranging my head on the stone so that my neck was in the middle, facing the other thegns. A humming sound started from where they stood. I writhed in vain as a soldier pressed my head into the stone harder. Hot tears rolled across my face and hoped that I had bought Haldrek enough time.

A hand grasped my head beneath my jawbone, pressing on old bruises my mother had given me and pulling it up to reveal my neck. The soldier behind me rasped out with a deep, gravelly voice: "Looks like we weren't the only ones after your throat."

I froze as I saw the large, muscular executioner walk out from a nearby tent, surveying us prisoners. A moment passed before he checked his blade. He shifted to me, grinning with a mouth near void of teeth, and walked behind me and out of my sight. My gut churned with fear as soon as I lost sight of him.

*I'm going to die.* My mind went blind with panic as I jerked against the soldier's grasp again, and my sight blurred with tears.

Then the thegns began to chant. It was a song I knew. *A Plea to Tenelth.*

The soldiers began murmuring, grabbing for their swords. The thegns ignored them. Even the soldier holding my head loosened his grip. Pulled in by the sound, I started singing along, keeping in tune with them and speaking the words as the song grew louder and louder.

"Silence! Silence them, men!" The commander pulled out his blade and pointed it at Haldrek's throat. Both the soldier holding me down and the executioner ran toward the thegns.

Then the first screech came. Our song finished, and I heard Haldrek's voice above the ensuing fray.

"Cover your ears, Ina!"

With no one holding me to the stone, I twisted off of it and onto my back. I was faster now than I was in the game, but despite plugging my ears as best I could, I heard a muffled but louder screech as a massive, familiar-looking dragon flew overhead. I watched as it took a breath above us, and I braced for the next screech. The ground shook from the sound as I shut my eyes, curling up as tight as I could. Then silence before a feminine voice spoke.

*Welcome home, little one.*

The surrounding noises returned, this time including screaming and gurgling. I fought the urge to heave from the vibrations of the screeching and held my breath until everything was silent.

Silent except for the plodding of feet in my direction. "Keep your eyes closed, Ina!" Haldrek sounded calmer now, but I did as he said, until he stood me up and started slicing the ropes from my wrists. I opened one eye to catch him grinning.

"Hearing a dragon's war cry can be a life-altering experience. How did you recognize the summoning song?"

I stared at the surrounding scene, just now seeing the carnage. All the Blodnar soldiers lay dead despite no outward injuries, except for blood dripping from various orifices. However, the air above their bodies shimmered unnaturally. The urge to vomit came quick and violent. Haldrek turned me to the side as I began dry heaving. I was shaking and weak by the time it stopped.

"Told you to keep your eyes closed." His voice was soft, his words more a statement of fact than a chastisement. He guided me to where the other men stood, cutting the ropes off of each other's wrists.

Haldrek's uncle smiled at me. "You are your father's daughter, for sure. And you sang the summoning song perfectly. Did your father teach it to you as a child? I believe you singing it brought the dragon to our aid more quickly."

I groaned as I tried to keep my balance, not having the energy to explain the real reason I could sing the song.

Haldrek tightened his arm around my shoulders and said, "I need to find Hrimfax and determine if any of the horses here are worth taking." He steered me over to another young man who had gathered up six agitated horses, trying to soothe them. Once he had calmed them enough, he turned to us and smiled.

"We're lucky. These are war horses. And good ones, too. They were jittery." Hrimfax shrugged. "Any animal would be around dragons. But we'll get home without delay." He then cocked his head and stared at me as if gauging me, before glancing back at Haldrek. "Does she know how to ride?"

I shook my head and Haldrek replied, "Even if she could, I think she'll need a hot meal and some rest before riding. Today's been eventful for her."

"It's been memorable for all of us." Hrimfax grabbed the reins of two of the stallions, guiding them over to Haldrek, who tied one to another.

"Why weren't the horses affected by the dragon's war cry?" Despite still feeling weak, my curiosity prevailed.

Hrimfax grinned. "Legend has it that horses and dragons are related. So, while they get jittery, they have no ill effects from dragons." He nuzzled one horse, and it seemed to return the sentiment. "Which makes me happy. I can't bear to see horses suffer. They're smart animals, you know."

Haldrek put his hand on my shoulder, and I let him help me up onto one of the horses. He turned to Hrimfax and said, "Thank you, cousin. Your gift with horses has always been an asset."

Hrimfax shrugged again and said, "You could say the same for your gift. Either way, are you two headed back to Andrattür? Or…"

Haldrek shook his head as he got up on the horse behind me and wrapped a large horse blanket around the two of us. "Svartån. Ina needs to visit her thegn lands sooner rather than later."

I twisted around wide-eyed as Haldrek's cousin gawked at us and then turned to him. "So, the rumors were true…?"

Haldrek nodded. "Yes. And now it's time for Ina to take her father's place."

As we headed out, my mind roiled with the implications of Haldrek's comments. My dad was from this place—a place very much not Earth—and Haldrek made it sound like he was dead now. As much as I wanted to start spitting out questions, my tongue was too heavy to even make a sound. Plus, I still felt awkward and uncomfortable sitting so close to Haldrek. We were pushed together, my back to his chest, and as much as I tried to sit stiff and with space between us, I quickly realized that was impossible. I was weak as it was and sitting forward took too much energy. It also left me painfully exposed to the weather. Even by North Dakota's standards, the weather here was downright bitter, and I wasn't wearing my typical heavy winter gear.

I pushed aside my discomfort at being so close to someone I'd just met, and tried to think of a neutral question. Something that wouldn't cause me to vomit out all the questions in my head at once.

"How long until we reach Svartån?" I asked, as we navigated up a gentle hill and between tall pine trees. I ducked my head closer to Haldrek's, to keep my face from getting swatted by low-hanging branches. We had strayed away from the main path while still paralleling it, and the bit of sunlight that peeked through the clouds gave the surrounding woods a serene yet ominous feeling.

"It's not yet midday, so barring any foul weather or errant soldiers, we should reach the border with Svartån by tonight and the thegn's estate—Svangendom—in two days' time. We're in Svarhestån now, and there's a respectable inn just beyond the border with Svartån that we can stop at tonight."

"Thank you." I did my best to stay stable on the horse and not lean into Haldrek, but between nearly being beheaded, vomiting, and freezing to death, exhaustion crept into every bone, and I succumbed to slumping against him.

We continued through the dense fir forest for a while, the only sounds coming from our horses and the wildlife, before he asked, "So... How long was your father around after you were born? If I may ask? Did you have time to know him?"

I hesitated, wondering how much I wanted to tell him. "I... I was young when he left. Five, maybe? I have a few memories of him reading stories to me." I paused again. If this was really the Lohikärra of the video games, then the stories I remembered would be common knowledge, right? Or at least the characters? "About two warriors. Bjornulf and Freya."

Haldrek laughed. Hot air hit my neck and made the hair on it stand up. "So, he read some of the Epics to you. What else did he teach you about Lohikärra?"

"Not much. I didn't really learn about Lohikärra from him. Except for those stories. He... had a few weird knick knacks that he gave me, though. Like..." My chest squeezed tight as I remembered the book that my dad had given me as a child. Full of drawings like the ones I saw later in the Lohikärran video games. My mother had ripped it up and thrown it in the trash during one of her rages soon after Mattie's arrival. The memory still hurt, so I didn't like to think about it—or the book—too much. But now I wondered.

"What?"

"Nothing. Just a memory. About the stories he'd tell me. So... who was he here?" I asked.

"He was a warrior. One of the best in all of Lohikärra. You'd need to talk to Aallotar about that side of him. The thegn-heir of Heidrunefoss. He trained both of us in that regard. I hope she survived the battle." He sighed. "I hope all the other thegns survived the battle as well. Otherwise, Lohikärra will still be in a world of hurt."

I stayed silent as I struggled to imagine my dad being a warrior. Perhaps because my memories were mostly of my mother yelling at him and him never lashing back. Warriors were aggressive, but the father I remembered wasn't. My thoughts returned to the gift that reminded me the most of him. My dragon stone. The one that had broken just before I woke up here.

"What are you thinking about?"

"My father being a warrior... And a gift he gave me before he left. He called it a dragon stone. Told me it was special." My mind raced as I tried to connect the dots, but the harder I tried, the harder it was to concentrate.

"If it really was a dragon stone, it was special. And that was likely how you got here. But I wonder how your father got one? Those... are difficult to get."

I leaned back into Haldrek's shoulder as my head swam, and my mind switched to the present with a heavy realization. All the questions I'd been trying to keep from bubbling pushed to the forefront of my mind. "So, if I'm here and here isn't a dream—and I'm the new thegn of Svartån... that means my father is actually truly dead now, isn't he?" Parts of my dream from the night before started coming back in full force, in particular the part where he laid dying, holding his pendant in his hand and calling out my name.

Haldrek nodded, his face beside mine, his beard brushing up and down against the side of my face. I sat up as tears formed in my eyes. Grief and anxiety washed over me, making my head swim even more as I fought the desire to hide. "What am I going to do?" I tried to steady my voice. "Are the people of Svartån going to expect me to be some amazing warrior, like my father, when we get there?"

"No. For now, what they need is a leader. Someone who will protect Svartån. I hope the Blodnar haven't reached it or Andrattür yet, but with the defeat at Drattüjert, they may soon be there. Plus, Svartån—and my thegn lands—have another enemy. The Isillas elves to the north. And even before Drattüjert, there were reports of their ships coming within sight of our coasts."

I shuddered. Both at the idea of the Isillas and at leading people. How was I supposed to be the thegn of Svartån when I had no idea how to be in charge of anyone? I had never led a club or a team or a group project. I had avoided the spotlight. My mother's voice popped into my head, reminding me of how I could never be responsible for anything or anyone.

Haldrek squeezed me tight, and I gasped in surprise. He quickly released me from the hug as soon as I did. "However... before I return to Andrattür, I would like to help you learn how to be a thegn. As your father did for me."

I turned back to look at him, and saw that he wore a somber grin while watching the surrounding forest. "It is tradition here. Thegn-heirs spend a few years under the instruction of another thegn. We'd have to shorten your training, but that's not unheard of. Your father trained me, and it would honor me to do it for you. We... both seem to have some things in common." He stopped his vigil to look at me.

"Like absent fathers?" The words popped out of my mouth before I could stop them. I winced and turned away from his gaze. It sounded like that was a sensitive topic back in the wagon.

Haldrek paused, an awkward silence settling between us, leaving just the sounds of the horses and the forest. After what felt like an eternity, he said, "Keldan—my uncle—was right. My father wasn't happy after my mother's death. That's my guess why he took your father's offer to explore. I had—have a large family of aunts, uncles, cousins, and so on. I'm related to half the thegns in Lohikärra. So, it wasn't like he was abandoning me."

"But he was. Like my father did me." My voice came out harder than I intended.

"Your father didn't abandon you. He brought my father home after his death. And years later, as he was training me, he mentioned that he planned to go back if the High King had not demanded he stay when the Blodnar began pushing into Lohikärra. Goodness knows, he talked about you all the time." He paused again. "By the way, is the first day of May your actual birthday?"

I stared at him for a moment and nodded. "Yes. Why?"

"May first was a high holiday in Svartån while your father was thegn. All those who swore fealty to him had the day off from any responsibilities. When he was actually in Svartån, the people were very fond of him. Since his celebration coincided with Boldyyn, many other thegns just thought he celebrated it more than usual."

"Boldyyn?"

"Among the farmers and peasants here in Lohikärra, they consider it the first day of summer, despite being six weeks before the solstice. Boldyyn is also the day that the first High King—Bjornulf—fought and defeated Ryluth. They usually hold celebrations in the evening and at night. Bonfires, singing, and dancing, but always after the day's work. Your father, however, would give the entire day off—from sunrise to sunrise. And he said that was his way of celebrating his Inka."

My heart stopped for a moment and I all of a sudden felt very warm underneath the blanket. I turned around to hide my reaction from Haldrek. 'Inka' had been my father's nickname for me as a child. No one knew that nickname except him and me. Any doubt that I may have had was now gone. But a bitter anger filled its place. I loved my dad, but I hated that he had left me with my mother. "Was there ever a time when the Blodnar weren't attacking? In over ten years, he could have said, 'Hey, I need to grab my *heir*, be right back.' If he knew how to get to Fargo and back, he could have, right?"

"The Blodnar have been battling us since before your father's return. And as a thegn, you can't exactly tell the High King that you're taking a break from whatever he commanded you to do. I doubt your father ever wanted to leave you. If he could have returned for you without incurring High King Kalle's wrath, he would have." Haldrek rubbed my shoulder consolingly. "His last words were about you."

The image of the man who resembled my dad in my dream came back to mind. Had that actually been my dad? Anger and grief mixed inside my chest. "And now he's *dead* and I'm here. In a world I barely knew existed." I snapped. I knew I had reached my breaking point when tears streamed down my face. The only saving grace to the whole situation was that Haldrek couldn't see me crying.

"You aren't alone. Or at least you won't be. You are a thegn of Lohikärra. And Ingmar Svanunge's daughter. Your subjects will expect much of you, but there will be people around to help. Other thegns and your gesiths—high ranking warriors from various towns in Svartån, sworn to obey you as thegn. And those who served your father at his estate—Svangendom."

I took a deep breath. "Can I trust them, though?" I thought back to the smirking thegn—Gustav—in the wagon. Despite only meeting him briefly, there was something off about him.

"You can trust me. I owe too much to your father to do anything but help you. And there are others like Hrimfax, Aallotar, and my uncles, that I would trust my life with. As for the rest... hopefully. I won't speak ill of our fellow thegns, but I believe, and your father did as well, that if we were more unified, we wouldn't be having such a troublesome time with the Blodnar."

I stayed silent as more questions swirled in my head and more worries weighed me down. There was little I could do to fix any of those things in my current state. Giving in to my exhaustion once and for all, I leaned back on Haldrek's shoulder and closed my eyes, hoping things would get better once I opened them again.

# Chapter Three

Night had already fallen, and a snowstorm had moved in, by the time we arrived at the inn. It was the only building with light coming from it, and the surrounding darkness gave it a lonely feeling. Snow started falling before the sun had even set and once we arrived, there was easily an inch or two on the ground.

"They should still have room for us. The Svartån Inn is a popular place for travelers to rest without worry. Even in these troubled times."

"I'm surprised that anyone would travel, with the Blodnar and all."

Haldrek shook his head as he tied the horses to a post and helped me down.

"Life doesn't stop because war abounds. People just adjust and do what they can to survive."

As we walked into the inn, I felt like I had entered a small Anglo-Saxon tavern. I didn't understand why that specific image came to mind, but it seemed to fit. The man who I assumed was the owner of the place scrutinized us as soon as we stopped. Then his eyes widened, followed by an equally wide smile.

"Thegn Andrattür?"

Haldrek grinned. "I'm more difficult to kill than those Blodnar bastards expected. Plus, I had some help." He rested his hand on my shoulder, and I felt a little too visible. "This is Maja Ingmar Svanunge—thegn-heir of Svartån. She helped summon the dragon that destroyed the Blodnar who would have us dead."

The innkeeper now gaped; his eyes wide as he surveyed me. I closed my eyes as if to disappear. I could hear a few whispers near us before Haldrek cleared his throat.

His hand tightened around my shoulder in comfort. "It has been a long day fighting Blodnar. Do you have a room for us?"

I opened my eyes to see the innkeeper nod. He motioned to a burly man drinking near us. "You know the drill. Check on their horses as well, will ya?"

"Aye. No complaint from me." The burly man, who was at least a head taller than me, put his tankard down, and walked up the stairs on the other side of the building.

The innkeeper turned to us. "Gunnolf keeps this inn peaceful and the coin coming. So, he gets a free room. But if honored guests come to visit, he's the first to move."

After the man returned and slipped outside, Haldrek led me up to the room and gestured to the bed. "You're probably more exhausted than I am. You can have the bed tonight and I'll see if they have any attire for you and extra blankets for myself."

He left me in the tiny room, staring at the bed. It was awkward taking someone else's room spur of the moment, but no one else seemed fazed by it. The bed took up half the space but was some ways nicer than what I slept on back home. There was an actual frame that held the mattress. The mattress was lumpy and well used, but it was off the floor. I gingerly sat on it, figuring out where to put my weight.

After a few minutes, I heard a knock on the door. I pulled myself to a standing position and opened the door. Haldrek stood in the hall with a dress draped across his arm.

"Hopefully this will fit. It's the only dress that the innkeeper had."

"Doesn't look too small." I tried not to imagine where the dress had come from as Haldrek handed me a set of thick leggings, socks, and a hooded scarf.

"The rest is men's clothing. It'll keep you warm until we reach Svangendom."

I laughed, gesturing to my jeans. "I'm used to wearing pants. That was normal for me in Fargo."

"Oh." Haldrek looked a little redder than normal. "Well, I'll let you get dressed. If you're hungry, there's food downstairs."

"I'll be out in a moment then." Closing the door, I put the clothes down on the bed and undressed. My underwear and bra had survived whatever travel I had gone through as well. It baffled me, but I wasn't complaining. The dress hung loosely from my shoulders, but was thick enough to keep me warm. The knit woolen leggings were long enough, but loose at the waist. I'd always been lanky, so it didn't surprise me that these clothes fit in height, but not otherwise.

Haldrek was waiting for me as soon as I opened the door. His eyes widened in surprise. "The clothes seem a bit... big."

I dropped the leggings I had been holding onto through the dress, so they puddled on the floor just below the hem. "I think I need a belt. Or some rope."

Haldrek let out a loud guffaw. "You'll definitely need something like that." He hurried downstairs and returned with two lengths of rope. I grabbed them and closed the door, only returning once I had figured out how to tie the rope in a way to keep the pants around my waist, and cinch the dress in.

"Ready?"

I hesitated. "The innkeeper and the others downstairs didn't seem too happy when you announced I was the thegn-heir…"

Haldrek shook his head. "I wouldn't worry. The Battle at Drattüjert only happened yesterday." He took a deep breath and exhaled, as if realizing something. "I didn't think of that. There is no way that they would already know of your father's death." He winced. "I should have thought of that before announcing you as thegn-heir. Either way, though… you will be their thegn soon."

I tried not to dwell on the news of my father's death too much. The idea of grieving outwardly around strangers was uncomfortable, so I pushed my emotions away as I followed him downstairs to a table in the corner next to the fireplace. My back against the wooden beams, I let the warmth relax me as someone served Haldrek and me a hearty-looking stew inside a hollowed-out bread loaf.

The eating area was full, yet I was the only woman in the room. They ignored Haldrek and me; the men tending to their food with hungry devotion. As soon as I tried the stew, I understood why. Whatever it was, tasted delicious and filled me up, helping me to focus on something other than my thoughts. I quickly finished my bowl and began nibbling on the edges of it.

"I take it you like the stew?"

"Yeah. I dunno what's in it, but I feel a lot better after eating it."

Haldrek opened his mouth to reply when the door burst open, letting snow in and a blond-haired woman toppled in, crashing to the floor. Gunnolf came walking in after her and smirked at the innkeeper.

"Look at what I found in the stables."

"What was she doing in there?"

"Dunno. Horse thieving, whoring, something. Whatever her kind does."

The woman glared up at Gunnolf and then the innkeeper and snapped, "I was trying to get out of the storm. You wouldn't rent me a room if I was the only person here."

"You're right. So why should I let you sleep in my stables? We might wake up and find all our horses gone."

"Because it's not right to let a person freeze in the storm blowing out there."

The innkeeper snorted and gestured to Gunnolf. He grabbed the woman by the arm and twisted it behind her, wrenching her into a standing position. The woman was very pregnant, and much to my surprise, she had pointy ears. She seemed almost elven from the ears, but everything else about her, including attire, was Lohikärran. I turned to Haldrek and saw that he was staring into his stew bowl intently.

"Haldrek?" I whispered, nudging him with my spoon.

"I'm not the thegn here. It's not my place to tell him who to let sleep at his inn."

"*What?*"

He shook his head and stared at me. "*You* are though."

I dropped my spoon next to my bowl, realizing what he was getting at. Looking up, I saw Gunnolf still holding her arm at a weird angle as the innkeeper examined her with an eager and smug expression that made me angry. My gut twisted with anxiety over staying silent or standing up for the woman. She was a stranger. *I* was a stranger. And I hated being the center of attention.

But... I was the thegn-heir. This was my job, right? To defend people? Plus, I hated seeing people get bullied. Even if it risked me getting in trouble.

"Hey!"

I stood up, and the room went silent, everyone's attention on me. My chest froze, but I stumbled from my spot anyway, despite trying to be graceful as I walked up to Gunnolf and the woman. Turning to the innkeeper, I asked, "Has she stolen from you before?"

He straightened up. "I... Not as far as I know. But her kind..."

"Her kind what? She looks as human as you or me." The words popped out of my mouth before I could think, and I leaned one hand against a nearby chair to steady my nerves.

There were a few whispers behind me as Gunnolf yanked her hair back, revealing her pointed ears again. The woman closed her eyes, as if humiliated. "She's not human. And no self-respecting thegn would defend an *elf*. This ain't Sodrporti. Svartån ain't Fosseån with its Ixafeans, Blodnar and other foreigners running around."

"Sodrporti?" It was a port city in the games, but I shook my head, trying to stay focused. "Never mind. She looks more human than elf to me. And... there are humans where I am from who have pointed ears. They *choose* to have pointy ears."

I pressed my lips together to keep from saying anything else. I was sure I sounded crazy.

Both Gunnolf and the innkeeper stared at me in disbelief. Maybe I had gone too far. I was still a stranger here, even if I was a thegn—or thegn-heir.

"What would you have us do, then? We have no extra room for her." A hint of sarcasm colored the innkeeper's tone.

I turned to Haldrek, who was still staring into his soup bowl. Returning my gaze to the innkeeper, I said, "She will stay with me and Thegn Andrattür."

The innkeeper sputtered. "That room is barely big enough for two people."

My heart beat faster as I tried to think of something convincing to say. But my mind blanked and panic flooded my body as I tried to think of something. Anything.

Haldrek's voice rose behind me. "I don't mind. More bodies, more warmth. We're all aware of how drafty your rooms are here."

Gunnolf stared at me. "You aren't afraid of her?"

I glared at him, summoning all the courage I had. "Not any more than I am of you."

He hesitated and then released her. She straightened out and rubbed her shoulder, giving me a small smile. I motioned for her to head upstairs and followed, wondering if I'd made the right decision.

My heart still pounded from the confrontation as I got upstairs and to the bedroom door with the woman. It was rare for me to bring attention to myself like that, and adrenaline still pumped through my body. I didn't even know her name, but now we were roommates for the night and a small part of me wondered if I was safe with either her or Haldrek. As I opened the door, I heard heavy footsteps behind me.

"Ina!" Haldrek called out. I ignored him and gestured for the woman to go in.

He grabbed my shoulder, and I froze. The buzz from standing up for the woman downstairs was dying down, and I wondered if I had misjudged Haldrek. His grip on my shoulder didn't feel angry, but I knew that could change.

"Ina." His voice was softer and quieter. "Can we talk privately?"

"As privately as one can here." The door closed in front of me, leaving us the only ones in the hallway. Still, neither the doors nor the floor were soundproof.

Haldrek sighed. In a low voice, he said, "She's part elf. What kind of elf, I don't know, but the elven nations and Lohikärra have had a rough history. I don't know how much you know about that, but—"

"I know full well about the Isillas. But she doesn't look like an Isillas elf. At least the way I've seen—heard—them described. What she is, is alone, pregnant, and wanting shelter. She was going to sleep in the friggin' stable, but apparently that was too good for the innkeeper and Thuggy McThuggerson downstairs."

Haldrek's voice was gentle, but I still listened for any hint of malice. "Elves are known for being crafty individuals. You don't know if she is actually what she seems. I don't know if magic exists in Fargo, but—"

"It doesn't, but how is she going to magically be pregnant one moment and not the next?"

"Because it could be an illusion."

The door squeaked open, and the woman positioned herself in the frame, one hand over her belly, the other on the doorknob.

"May I speak for myself?"

Haldrek glanced at me, then at her, and nodded.

"Thank you, Thegn Andrattür."

"How do you know who I am?" Haldrek stiffened up and shifted his body in front of mine.

The woman gestured to me. "She referred to you as such downstairs. But I was born and raised at Svangendom as well. You trained with my brothers there while with Thegn Svartån. My name is Thandes. And I'm a Hethurin."

Haldrek took a deep breath and exhaled, as though embarrassed. "I'm sorry. I misjudged you."

"Exactly. Though I don't blame you, given the Isillas threat."

I glanced between the two of them, waiting for an explanation. Neither the games nor their lore mentioned anything about 'Hethurin' elves. When neither gave one, I cleared my throat.

"A little backstory would help me..." I turned to Thandes and said, "I just arrived here this morning."

She bobbed her head in deference. "Of course. The Hethurin are half Linvyl Elf, half Lohikärran. My father is Pephennas Gilormen. He advised Thegn Svartån in magical matters and diplomacy concerning a few of the different Elven nations." Thandes paused, looking back at Haldrek. "I overheard the man who dragged me into the inn mentioned that a thegn and a 'supposed' thegn-heir had just arrived… I know who you are, but…" Thandes focused on me. "Are you the thegn-heir he spoke of?"

"I… I am. My father is Ingmar Svanunge. And I'm Ina Svanunge."

Thandes's eyes widened as she glanced between us. "Thegn Svartån had a child then." She paused again. "If you are here with Thegn Andrattür… where is your father? And where have you been these many years? If I may ask?"

"I…" I faltered. How was I going to explain how I got here? I didn't even know how I got here.

Haldrek broke the awkward silence. "Thegn Svartån fell at the Battle of Drattüjert not two days past. And Ina arrived this morning from the lands that the thegn traveled to in his youth. Though I think she has been as aware of Lohikärra as we have been of her. Needless to say, she is the true thegn-heir. Gunnolf called her the 'supposed' thegn-heir?"

Thandes nodded. "I didn't ask what he meant by it, though. He was too busy finding me and dragging me out of the stable."

Haldrek sighed. "I am curious why he would say that. Even if they didn't know that Thegn Svartån was killed, there should be no question who the thegn-heir is."

"I am not one for politics, Thegn Andrattür. I only wish to be safe." Thandes glanced at me and rubbed her large stomach. "Thegn Svartån protected us Hethurin, even when others would not. If you are to be the next thegn, I hope you will continue in your father's footsteps."

Anxiety weighed me down as I realized that I knew nothing about having people rely on me. "I know little about what my father did as thegn. Or much about the Hethurin other than what you've just told me."

Haldrek pushed the door open. "Why don't we sit down? You two can sit on the bed, I'll sit on the floor."

Once we were comfortable, he continued. "Pephennas Gilormen was your father and grandfather's chief mage until a few years ago. He… he was very good at his job and honest. Given the history that Lohikärrans have had with the different elven races, their civil relationship with him was unusual."

"So, what happened? I'm getting the impression that the Hethurin are a group? Of people? Elves?"

Thandes piped up. "We are people. Pephennas was very attracted to Lohikärran women." She bobbed her head from side to side. "How much do you know about Linvyl Elves?"

I thought back to what the game lore had said about them. The Linvyl Elves had never been a big part of the games. While you could play as one and that character would have some perks based around nature and wild animals, beyond that, I had never read much about them. "Not much. Don't they live in the thick forestlands that are southeast of here?"

Thandes continued, "They are known for their healing and growing magic. Any place that Linvyl Elves settle won't stay desolate for long. And... they also are known for having enormous families, and the wealthiest elves often have harems. Both men and women. Or so I've been told. I have never been outside of Svartån. Needless to say, my father had many children. Just not all with one woman."

I groaned. I could see where this was going.

Haldrek turned to me. "As soon as your father became thegn, men would come with their wives or daughters, complaining that Pephennas had bedded them. They had either borne half elf/ half human babies or were about to. This had been an issue under your grandfather, but he left the men and their families to deal with the children as they saw fit. Your father, however, said that if they were not wanted, the Hethurin would be raised at the estate, trained into a profession, and then sent off at the age of maturity."

"How many Hethurin were there?"

Thandes cleared her throat. "At least one hundred while I was there. But there are more. Some people kept their children or sold them off at a young age. And we were not just Pephennas's children, but also grandchildren or great-grandchildren. If someone is his descendant, no matter how many generations removed, they are Hethurin."

I cringed as I tried to do the math. "How did he end up sleeping with so many women? Wouldn't people hide their wives and daughters when Pephennas was around? Or..." I grimaced. "Did anyone ever try to kill him?"

Thandes shook her head. "As an esteemed member of the thegn's court, both your grandfather and your father protected my father. Not that many men didn't try to keep their women away from him. But inevitably, you'd have newcomers. Like my mother. She was from Svarhestån. Came here to find work and my father found her."

"Is Pephennas still at Svangendom?" Would I have to interact with him much when I arrived there? "And if you grew up there, why didn't you stay?"

"He left a few years ago. The lands of the Linvyl were attacked, and the rulers there called him back. As for me... my husband sent me to help relatives of his in the high mountains east of here. They needed help with tending and mending, and I've always wanted to see what the world outside the estate was like."

"Why are you here, then? Were..." I wondered if Thandes' life with her husband's family had been unpleasant, given what I'd been told so far.

Thandes shook her head, wiping her eyes as tears threatened to fall. "His family are good people. But they were attacked. The village where his family lived. I only saw a few people escape."

Haldrek straightened up. "What? Who attacked?"

"Isillas elves. After escaping to the woods, I overheard them talking about Svangendom. I'm afraid to go back, but where else am I to go? The village is my only home."

Haldrek exhaled and faced me, the color drained from his face. "We may arrive to find Svangendom is in worse condition than I thought. I pray to Tenelth the soldiers your father left at the estate were not caught unaware."

I grimaced and turned to Thandes. "We're headed to Svangendom in the morning. You can ride with us if you wish."

"I fear I might slow you two down." She cradled her stomach.

Haldrek cleared his throat. "We can figure that out tomorrow. For now, we should probably get some rest. Especially if we need to be on the lookout for Isillas." He wrapped a blanket around himself and leaned his head back. Immediately, Thandes stood up and offered the bed to me. "I can find a corner for myself in here. It's warmer than outside and I have my cloak."

I shook my head. "There's plenty of room for the two of us, if we sleep on our sides. I would feel bad if I made you sleep on the floor." I gestured awkwardly towards her stomach. "With you being pregnant and all."

"Are you sure?"

"Yes. Plus, it'll keep us both warm. It's colder here than it is in my hometown, and that's saying something."

"My thanks." Thandes curled up on the far edge of the bed and wrapped her cloak around herself. I laid down on the bed, my back to her and facing Haldrek.

His eyes were closed and after a few minutes, I dozed off, wondering what awaited us at Svangendom.

I opened my eyes to find myself standing in a grand stone hall where men and women in fancy robes and dresses walked around mingling with each other. The hall itself had two carved stone chairs in front of me. It was the throne room at Drattüjert. But the lightness of the room, compared to the last time I'd seen it, confused me. The people in the room were ignoring me or oblivious to my presence. A large hand gripped my shoulder and I jumped forward. I spun to see my father staring at me in surprise. He no longer wore the armor from my dream, instead only a stained tunic, dark pants, and thick socks. What struck me most, however, was his large, well-trimmed beard. He was clean-shaven in all of my childhood memories. But now he looked identical to the man from my most recent vivid dream.

"Dad?" I didn't understand what to make of him. If Haldrek was right, he was dead.

He smiled in hesitation. "I hope your trip here wasn't too eventful. I'm glad to see you. You've grown into a fine young woman, it seems."

I stared at him, then shook my head. "The Blodnar—video game villains—tried to behead me when I got here. You're dead... maybe? And there are elves and dragons here. I feel like I'm in a strange dream."

"Well, currently you are in a dream. Sort of. Sleep allows you to shift between planes of being. But being in Lohikärra is very real. As are elves and dragons."

I spun around—the others still moved, their murmurs adding to the background noise. As I watched them, I realized they were floating, not walking. When I turned back to my father, he continued, "Right now, you are in the Realm of Ghosts. It's where those of us who have died but have not gone on to the afterlife reside."

"Wait, so you *are* dead?" A large lump swelled in my throat as he nodded. Rage, frustration, sorrow, and disappointment all joined together inside my chest at the same time, squeezing the air out of my lungs. I lashed out at him, hitting him as hard as I could in the shoulders. It surprised me that he felt so solid. "You left me alone with *her*. Why didn't you come back? There *had* to have been moments of peace where you could've come back."

My father winced. "She is your mother. For all her flaws, I thought you would be safer there than here. I see now that I was a fool in that regard. That said, if I had left without High King Kalle's permission, our return would have endangered both our lives. He was not happy when I left with Svante."

"Did you even know? How could you *not* know? I remember the fights between you two. You *had* to know." I trembled as hurt bubbled up inside me. I loved my dad. He was the opposite of everything my mother was. Therefore, he was good, and she was bad. Yet my anger hardened inside of me and jumbled my thoughts. If he had really returned here... if Lohikärra wasn't a hallucination, why leave me?

"There... there were clues. Things I only realized once I returned. I wanted to take you with me to Seattle. Your mother refused. I believe now, it was another attempt to control me. As for her lashing out at me, I understand why she acted the way she did. Your mother and I had a complicated relationship, but... she always took her rage out on me. I never thought she would hurt her own daughter."

"Instead, she told me I was the worst mistake of her life. Tossed away anything she could find with a connection to you and told me you left us because of me." I scrunched my face tight to fight off the tears. When that didn't work, I brushed my hand roughly against my face.

A flash of annoyance crossed my father's face, and I stepped back in fear. His expression softened, and he held up his hands as if to calm me. "I would never leave *because* of you, Inka. She knew that. She knew the items I left behind were important. One of them is the reason you are here now. The dragon stone. I was learning how to harness its powers when I got pulled into your mother's world. It's how Svante traveled to Seattle and how I returned here with his body."

"Mattie's dad?" Now I wondered where she was. Had the stone transported her here too?

He nodded. "Which is why I'm curious to find out where she landed. Dragon stones don't allow you to teleport two or more people at a time to the same spot. I went to Fargo and Svante to Seattle. So, Mattie got pulled to Lohikärra when the stone broke, but I don't know where."

"*What?* How do you know Mattie got pulled into Lohikärra? And if she is here, you're saying she could be anywhere? And why are we here, anyway? Mattie and me? I thought this whole place was some made-up fantasy world."

My dad smiled grimly. "Svante has always been very smart. Not creative enough to devise a world like Lohikärra from scratch. However, he could always discern a good idea when he saw one. No, he created those games based on the history and lore of Lohikärra. As for how I know, even in death I'm still connected to the dragons. They told me when you and Mattie arrived." His face grew somber. "I expect the dragon stone sent you here because I died and Svartån needed a thegn. I studied those rocks my entire life, and I still have more questions than answers. Even with Pephennas's help."

"The elf guy who slept with half the women in Svartån?"

My father looked away, annoyed again. "His actions didn't please me when I learned of them. But there was little I could do to persuade him otherwise."

"You didn't tell him to knock it off or someone would try to kill him? You didn't think that you should have protected the women of Svartån from him?"

"Hindsight is the clearest vision we have. Unfortunately, it's the vision with which we can do the least." He turned back, looking me straight in the eye. "I am not a perfect person. I did things I shouldn't have. I ignored things I should have paid attention to... Including Pephennas's actions. But I tried my best. I doubt your mother spoke well of me and I can see your anger, but I wish I could have been a better father. There wasn't a day that I didn't think about you."

I *wanted* to believe my dad, despite everything. I *wanted* him to be the good guy. I *wanted* there to be some kind of goodness I could rely on in my life. But I didn't know if I could trust him. The only person I honestly trusted was Mattie. Still...

"Haldrek mentioned that you made my birthday a holiday here?"

My father's face lit up. "Technically, it was already a festival day, but yes. I wanted a way to celebrate your birthday and the best way was to make the day even more festive than it already was." His smile disappeared. "Did your mother at least celebrate your birthday?"

My eyes burned, and I glanced down at my feet, not wanting to cry again. "No. She's told me more than once that the day I was born was her worst."

My father wrapped his arms around me, squeezing me tight, and whispered, "Oh, Inka... I should have brought you here. Kalle's approval or not."

Tears started streaming down my face, and I took a ragged breath. As he stepped back, he said, "I might not be in the Realm of the Living now, but you can make Lohikärra your home if you wish."

I shook my head. "How do I figure out if it'll be better here or worse?"

"That is for you to decide. If the dragon stone brought you here, then there is a reason."

"To be a thegn?"

"I believe so." My father sighed. "I'm no longer around to protect Svartån. So as my heir, my—our—people will need someone to protect and lead them. You."

"How on earth am I supposed to be a thegn? I hate being the center of attention. I've never been in charge in my life. And…" I didn't want to think about my mother being right. What if I wasn't capable of being responsible? For myself, much less others?

"I believe you have it in you. You are a Svanunge after all. And you will have people to help you."

"Like Mattie?" My mind went back to the fact that I still had no idea where she was. "Is there any way to find out where she is?" I hoped I'd be able to find her. If the stones tossed our dads fifteen hundred miles apart, who knows where she was?

"You'll be able to find her. I doubt the dragon stone would have sent her far. She's somewhere in Lohikärra. And yes, you'll have Mattie to help you if she chooses. And Haldrek. You and he have more in common than you realize." He paused. "In fact, all three of you have more in common than you realize."

Without thinking, I responded, "Like growing up without a father?" Now standing in front of him, it hit me how much I hurt when he left, and I realized he wasn't coming back.

My dad grimaced, pressing his lips between his teeth. "You, she and Haldrek have fathers who regretted leaving you."

"And who we'll probably never see again?"

"You'll see me again. I promise you that. I'm stuck here in the Realm of Ghosts until I can be properly interred. And I plan on helping you while you are here in Lohikärra."

"Wait. So, your body is lying around?" I thought back to my dream. "Is it still in the throne room?"

My father nodded. "Barring anyone moving it, it will be right where I fell."

I grimaced. Had I really watched my father die in a dream? Or what I thought was a dream?

"You don't have to go looking for my body yet. It won't decompose while I am still attached to my dragon soul. What is more important is Svartån. You need to rebuild my—our—lands now." He paused. "The village of Svangendom—below the estate—was attacked at the same time as Drattüjert. By the number of spirits

I have seen here... they caught most of the villagers before they had time to escape or protect themselves."

"Who are 'they'? The Blodnar or..." Thandes's story of the Isillas attacking made me wonder if the Isillas had gotten to Svangendom yet.

"The Isillas." My father's tone softened. "Svangendom needs you. Svartån needs you. And I fully believe that you will be the thegn to restore and strengthen Svartån."

"I..." My stomach churned. That I was supposed to take charge of a place and people I barely knew made my head spin. "What if I can't do it?"

My father smiled. "I believe you have it in you. And like I said, you will have people to help you. Now it's time to go. I'll be watching over you." He grabbed my shoulders, and everything went black as a pulse of energy pushed me back.

When I opened my eyes, I saw Haldrek leaning over me, his hands gripping my shoulders like my father's had been, eyes wide with panic.

"Ina!"

I sank my nails into Haldrek's arms and jerked myself upright as I pushed him away. What had happened while I was asleep?

Haldrek stepped back, exhaling. "Thank the dragons you're alive! I thought you were dead."

I turned to see Thandes curled against the wall, wide-eyed.

"What on earth is going on?" I shook my head, still woozy from sleep, but my heart now raced. Had I been an idiot to trust him? Them?

"It's mid-morning. I thought... Are you all right?"

"I feel fine. Why... why were you hovering over me?"

He stared at me in surprise. "You looked like you were dead. Thandes woke me up just now, and when you didn't respond..." He exhaled, the muscles in his shoulders relaxing. "I was afraid."

I faced Thandes. "Is that true? Did I look like I was dead?"

"Yes. I woke up because I had to pee. When I saw how you looked, though, I tried to wake you up. But that didn't work, so I woke up Thegn Andrattür."

Haldrek focused on me. "Do you remember anything from your sleep last night?"

"I dreamt that my father dragged me into the Realm of Ghosts to talk to me."

"The Realm of Ghosts?" Thandes and Haldrek spoke at the same time.

"That's what he called it."

"I suppose... that makes sense. It's not been two days since the battle." Haldrek sat on the bed frame next to where I sat, making it creak.

"He said something about being interred. But he also said not to worry about it. That I needed to rebuild Svartån before dealing with his corpse. It was a weird dream."

Haldrek was silent, and Thandes whispered, "The Realm of Ghosts?" She met my gaze and said, "You are Thegn Svartån's daughter for sure then."

I turned back to Haldrek. "If it's mid-morning already, will we be able to make it to the estate tomorrow? My father mentioned... that we needed to get there."

"If we ride hard." He stared at Thandes.

"I was planning on walking, anyway." Her voice was quiet as she spoke. "I wouldn't want to slow you two down any."

I turned to her. "Can you ride a horse?"

She glanced down at her belly and then up at me. "I could, before I was with child. I doubt it'd be comfortable now, though. And I've walked all this way. I think I can make it back to Svangendom on foot."

"Are you sure?"

She nodded. "I'll be fine. If I rode, what would you ride?"

I hesitated, trying to ignore the anxiety still buzzing around inside me. "I've actually never rode a horse. Before yesterday." I gestured to Haldrek. "I was going to ride on the same horse as him. That's what we did on our way here."

Thandes's eyes widened in surprise.

"Perhaps I can begin training you on how to ride." Haldrek began gathering up his blanket from the night before. "You'll be doing a lot of it now that you're here."

I groaned and turned to Thandes. "Are you sure?"

Thandes bowed her head in deference. "I'll be fine. Plus... if you were to arrive at the estate on foot, I think people might..."

"Might not take you seriously as thegn." Haldrek finished her thought as she grimaced.

"Not to say you aren't the thegn-heir. Just..." She averted her gaze.

"I need to look the part." I sighed. "Fine. We'll see you at the estate then?"

She turned back to me and bowed again. "Of course, my thegn. I'll see you there."

After parting ways with Thandes and leaving the inn, Haldrek and I set off for the estate—he on one horse and I on the other. He had given me a quick overview on how to ride a horse, but we still kept a slower pace than the day before. Or at least it felt like it.

As we got to the top of the hill beyond the inn, Haldrek stopped his horse until both were neck and neck. "So... what... what did your father tell you in the Realm of Ghosts? About Svangendom?"

I glanced at him before focusing back on my horse. "The Isillas attacked Svangendom at the same time that the Blodnar attacked Drattüjert. He made it sound like... like many people died." My throat tightened up as my mind wandered to the dagger at my hip. Haldrek had purchased it from the innkeeper this morning and told me that while he doubted I'd use it soon, it was always better to have *some* kind of weapon on me.

My mind churned with worry as different scenarios ran through my mind concerning Svangendom.

"Damn Isillas." He urged the horse on faster through the deepening snow, and I struggled to keep up. "I'm afraid to see what we'll find when we arrive."

# Chapter Four

By mid-afternoon of the next day, we reached the end of the main road. Beyond was a long stone wall with a metal gate in the middle, in front of it was another road running horizontal to us. Two pine tree-covered hills rose from beyond the walls on either side of the gate and a small but well-used path split the hills as it rose into the plateau above. A pointy roof and spire poked out above the plateau's tree line. A familiar sight from the games.

"And this would be Svangendom. Your estate, Ina, and the village that bears its name." Haldrek slipped from his saddle and surveyed our surroundings before testing the gate.

One of the gate doors creaked forward as Haldrek inspected it.

"This makes no sense. There should be guards here."

"What? If the Isillas attacked Svangendom..." I paused as I realized that even my thoughts made no sense. If the Isillas attacked through here, wouldn't they have damaged the gate at least?

"It doesn't look like they came into the southern part of the estate from here. But I would think that there would be estate guards still patrolling around if the Isillas attacked in the last few days. At least *someone* to guard against any other attacks." Haldrek rubbed the bridge of his nose and groaned. "I think this gate is unlocked because people used it to flee."

Haldrek pulled one of the gate doors away enough to lead the horses inside before closing it again.

"I have my work cut out for me, I guess." My voice sounded less certain than I wanted it to.

"You'll have people to help you." Haldrek pulled himself back on his horse. "If there are any survivors in the village, they'll be pledged to you as they were to your father. As will your people at the estate itself. When that Hethurin girl actually comes back, I believe she'll do the same."

"How many survivors…" I stopped as sudden movement directed my attention elsewhere. Ghostly, near transparent, blue figures walked out of the woods on either side of us and down the hill on the path we were on. Men, women, and children peering up at us. A few of the men holding weapons saluted us. Unlike the people in my dream, these figures were fully aware of Haldrek and myself.

"What are you looking at?" Haldrek's voice was one of concern as he focused on me.

"Um…" I tried to keep my voice calm and my heart from racing as I surveyed the people. My stomach grew heavy as I watched the group surround us. "Tell me what you see. Around us. On the path."

"Trees? Dirt? Snow and rocks? What do *you* see?"

"People. Lots of people." I stared at one woman as she approached us. She curtsied and tucked her hair back behind her ear. It was pointy.

*Hethurin.*

It was a few moments before Haldrek responded, a slight quiver in his voice. "You see the… dead then. Your father had that ability. He was always insistent on burying them as quickly as possible."

I shuddered. "Does this mean we'll see dead bodies?" It was a stupid question, but the realization hit me hard as I stared at the people around us.

"In the village? It would surprise me more if we didn't."

I shuddered again, still watching the spirits as they walked toward me. Fear flooded over me as my chest tightened. All I could think about was escaping. "I don't know if I can do this." Panic swelled through me as I stumbled from my horse, legs aching, and ran for the gate. There was no way I could deal with the corpses of the people who were now haunting me. Not right now. Haldrek ran in front of me and blocked my path. As I ducked to one side, my legs gave out from under me. He knelt down in the snow and dirt as he grabbed my shoulders to catch me. I flinched.

"As thegn-heir of Svartån, it is your duty—"

The spirits enclosed on me, and it sounded like they were begging '*please*'.

"I can't do this, Haldrek!" My voice went higher as I pleaded, pushing him away. The last few days of travel had been exhausting—emotionally, mentally, and physically—as I'd tried to prepare myself for what was ahead. But the intensity of my feelings was *not* what I'd expected. Seeing ghosts was *not* what I'd expected. "I'm not a warrior. I've never seen a dead body before. Or ghosts. How am I supposed to help these people when I don't know what to do?" My mother was right. How could I be responsible for anything? I had no idea what to do.

"I'll help you. There are certain rites that need to be done, but I've done that before. And there will be others at the estate who can do the rites. You can't run away from this, Ina."

"I don't know if I can look at the bodies. Not while their spirits wander around as well..."

"I'll... help with that. At least the bodies." Haldrek relaxed his posture. "And if there are survivors... we'll see what we can do."

I desperately wanted to march past him and out the gate. To make this all disappear and hide away, like I always did. I didn't ask to deal with corpses. Or ghosts. Not real ones at least.

But I was the thegn-heir. I thought back to my conversation with my dad. If I didn't take care of these people, who would? As my anxiety climbed and I fought between my fears and my new duty, the ghosts hovered in my periphery, giving me space.

I brushed angry tears from my face and gave Haldrek my hand to help me up. "Fine. But I'm no hero, so don't expect me to be one."

Haldrek grinned as he helped me stand back up and then into the saddle. "Not yet. But if you are anything like your father, you will be."

Sure enough, as we rode through the village, blackened corpses covered the ground. A few people tended to the bodies and watched us as we rode up the main street. I gagged on the unfamiliar smell that hung in the chill air. The closest thing I could think of was the smell of freezer burned meat left out to thaw. It was a grim thought, and I hid my face in the collar of my clothing the best that I could, both to keep the smell out and to hide my tears.

"Vile Isillas. They'll pay for what they've done." Haldrek inhaled stiffly. "I fear what they plan for Andrattür."

"How do we fix this?" I glanced up as we stopped. More spirits ambled toward us as I tried to suppress my nerves. Were these new spirits, and if so, how many people lived on this estate? Both Hethurin and non-Hethurin? So far, the spirits seemed docile, but would they remain that way? Or would I have to worry about fighting off ghosts too?

"First, we need to—" The sound of shouting interrupted Haldrek as we heard weapons being unsheathed above us where the street's incline flattened. A few of the spirits even looked in the sound's direction. Haldrek slipped down from the horse and put his hand on the sword hilt at his hip. I followed him on horseback a few paces and my chest seized up at the scene in front of us.

Two men stared at each other, ready to fight. One, to our left, in chainmail, helmet and everything, but wearing an unfamiliar insignia on the cloth covering his armor, and the other, on our right, in only a thick jacket like the one I wore over my dress.

The man in chainmail snapped, "You stupid half-breed! Your kind need no rites! The thegn-heir has given your kind their tasks. Do as he says or I'll cut you down."

"He has no authority here. I'll go to Camroth before I take orders from anyone but the true thegn of Svartån."

The man in chainmail swung at the other man, making him jump back. A few of the surrounding people started screaming and moving out of their way.

"Stop it! Leave him alone!"

I turned to see a familiar face running toward the fight. Mattie swung a broom handle at the threatening soldier from behind, hitting him squarely in the neck. He staggered for a second before spinning around. The broom handle caught in between the layers of his armor and jaw, jerking out of Mattie's hands. Her eyes widened as he faced her.

"Mattie!"

I stumbled off my horse again and grabbed at my dagger as the other soldier—loyal to Svartån—tackled him from behind, pushing him to the ground. As they tussled, Haldrek ran over and pointed the tip of his sword at the offending warrior's neck. He froze, dropping his sword to the ground.

"What. In the name of Tenelth. Is going on here?" Haldrek's tone was deep and commanding. Enough that I straightened up, and even the Svartån soldier backed away.

The foreign warrior said, "This *half-breed* won't listen to the orders that his thegn gave him and his kind. Instead, he says the *Hethurin* need burials. What's it to you?"

"*His* thegn?" Haldrek's tone deepened with anger. "*You* wear the emblem of Lansiranikä. What is it to you what a subject of Svartån does?"

The soldier crinkled his nose in disgust. "You been under a rock these past few days, stranger?" He paused as Haldrek pushed his sword further into his chain mail. "Blodnar took Drattüjert. Killed the High King. His family. Thegn of Svartån, too. My gesith, Hardbein Hoskuldsson, is the new thegn. He's the old thegn's cousin and the old thegn had no heir."

My chest tightened as I realized what was going on.

"The Thegn of Svartån died not three days ago. I fought beside him and High King Kalle. Unless Hardbein fought at that battle, how does he know that the Thegn of Svartån fell?"

The soldier's eyes went wide. "I... I only speak of what I've been told."

Haldrek growled, but pulled his sword away from the man's throat. "Get up and tell your *gesith* that the Thegn of Andrattür has questions for him."

The man scrambled to his feet. He disappeared, leaving Haldrek, me, the Svartån soldier, and Mattie in the center of the intersection.

"Ina?" Mattie gasped, eyes wide. She rushed forward, squeezing me into a tight embrace. "We're in..."

"Lohikärra. I know. I thought..." I hugged her back as I started laughing. From joy at seeing Mattie or from frazzled nerves, I had no idea. "This place is *real.*"

"Is it? We're not in some coma dream or something?"

I shrugged. "No. I've never had a dream like this. This feels real. And it's still better than Fargo."

"This is your friend?" Haldrek stared at Mattie wide-eyed as I glanced back at him.

I nodded. "Her father was the one who told us stories about Lohikärra."

Haldrek glanced around, then focused on Mattie again. "You're also from Fargo? How did your father know of Lohikärra?"

Mattie scrutinized him for a split second. "Kinda? I grew up in a place called Seattle. Then moved to Fargo. As for my dad... I'm guessing he knew because he was from here?" She hesitated. "He told my mother he was from Andrattür."

Haldrek blinked and then shook his head. "Forgive me if I'm blunt, but... Seattle? Is it like the Raycana Isles? Are all the people there dark skinned like you?"

Mattie shook her head and grimaced. "No. Seattle is only slightly less... white... than Lohikärra. Or at least Svartån. My mother was born in another place. Somalia. She and my father met in Seattle."

"Somalia..." Haldrek frowned and scratched his beard, as if thinking. "Is *that* much like the Raycana Isles? I only ask because you look... You could be mistaken for being Ixafean. But I know little of yours and Ina's world."

"I don't know. Only that her family fled the fighting going on there. That's how they ended up in Seattle. But yeah... I don't look like your run-of-the-mill Lohikärran." She stretched her arm out, showing the stark difference between our skin colors. Hers a pleasant brown, mine a sickly white.

Haldrek cocked his head. "How did... I assume you came here the same way that Ina did?"

Mattie shrugged and looked back at me. "Did we seriously end up in my father's... er... stories?"

I grimaced, shaking my head. "We're not *in* the story. We're in the world that inspired it. How crazy do you think I'd be if I told you that my father reached out to me from the Realm of Ghosts?"

"Not any crazier than I feel right now." Mattie glanced left and right, surveying the area around us, before focusing on me. "I woke up pinned under some charred timbers here in the village." She gestured at the Svartån soldier next to her. "Llamryl helped me out. After I started thinking I was going to die under that rubble."

He grinned, taking off his leather helmet. Despite his head being shaved on both sides, and having a middle section tightly braided to his scalp, he resembled Thandes with his fair skin, blond hair, and pointed ears. "Only doing my duty."

I returned my focus to Mattie and said, "My dad—or his ghost—told me that this is an actual place. You remember the stone I had? Apparently... it sent us here. But they're sketchy at teleporting more than one person at a time."

Mattie sighed. "Good grief. So, I got transported here, and you got transported... where?"

"A... caged wagon. Like the way the vi- story starts out."

Mattie surveyed the burnt and crumbled buildings around us once again. "This *is* crazy."

I nodded. Our conversation lulled until I noticed Llamryl staring at me.

He shook his head as soon as he realized I was looking at him. "My apologies. But... By the dragons... you look like the thegn reborn as a woman."

I raised an eyebrow as Haldrek cleared his throat in annoyance.

"She *is* Thegn Svartån's daughter and *true* heir."

Llamryl stumbled back in surprise before bowing to me on one knee, "My apologies, my lady."

Haldrek cocked his head before turning to me. "Llamryl is... was part of the Svangendom guard under your father, I believe." He turned back to Llamryl. "If I'm remembering you correctly? The thegn held you and your fellow warriors in high esteem."

Llamryl bobbed his head in agreement and looked up at us. "And we did our best to protect those in the village when the Isillas came. Thegn Andrattür... They came as the sun was just lighting the sky." Llamryl stood up and shuddered as if trying to keep his composure. He focused on me and said, "We did our best. But there were too many."

"Do you remember how many?" I asked, despite my genuine reluctance to know.

"A full *sattar* or two. My men and I took down as many as I could, but they only retreated once it was clear they couldn't breach the estate's central walls."

"How many is a *sattar*?" I'd never heard that term in the games, or if I had, I didn't remember it.

"One hundred men, my lady. And not a day had passed before," Llamryl jerked his head backward and toward the estate, "your father's cousin came in here and proclaimed himself the new thegn."

"And you let him into the estate?" Haldrek's expression turned dark.

Llamryl shook his head. "The head of the Svangendom guard challenged the man, telling him he would bow to no other until he knew for certain Thegn Svartån had passed." His grimace turned to a scowl. "For that, the gesith killed him and 'disbanded' the guard, threatening the rest of us with death if we dared to challenge him."

My stomach squeezed tight as I thought about confronting this cousin. If he was a gesith and he was willing to kill those who challenged his claim, then what was I supposed to do? Did I need to fight him?

I turned to Haldrek with a grimace. "First the Blodnar, then the Isillas, and now this?"

He shook his head. "I had hoped that you might have a more gradual tutoring of your life as a thegn, but... it is what it is." He sighed and stared at the sky before returning his focus to me. "I believe there is a peaceful way to remove your father's cousin from the estate. But it will involve some courage on your part. While you'll have me as an ally, you must convince your people. It's important to present yourself as honorable and confident as your people would expect of a thegn. At least in public."

I grimaced as the weight of everything hit me, and I closed my eyes to think. Hardbein, the Isillas, the ghosts, and everything else. There were so many things I needed to do. It terrified me. That I might fail terrified me. And the one thing I knew I needed to do now—confronting Hardbein and his men—was so far out of my comfort zone that anxiety made my head swim just thinking about it.

I groaned and looked toward the main estate. "Thegn hall, then?"

Mattie nodded as we started walking in that direction. "That's my guess. If I were him, I'd be guarding that place."

Wiping my now clammy hands on my clothes, I tried to brace myself for what was inside. I hated confrontation of any kind, but if I was to deal with the Isillas or Blodnar in the future, I needed to deal with Hardbein now.

As Haldrek and I pushed open the doors to the hall, I could hear loud voices at the far end of the room. Mattie and Llamryl stood behind us, and I wondered if the real-life hall was anything like the hall in the games. At first glance, it seemed so. Only... grander in scale. The roofs arched up high so that the room's ceiling was two or three stories above us. Stairs took us up several small terraces to the main floor, where long tables with benches and chairs framed a rectangular fire pit in the center of the room.

At the far end stood a familiar, ornate chair. The back was carved to look like a swan taking flight, wings extended. The Svartån thegn's chair.

In front of it stood a large, heavyset man with a half balding head. He wore a long tunic with detailed embroidery that extended to his ankles, and a few pieces of gold jewelry. A large sword hung at his side, hooked into a belt below his gut. He was someone of importance, or at least dressed like he was.

"Thegn Andrattür!" The man raised his hands in greeting. "It pleases me to see you alive. It grieved me to hear of my cousin's passing at the Battle of Drattüjert."

Haldrek stopped at the opposite edge of the fire pit—its embers glowing ominously—from the heavyset man who stood in front of the thegn's chair. A growing sense of indignation surprised me as I tried to keep my expression blank.

"How did you hear of Thegn Svartån's passing, gesith Hardbein? If I may ask?"

Hardbein's face reddened as he hesitated.

"I... I was at Drattüjert fighting, Thegn Andrattür. Thegn Lansiranikä told me the news himself."

"I remember seeing Thegn Lansiranikä being bound and gagged along with the rest of the thegns before the Blodnar carted us off. I *don't* remember seeing you or any other living Lansiranikän soldiers around."

"He... he told me before they captured him."

"Before the battle?" Haldrek's voice hinted at disbelief. "How would he have known? Thegn Svartån was still alive at that point."

Hardbein ducked his head, placing his hands on his belt before looking back at Haldrek. "I don't know. Only that I was told as much. That said, Thegn Svartån died at Drattüjert, did he not? Without an heir? So, I am here to take his place and protect Svartån from its enemies. I hope that we may be allies, as Svartån and Andrattür have long been."

"No." Haldrek crossed his arms across his chest.

Hardbein blinked as if stunned. "I'm... sorry, what? You are rejecting an alliance? In this time of war?"

"No. I am disagreeing with you. Thegn Svartån did not die without an heir. He had a daughter by the name of Maja Ingmar Svanunge." Haldrek gestured to me. "*She* is the true thegn-heir of Svartån."

Hardbein glanced at me for a moment and then threw his head back in laughter. "*A woman?* A woman thegn?" He continued to laugh as my cheeks burned. When he stopped, he looked at Haldrek. "I doubt anyone of sound mind believed my predecessor when he came back stating he had a child with a mysterious woman in a mysterious land. No, the previous Thegn of Svartån had no children, for he had no natural affection toward women."

Haldrek narrowed his eyes. "I believed Thegn Svartån when he spoke of having an heir. As did many of my kin. Do you question the soundness of my mind?"

Hardbein scowled, hesitating. "What proof do you have that this piss wench is Thegn Svartån's daughter? Or did you just fetch some local girl and tell her to play a part?"

The hall was silent as Haldrek glanced at me, and then back at Hardbein. "The dragons told me."

Hardbein's face reddened as he narrowed his eyes at Haldrek. "I... Well..."

"Just leave. Go home." The words popped out of my mouth before I could think. "Unless you are here to help me, leave—because I have work to do."

Hardbein turned to me in surprise, his expression then hardening. "Thegn-heir or not, the people of Svartån would accept a Lansiranikän gesith before an outsider wench like yourself. This is *not* your home, and you'd be wise to return to whatever cursed place that is." He gestured to the soldiers who stood on either side of the hall as he began walking toward our group. Haldrek placed his hands on the sheath of his sword. But I noticed that neither Hardbein nor his men had unsheathed their weapons. "When your pathetic incompetence gets you cut down by one of your many enemies, I'll be back to take my rightful title." He knocked his shoulder into mine as he passed, making me stumble into Llamryl and Mattie.

I scrambled to my feet and watched the group leave, still heady with panic over my retort to Hardbein. I glanced at Haldrek, hoping for some sign that I'd done the right thing. Instead, a grim frown crossed his face.

"That *churl* was lying through his teeth the whole time. He's not going to just sit back and watch you become thegn."

"What do I do then? I mean... I did the right thing by telling him to leave, right?"

Haldrek turned to me. "You did. He wouldn't leave unless one of us forced him to. You standing up to him did that. However, it means that you will need to search for allies sooner rather than later. Rally the gesiths of Svartån behind you before Hardbein rallies them behind him."

My stomach squeezed tight at the thought of more confrontations. With Hardbein or anyone else. "Is there a chance that he'd keep me from becoming thegn of Svartån?"

"There's always a chance. There's always someone who wants what position you have. I had distant relatives try to claim the title of Thegn Andrattür before I came of age and after my father's death. The only difference is that few people gave them any heed. In that regard, Hardbein is right. Many in Svartån would accept a proven gesith before an outsider. And... the last female thegn of Svartån was Ottkatla herself. The first thegn of Svartån."

"So, I need to prove I can fight when I've never done so in my life?" I tried to hold the panic back from my voice.

Llamryl bowed again out of the corner of my eye. As he rose, Mattie held him steady. He looked up at me and said, "It would honor me to teach you what fighting skills I know, my thegn."

Haldrek faced me with a smile. "I'll teach you as well."

Mattie grinned at me. "I have a few tricks too..." A globe of fire emerged from her free hand.

I gaped. "How'd you figure that out?" Given Mattie's style of fighting in the games, it didn't surprise me that she'd figured out a way to do magic here.

"I just tried the same spells that my dad noted down in his lore journals. They actually work. Here, at least."

"You are a mage?" Llamryl stared at Mattie wide-eyed as she made the fire disappear. I couldn't tell if that was a good thing or a bad thing by his expression.

"You could say that, I guess. I... always imagined I'd use magic over weapons. If I was ever... here."

Llamryl turned back to me. "You have many people who will teach you, my thegn. You are from a land foreign to us Lohikärrans, but that may benefit you."

He had a point, even as the voices in my head tried to tell me otherwise. I had a title but was, otherwise, a nobody in this world. I could create my story. No one here, except Mattie, knew of my life back in Fargo. Which meant this could be a fresh start for me. My lips curled into a small grin.

"Then what is the first thing that I need to do?" I turned to Haldrek. "You mentioned rallying gesiths? Which... how many gesiths did my father have, anyway?"

"Fifteen, I believe." Haldrek paused. "And when two or more people claim the title of thegn, the victor is often the one with more gesiths behind them."

My smile disappeared, and I asked, "How do I get gesiths behind me?"

"Prove to them that you will be an excellent leader. There are a few nearby... Eldingheimr, Bolvo, and others that will readily accept you. They were loyal to your father, and I see no reason why they wouldn't follow you as well. My plan was to visit them sooner rather than later. Though, if you are amenable to it, I need your thegn stones currently."

"Those are real?" Mattie gasped.

I frowned in confusion at her. Whatever thegn stones were, they hadn't been in the game. "What...?"

Haldrek nodded. "They're a way for thegns to communicate with each other, even if they are in different places. I allow my *husceorl*—my steward—to use the main one at Mirratoft when I am away and so I can deal with matters back home through him. But I need to let him know I am alive and issue orders to protect Andrattür."

I shrugged. "I have no problem with you using them."

Haldrek bobbed his head quickly and left to wherever the thegn stones were.

Llamryl groaned, sinking into a nearby chair. As he sat, he looked up at me. "My apologies, my thegn. I've been running around since the Isillas attacked."

"Rest, then. It's hard to do anything when you're not rested."

"Spoken like a true thegn."

Mattie and I turned around to see an older man with a trimmed gray beard walking down the staircase on the far side of the hall. As he reached us, he continued, "You look like a Svanunge, that's for certain."

"Master Skuti." Llamryl bobbed his head in deference to the man before looking up at me. "He was your father's *husceorl*. Been here since before I was born."

Master Skuti smiled. "You are? A Svanunge, I can tell, but which one?"

"Maja Ingmar Svanunge. I go by Ina. How many Svanunges are there?"

"A few are still here in Svartån. Most outside its borders. Your great-grandfather had many children. Married them off to other members of the *abthanry*. Which resulted in descendants such as Hardbein."

"*Abthanry*?" I frowned at the man. Haldrek had used the term, but I still wasn't familiar with it.

"The elite and noble of Lohikärra. If one can claim a thegn or the High King as a direct relation within three generations, then they are part of the *abthanry*."

Now it was Mattie's turn to frown. "Are there only so many people who can be part of the *abthanry*?"

Master Skuti shook his head. "It is something that both legitimate and illegitimate heirs may claim. Though in times past, that has caused quite a bit of conflict." He paused. "Your father's cousin—Hardbein—is such a case. His grandfather—your great-grandfather—was the Thegn of Svartån. Hardbein's father, however, was a common *ceorl* from Sigreykir. A tryst, so to speak, and records speak of great discord over the whole situation."

"Spreading gossip again, Skuti?" Haldrek walked up next to me. I jumped, despite his tone being light and playful.

"Thegn Andrattür! It isn't gossip if it is true. And it adds weight to the lady's claim. A legitimate child trumps an illegitimate grandchild." Skuti turned back to me. "Given how your father spoke, I presume your parents were married, even if only in your homeland?"

I nodded.

"Then you have a better claim than Hardbein. Thank the dragons for that."

Haldrek chuckled under his breath. "No desire to serve the gesith?"

Skuti shook his head. "I hid myself away in the library to avoid him. He seemed not to be the reading kind." He focused on me again. "Do you read, my lady?"

"Uh... not Lohikärran. I know the language of my homeland though."

"It's a start." Skuti bobbed his head.

"I..." I looked around the hall, avoiding eye contact with him as I collected my thoughts. "I'll do my best. At being a thegn. This is all new to me. But... I don't want to let people down."

Llamryl sat forward in his seat. "Your father was a great and honorable man. I was proud to serve as one of his guards. Even if you are half the person he was, you will be a better thegn than that Hardbein man."

I gave a little smile but said nothing. People like Llamryl, Haldrek and my father may have had faith in my abilities, but with three enemies vying for Svartån, I knew I needed more than just other people's belief in me. I needed to show my capability for being a good thegn.

# Chapter Five

"Too-Weli!" I waved my hand over the coals as I sat on the ledge of the firepit with Mattie. A few flames popped up from my fingers and then disappeared.

Mattie laughed. "Try imagining a larger flame. That's what's worked for me." She closed her eyes and waved her hand over the pit. A steady flame popped up from her palm and fingers.

"How come you can do it without saying it out loud?"

"I'm saying it in my head." She pursed her lips thoughtfully. "Try shouting it in your head while imagining a large flame."

I closed my eyes and put my hand over the fire pit. In my mind, I imagined a raging fire bursting from my hand as I shouted *Too-Weli* in my head.

"There you go." Llamryl's attempt to contain his laughter failed. He had stayed in the hall, resting and peppering Mattie and I with questions about our homeland.

I opened my eyes to see a large flame spurting up from my hand. The heat from the flame tickled, but it didn't burn. At least for the first few seconds.

Shaking out my hand and making the flame disappear, I grinned. In the few hours since we'd arrived, Skuti had arranged for Mattie and me to wear better clothing than the rags we had arrived here in. It made practicing spells with Mattie much easier.

The sound of books falling on a table made me jump, and I turned to see Skuti placing a small pile of books on the table behind me. "My thegn, some tomes I believe will help you." He grabbed the one on top and handed it to me as I stood up. "I remember you mentioning that you were not familiar with the Lohikärran written language. Here's an old primer that you may find useful. I apologize though, it is geared toward younger students than yourself."

My chest tightened in surprise as I stared at the book that Skuti gave me.

Mattie stood up and asked, "Is that...?"

"It *looks* identical to the one my dad gave me as a kid." I bit the inside of my lip to keep from crying. Flipping through the pages, I tried to stay composed as I stared at the familiar pictures and remembered my dad reading about some of them to me. My throat and chest squeezed even tighter as I realized how I would never see him again. At least alive.

"It seems this book means something to you?" Skuti asked.

I nodded. "My dad... I had a copy of this exact book as a child. Until... it got destroyed." Looking up at Skuti, I said. "I have no idea how to read it, but I remember my father telling me stories about Bjornulf and Freya from it."

"It will be a good place to start then." Skuti continued, "It's good to hear that your father introduced some of your heritage to you, if only in your youth."

I began flipping through the book again with Mattie, but a sound made my head snap back up. Thandes ran down the stairs on the far side of the room, tears streaming down her face, and a strangled sob wrenched from her throat. She had arrived at the hall earlier, hurrying to the armory after a respectful curtsy to Mattie, Llamryl, and me.

"Sister!" Llamryl ran over to her, pulling her into a hug. I put my book down and hobbled over, my legs still aching from all the horse riding I'd done over the past few days.

"Where is he, Llamryl? He wasn't in the village or the barracks or the armory. Where is Thyre?"

Llamryl held her tight. "I'm sorry, Thandes... He fell. Fighting the Isillas."

Thandes looked up at her brother. "No... None of his family survived the Isillas attack. I had hoped..." She leaned her head into her brother's shoulder, her body still shaking from her sobs.

"It doesn't help that our family has sustained losses from the Isillas as well," Llamryl said, rubbing Thandes's back as I reached them.

"I'm so sorry. How... how many..." I hesitated, not wanting to come off insensitive. "Are you two the only ones left of your family?"

Llamryl shook his head as he led Thandes over to a table to sit. "My mother bore eight children. Thandes is my twin. And the eldest of us all. Two of my younger brothers stood with me to protect those in the village. They were the reason I was arguing with the Lansiranikän today. They fought and fell, protecting both

Hethurin and non-Hethurin alike, so I demanded both their burial, and for them to get the proper rites.”

“I’ll make sure that happens. What about the other four?”

“Our sister left the estate last summer for adventure. I hope she is well, but I don’t know where she is. The three youngest… fled as soon as my mother sent them away. I don’t know what became of them. Other than they are no longer in the village.”

The hall went quiet except for the crackling of the fire pit. Thandes leaned into her brother’s shoulder. He held her, muffling her crying.

After a few minutes, footsteps broke the silence as Haldrek walked down from an upper floor. He stopped and cocked his head.

“What happened?”

I grimaced a little at his bluntness. “Thandes just returned from the armory. She…”

“She’s mourning the loss of her family.” Mattie snapped.

Haldrek stared at her in surprise and turned back to Thandes. “My grief is with you. May they all reside in Mirroth.”

She smiled as she wiped her tears. “Thank you.”

I turned to Haldrek. “It sounds like the Hethurin still need their rites done.”

He grimaced. “The priests of Tenelth have long argued whether those of elven descent have souls to send to Mirroth.”

“That’s stupid.” I snapped. “*Those* were the spirits I saw coming into the village.” The priests’ theories sounded more like an excuse than a reason. “Are there priests of Tenelth here at the estate or is this something else I need to learn?”

Skuti shifted behind me, and I turned to him. “The answers to your questions are yes, and most likely. The priests here were quick to do the rites for others, but they have been slothful in doing it for the Hethurin unless your father upbraided them. A regular occurrence.”

I groaned. “So, I need to confront them?”

Skuti nodded. “Their quarters are close by. Go introduce yourself. And continue your father’s tradition of upbraiding their lazy bottoms.” A small grin colored his expression as he studied the books on the table.

“We should go visit them.” I turned to both Haldrek and Mattie. “You two want to come?”

“Right now?” Haldrek’s eyes widened in surprise.

Mattie shook her head. "As much as I would enjoy seeing this conversation, I've had my fill of people today. I'm more curious about some of these books and scrolls that Skuti's brought out." Mattie cocked her head to look at some of the spines.

I turned back to Haldrek. "I was hoping for right now. As tired as I am, if I can get these priests to do the rites for the Hethurin, then that means I can deal with other stuff tomorrow."

He nodded. "Very well."

Once outside the safety of the hall, Haldrek walked as close as he could to me, his arm bumping into mine with almost every step.

As we reached the edge of the courtyard, he asked, "Are they out here? With us?"

I stopped and blinked at him. It dawned on me that Haldrek was referring to the ghosts that stood nearby, their presence giving the courtyard a blue glow. "There are a few here. I'm guessing members of my dad's Hethurin guard." The whispers of '*Please*' still echoed in the wind, just as they had when we'd been walking in. While I wasn't afraid of them, their presence made things a bit more eerie.

"What are they doing?"

"Just standing around, watching us. They keep saying '*Please*' though."

"Are they just frozen in place? I thought ghosts could move?"

"They can and they are, but they're waiting right now. At least the ones in the courtyard."

Haldrek's posture relaxed. "Waiting for burial?"

I nodded. "That's why I want to talk to the priests here." I continued, "The Hethurin shouldn't have to beg for burials."

Haldrek sighed. "They shouldn't. It's not their fault they're related to Pephennas, or that he stirred up such anger among the people here."

"Are the priests of Tenelth not doing their rites just because they don't believe the Hethurin have souls? Or something else?"

"The former, for the most part. But there are also rumors that the Hethurin do not worship Tenelth or his kin. Many elves have their own ideas on who rules us and where one goes when they die. So, there are those who fear treating the Hethurin the same as Lohikärrans would invoke the wrath of the dragons upon them."

"Like the priests of Tenelth?"

"Some of them." Haldrek gestured at a squat stone building in front of us, near the gates leading down into the village. "That would be where they reside."

It was a very plain building from the little that I could see. Large candles inside lamps stood outside the one door, and the bit of light from them showed minimal decoration. Nothing to denote that the building was anything special.

"How many priests are there here?" I asked, as we stopped in front of the building.

Haldrek shrugged. "Half a dozen at most in this building. There are a few smaller shrines in the village and one priest attends to each of those, but these are the chief priests for the estate."

"Hmm." Six priests were less than I expected, given that Svangendom was the thegn's estate. In the games, there always seemed to be dozens of priests milling around each of the estates. Though, that could have been creative license at play. As we stood there now, in front of the door, I wondered if I'd be more nervous, if there were more priests.

"Are you going to knock?"

"Yeah…" I shook my head to clear my thoughts. I was the thegn-heir of Svartån, and these priests needed to do the rites for the Hethurin whether or not they liked it.

I pounded on the door until it opened. A young, beardless man faced me. He glanced at Haldrek and then back at me with a frown.

"Can I help you?"

"My name is Ina—Maja Ingmar Svanunge—and my father was the Thegn of Svartån. I hear the rites for the Hethurin aren't being done."

The man's face darkened in the candlelight. "I heard that Ingmar Svanunge, Thegn of Svartån, passed. His heir spoke to me this morning. I don't know who you are, but you have no reason to speak with me or my fellow priests about the half-breeds in the village."

He began to shut the door in my face, but Haldrek put his hand on the door and leaned into it, keeping it open.

"That is *no way* to speak to a thegn-heir."

"Who are you?"

"I am Haldrek Rodreksson. Thegn of Andrattür."

The man paused for a second. "Prove it."

Haldrek grabbed a small chain from around his neck and pulled out a pendant. "What insignia do you see?"

The priest squinted. "Andrattür. But how do I know you are the thegn and not just part of the *abthanry*?"

Haldrek growled. "You little—"

"Let the two in, young one. No need to agitate people." A gray-haired man stepped up behind the ornery priest and waved us in. "I apologize for his behavior, Thegn Andrattür."

We stepped inside as the young priest slammed the door behind us.

"You seem more distempered than normal, my friend." The older man glanced at the younger priest. "Why don't you rest, and I will speak with our guests?"

The young man grumbled and disappeared into a back room.

Once we were alone, the older man gestured for us to sit at the small table in the center of the room. It was almost as plain as the exterior. A fireplace built into the wall behind us and an ornate shrine behind the old priest and beneath a small staircase were the only decorations.

"You look like the late thegn. Though that doesn't mean you are his daughter. Have you any tokens from him revealing you as such?"

"I..." I shook my head. "No. Not right now. But I spoke with him. Last night. In the Realm of Ghosts."

The old priest's lips tightened as he studied the table. "And I have spoken with the late thegn many times in my life, but that doesn't make us related."

My face heated up as anger and embarrassment made my chest tighten.

"Has he dragged you into another realm since his passing?" Haldrek snapped.

The old priest looked up at Haldrek. "No, of course not. But—"

"Then Ina is someone of importance to him. And I remember him swearing up and down that Hardbein would never be his heir."

"Of course." The old priest bobbed his head. "I remember you, Thegn Andrattür. I am glad to see you are alive and well, given some of the other news that has come out of Drattüjert. But even if the late Thegn did not wish Hardbein to be his heir, Hardbein is still the nearest blood relation to him."

"Not according to the Svanunge Annals."

"The..." The old priest gaped. "Is she in them?"

Haldrek nodded, and I stared at him in surprise. What were the Svanunge Annals?

"Ingmar had an heir, did he then?" The old priest focused on the table before facing me again.

"Welcome to Svangendom, my lady. My apologies for my earlier dismissal. I have only once seen the contents of the Svanunge Annals, but I trust that Thegn Andrattür speaks the truth."

I blinked in surprise and turned to Haldrek.

He raised his eyebrows at the old priest before grinning at me. "The Svanunge Annals are a genealogy of your family. Each thegn family has one. It *usually* makes it easy for families to figure out who should be thegn."

"Usually?"

"Sometimes people will fight over whether an heir is deserving of a title they've inherited."

Like what Hardbein was trying to do. Turning back to the priest, I said, "I heard the Hethurin aren't getting their rites." I paused, trying to pull back at my annoyance with the whole situation, but failed. "That *is* your job, right?"

The priest sat in silence for a moment, looking down at the table. "It is. My fellow priests and I have been doing so. Since the Isillas attack. I don't know if there are elves where you come from, but... it is common knowledge that those sired by elves do not have spirits and that it is an affront to Tenelth to send them to *any* of the realms of the dead. Even Lyrroth."

"Lyrroth?" The name sounded familiar, but I shook my head. That was something I could figure out later. I focused on the old priest and asked, "So, how do you explain the spirits I see walking around the estate? That I saw in the village today?"

The priest leaned back in his chair; hands still clasped in front of him on the table. "That you see spirits... I suppose more proof that you're the late thegn's daughter." He paused, letting his gaze wander around the room. "There are still some non-Hethurin who need their rites done. Perhaps those were the spirits you saw?"

"They had pointy ears..." I crossed my arms across my chest, feeling as though this conversation would not end well.

"Perhaps some kind of elven magic? Some kind of illusion. Not true spirits, but something created to trick those of us who worship Tenelth."

I pursed my lips and looked at Haldrek for some kind of backup. He shrugged.

Turning back to the priest, I snapped, "You won't do your job unless you're forced to, correct?"

"No, my fellow priests and I will do the job the dragons gave us. Send the spirits of those who have passed on to one of the three realms of the afterlife. But we will *not* defile Tenelth's name by doing rites for those who will never tread in those realms." He stood up and glanced toward the room where the other priest had gone. "With all due respect, *thegn-heir*, it is late, and I expect tomorrow will be another long day of *work* sending spirits into the afterlife. I am tired and if you are so intent on dealing with the half-breeds here, do it yourself. I will not doom myself or my fellow priests to Tenelth's or his kin's condemnation." He walked out, leaving Haldrek and I alone in the front room.

My chest burned with humiliation. Haldrek put his hand on my shoulder and said, "We should go."

I faced him and whispered, "He *did* the rites for my father. Why is it forbidden now?" I wondered if Haldrek felt the same way as the priests. If he was only placating me because of who my dad was or who I was supposed to be.

"Let's talk outside." Haldrek opened the door and gestured for me to head out.

As soon as we were outside and he had closed the door, I spun around and faced him. "Now what? Do we just leave the Hethurin to be ghosts? They *have* spirits. Even if the idiots in there are too… idiotic… to know any better." I kicked a small, nearby snow mound and regretted it as soon as my foot met the rock underneath. Swear words hissed out under my breath as I turned back to the priests' hut. "I hope the Hethurin spirits haunt you all tonight and every night until you learn to do your job."

"Easy, Ina."

"Easy?" I turned my anger on Haldrek. "They refuse to do their job because of some stupid tradition that I *know* is incorrect. They're… they're being bullies to the Hethurin, rejecting them because of something that the Hethurin can't change. And you're like… 'Easy, Ina'. No, I won't be easy. Screw them. You were willing to defend me to the priests, why not the Hethurin?"

A small grin popped up on Haldrek's face. "I like your fire, Ina. You don't back down without a fight." He gestured to the priests' hut. "The priest in there is trying to throw his weight around. We know that he and the others never enjoyed doing the rites for the Hethurin. And now that you're here, he's trying to make it seem like he *can't* do it, when he *won't*."

My anger faded, and I sighed. I felt stupid now. My emotions had controlled me for a moment. "What now, then? I can't force them to do the rites, at least not yet, and I'm sure if I were to kick them out of the estate, that wouldn't help anyone."

"It wouldn't. But there is something you can do. A few things. First off, the priests of Tenelth aren't the only ones who can do the death rites. Anyone who is a member of the *abthanry* can. So, both you and I can. Most thegns just delegate those tasks to the priests of Tenelth." Haldrek grinned before continuing. "Also, you can tell Skuti that the priests of Tenelth are to be treated like any other person on the estate. If you wanted to be vindictive, you could say that they should be treated as less than the Hethurin."

"What would that do?"

"For most priests of Tenelth, working at a thegn's estate is a choice position. It comes with certain privileges, such as eating with the thegn and his—or her—advisors and having free rein to move about the estate at their leisure. However, if they were treated as anyone else on the estate, they would no longer have those benefits, among others."

"And if they were treated as less than the Hethurin?"

"Not only would they be required to do their current work, but they'd be required to do whatever manual labor the Hethurin must do to survive. Housing would no longer be within the walls of the estate, but in the village. And food, if they didn't make their own, must be taken from whatever is leftover—either in the village or at the estate. Not even the Hethurin had to beg for food here. At least under your father."

A small bubble of excitement formed inside me. I could punish those who were misbehaving. At the same time... it was strange to wield that kind of power over people. I worried that I wouldn't be able to wield it well.

"You don't have to choose now. We can go back inside the hall. Warm up. Eat."

I shook my head. "You said we could do the death rites?"

Haldrek's focus darted away from me as he pressed his lips into a thin line. "Technically yes, but..."

"You're afraid of ghosts." I slipped my hand in his and squeezed it.

He groaned. "Yes."

I smiled. "If we do the rites for some of the Hethurin, there will be fewer ghosts."

"True... How tired are you feeling, though?"

"Not very, why?" I lied.

"The rites require a lot of emotional and mental strength. Each time you do it, it wears you down. I've only done a few in a row myself, and that's because I couldn't do any more. Another reason that thegns have the priests of Tenelth to do it. They train to have the strength to do many more rites than you or I ever could."

I bobbed my head in agreement, considering how tired I felt. And I knew going through the village meant that I'd have to deal with some uncomfortable emotions. Ghosts in the village meant I would see more of the massacred, as opposed to those who went down fighting.

"You still want to try doing the rites tonight?"

I nodded again. "No one's going to do the rites for the Hethurin except for me. And maybe you." My legs were stiff again from being still for so long, but I hobbled toward the gate anyway, and waited for him to join me. He grabbed a lamp like device from a soldier at the gate. Not that it made any difference to me. The village was lit with an eerie blue light now, and I got the sinking feeling that the brightness of it was because of how many ghosts were in the village.

As we got closer to the glow, I asked, "What do you see?"

"Just darkness and the moon above. Why?"

"I guess only I can see the blue glow up ahead." I hesitated again.

Haldrek grabbed my hand, interlacing his fingers with mine. His touch surprised me at first and then comforted me. "Are you afraid of the ghosts?"

"No. Not the ghosts, but the bodies. Knowing how they died. And I'm not afraid, I just... I want to conserve my energy for the rites."

"Would it help if you closed your eyes until we got into the village proper?"

"It... It would. I know that as soon as I see the bodies or the spirits, I'll get angry." My voice turned sharper than I intended. "My emotions make me weak. Too sensitive. I was always told to build a thick skin. Suppress my anger." Tears began dripping down my face, and I brushed them away. Despite my attempts to suppress my emotions, my anger was automatic at times, like now. Especially after my outburst at the priests' hut.

"Why aren't you allowed to feel angry? The Isillas are evil. What they did was evil. I'm angry and Svartån isn't even my thegn-land. And as for the priests... Their stubbornness is making your job more difficult. You have every right to be angry with them."

"Anger is a weakness. And if you're weak... you're worthless. Not responsible enough. Other people have to take care of you. And nobody enjoys dealing with a weak person. At least, that's what my mother always told me."

Verbalizing those thoughts made them sound *insane*. But I had been taught that my entire life. I was weak, irresponsible, a liability—so who would want to be around me? Who am I to be thegn? The thought popped into my head, and I shuddered.

"Your mother... sounds like a strange woman. I wonder what magic she possessed... that your father would be with her?" He shook his head. "That sounds insulting out loud. I apologize. You are your father's daughter and Svartån will be blessed for that."

"Thank you. I... I'm not offended. That is a question I have asked my entire life. And one I can't answer." I hesitated to say what I was thinking out loud. "But what if my mother is right? What if I'm weak and worthless and... what if I'm a failure?" Hardbein's words from earlier only fed my insecurities, adding to the voices inside my head, and I shuddered.

"She's not. You are taking on your father's mantle as thegn very well. At least in my opinion. Especially since you've been here for only... three days?"

A small smile crept onto my face. I guess hours playing as one of Lohikärra's mythical heroes *was* good for something... My smile disappeared as my insecurities around being thegn and protecting the people here pushed back into my mind. I changed the topic in an attempt to ignore them. "You said something interesting today. To Hardbein. You told him that the dragons spoke to you?"

Haldrek squeezed my hand. "Yes. It is a gift that every thegn of Andrattür and his children receive. The ability to converse with dragons. Just as we are conversing right now."

"So did the dragon who came to our rescue actually tell you who I was?"

He laughed and shook his head. "No. That was a lie. But I heard it speak to you. At least, you're the only one who I'm guessing Rhaegos was speaking to."

"Rhaegos?" The name sounded familiar, but I couldn't quite place it.

"The dragon who bonded with Ottkatla herself. And a very ancient and powerful creature in her own right. That's who we called to with our song."

I let the information sink in. "So, you're on a first name basis with the dragons here?"

"I guess? It's been something I've dealt with since I was a child. A few of my father's sisters also have the gift. But I don't know how often they speak to dragons."

Haldrek tugged my hand forward, and we began walking again. I kept my eyes open as we walked. I saw people—ghosts—run up to me. Women and children. Just like this morning, some waved as if they didn't know anything was wrong and others seemed very aware, expressions somber as they followed me back to the village. I heard them saying *please* again, and I cringed with the thought of the ghostly crowd behind me. I squeezed Haldrek's hand and leaned into him.

"Just close your eyes if you need to."

I did so and let Haldrek guide me. The blue glow of the ghosts disappeared immediately, and my shoulders relaxed. He turned both left and right several times until I couldn't tell where we were in the village, but after a few minutes, I heard him gasp.

"By the dragons..."

"It's bad, isn't it?" I could hear the word 'please' even louder.

"Curse those priests for their slothfulness."

My throat tightened as I squeezed my eyes shut. Why did I think I could do this?

"Would it be easier for you to see the spirits?"

"I think so."

Haldrek turned me around to face the way we had come. "You can open your eyes now. The bodies are behind you, so you don't have to look at them if you don't want to."

I opened my eyes and gasped at how many spirits faced me.

"Llamryl mentioned earlier where they have been laying out the bodies for burial. I... was thinking of us coming here tomorrow, but with you wanting to do the rites tonight... I thought this would be the best place to start. If it's too much, we can go back."

I shook my head. "Tell me how to do the rite. Please. Before I get too angry." Or lose my heart. There were so many people, and the sound of their pleas made me want to cry.

"Choose a person to focus the rite on. You can do only one person at a time."

I surveyed the crowd for a single person to focus on. The crowd split apart as I saw two young men walk forward with an older woman between them. She resembled a Lohikärran rather than Hethurin, making me wonder why she hadn't had her rites done yet. As I focused on her, I heard the crowd's murmur change from '*please*' to '*Geirny*'. She bowed low before straightening her shoulders and nodding to me. The two young men—teenagers—wrapped their arms around her as if to support or comfort her.

"I'm ready." I tried to steady my voice.

"*Tenelth, Lohikärras første drage,*" Haldrek's voice deepened as he closed his eyes and lifted his arms to the crowd.

"*Tenelth, Lohikärras første drage,*" I copied him, closing my eyes and lifting my arms. Much to my surprise, while the rest of the crowd faded out, I could still see the older woman—Geirny—in my mind's eye.

"*hastighet denne sjelen,*"

"*hastighet denne sjelen,*" Geirny's spirit focused on me and a whisper of air—or something—brush past my arms toward her. It tickled me, and I tried to focus on Haldrek's voice.

"*ærverdig i døden,*"

"*ærverdig i døden,*" The pull of the air or energy grew stronger, but now I sensed something different. Gratitude. Something I hadn't experienced in... forever.

"*til den høye salen,*"

"*til den høye salen,*" I focused on Geirny in my mind's eye as a brief smile touched her lips.

"*til Mirroth.*"

"*til Mirroth.*" I opened my eyes to see the bluish tint of her spirit change into white. She mouthed something, and I swore I heard '*thank you*' in the air. She disappeared, and it was as if an immense weight fell on my chest. My knees buckled and Haldrek grunted as he caught me.

"Easy." He helped me sit on the ground as the heaviness faded away and I gasped for breath.

"Like I said, each rite wears on you. How are you feeling?"

I stared at the two young men who had been with Geirny. They bowed and faded back into the crowd.

"I could do a couple more tonight. There are two boys? Men? With the spirit, I just did. I think they're related to her. Could you help me do theirs?" Fatigue seeped through me, but I tried to push through it.

"Of course." Haldrek helped pull me up to a standing position. I closed my eyes and lifted my arms once again, focusing on one of the young men.

"Ready?"

"Ready."

◈

That night, I found myself back in the Realm of Ghosts.

Instead of the palace at Drattüjert, I was in Svangendom's great hall, sitting on the edge of the fire pit and looking up at where the thegn's chair should have been. Instead, there were twelve stools in a semicircle and a much more ornate chair than I had ever seen, in the middle, with jewel encrusted staff beside it. Behind me, the fire pit glowed with a bluish fire, giving an eerie tint to the entire area.

"I know she is your daughter, Ingmar, but I must agree with the other thegns. Hardbein would have been a more fitting heir."

My stomach twisted into a knot as I saw my father walk into the light of the fire pit with another man. Both dressed in fine attire and decked out with various baubles, which glinted in the bluish light.

"No. Hardbein is loyal to Thegn Lansiranikä and would never put Svartån first. If I had named him heir, I might as well have given my lands to Bjorn."

Another man snorted as he met them at the half-circle. "And who will take the title when your daughter gets her head lopped off in her first battle? At least if Hardbein was thegn, he could defend Svartån."

My father glared at the man. "He could, but he wouldn't. I stand by my decision."

More men joined from the shadows until they filled the twelve stools.

Their muffled conversations came to a halt, and each man stood up posthaste. A tall woman dressed in ornate gold-lined robes and brown hair braided into a crown around her head walked past me. She didn't acknowledge any of the men. She just took her place at the center chair and grasped the staff that stood next to it. Only then did they sit down.

"Ingmar." Her tone rang out, and while it was firm, I didn't fear it. Instead, a strange comfort filled me.

My father stood up and bowed low to the ground. "Fairest Ottkatla, mother of Svartån."

"Your daughter ascends to my throne, now does she?"

"Yes. I—"

"And with no training in the ways of the thegns or Lohikärra?"

A few of the men held their hands to their mouths to suppress laughter. They fell silent as soon as Ottkatla glared at them.

My father straightened up and said, "She has knowledge of this land. I tried to give her what little I could. Before I brought Svante's body back. I had every intention of returning for my daughter if Kalle allowed it."

"Yet what little she has, was given to her by Svante. Even after his death and return here."

Awkward silence, and then my father bowed his head. "I would have brought her here if I knew I could do so safely. I have erred, Mother Ottkatla."

"She is not worthy then!" One thegn stood up abruptly. Ottkatla stared at him, not blinking, as he continued, oblivious. "We have no knowledge that she is a true heir and not some wench's offspring. Ingmar himself declares that her mother was a mage. A practitioner of wicked illusion arts at that."

"No, I said, she *beguiled* me. There is no magic in the world I went to. Sigyn had a way with words. No different from some thegns Lohikärra has seen through the ages. And we *were* married. I claim Ina as my legitimate daughter and heir, whether or not anyone disputes it with me."

Another man on the other side of the half-circle stood up as well. "Why not marry and produce an heir here, Ingmar? Then there would be no question of your heir's lineage."

"In case you didn't notice, there is a bit of a war going on, Ketill. Once High King Kalle ordered me to stay and fight, I had no time, nor any desire. *Given that I already had an heir.*"

Yet another man stood up, this time next to my father. "I trust Ingmar. Despite being a bit unconventional, he holds true to Lohikärran culture, and he has proved himself in other ways. If he says the girl is his heir, so she is."

"And there is that!" A young thegn near Ottkatla stood up. "Never has Svartån had a female thegn since fairest Ottkatla herself. How are we to know if she is not only worthy, but capable? She has no fighting skills. She'll die the first time she sees combat. So why put Svartån into chaos twice?"

"If not Ina, then who?" My father's voice boomed and, in an instant, the room was chaos, with all the men arguing and shouting above each other.

"Enough!" The floor shook with Ottkatla's command, and the men went silent. My father bowed to her once again as she glared in disapproval at all of them.

"Maja Ingmar Svanunge is weak. *For now.* But she is capable of far more than even she knows. My dragon sister Rhaegos tells me she seeks the girl. 'Ina', as she is called, will not only become thegn of Svartån, but much more. However, she must not let her fears impede her. If she conquers those fears, she will be a mother of Lohikärra, much as my mother Freya was and," Ottkatla glared at the young thegn who had questioned me for being female, "as many other female thegns have been."

The young thegn stared at the floor as the other men murmured. The first man to object to me bowed his head in respect. "If you accept her, Mother Ottkatla, then I shall as well."

"Then you all will need to help her from your positions as past thegns. Or at the very least, not impede her." She paused for a moment. "Ingmar?"

My father looked up at her.

She smiled. "Will you give her the pendant of Svartån?" Ottkatla held out her hand with a familiar-looking necklace.

"If you desire it, Mother Ottkatla." My father stepped toward her to take the necklace and then back to where he stood.

"I do. And tell her to find me in Aldinnvollr. If the gesiths and people of Svartån are to accept her, she must show them a token of my acceptance."

In a blink of an eye, they had all disappeared, except for my father. He came over and took my hand as he sat next to me on the edge of the fire pit. "I needed you to see that. So, you could understand—a little of what's going on behind the scenes."

I ducked my head down as he put the pendant and chain around my neck before pulling my hair out from under it. "What would have happened if she hadn't accepted me?"

"Rhaegos may have come to Svangendom to eliminate you."

I stopped and stared wide-eyed at my father. He laughed. "No. I am joking. I doubt that would have happened either way. Especially if Rhaegos seeks you."

"Rhaegos... I think she was the dragon that rescued me and the other thegns. If she's looking for me, why didn't she grab me then?"

My dad shrugged. "I don't claim to know the intentions of dragons. Nor do I question them. There is a saying from your world about that wisdom. Something about dragons and crunchy ketchup?" He frowned. "I just remember hearing it and thinking it sage advice. I doubt I was the first person to travel from Lohikärra, and now I wonder if perhaps that phrase originated with earlier travelers from here to there?" After a moment, he shook his head. "It doesn't matter."

He patted his pant leg and pulled another necklace from his pocket. "Before I forget... this is for Mattie. Her father, Svante, would haunt *me* if I forgot to get this to her."

I frowned. "Isn't he in Mirroth?"

"Yes. But it is a saying. He would be very upset with me if Mattie didn't get a pendant signifying her place in the house of Andrattür."

My eyes widened as questions piled up in my mind. If Mattie *was* of the house of Andrattür, that meant...

My dad continued, his thoughts on another track. "As a person fully of this world, when Svante died, his spirit was pulled back here. And that's why I had to bring his body back. So that his rite could be done. It would have reflected poorly if I hadn't. And he was my best friend."

I focused on the ground again, thinking about what my next steps should be before turning to my father. "Thank you. For believing in me."

"You're doing well so far. I saw what you did for the Hethurin and to the priests of Tenelth. I'm proud of you."

My thoughts went back to what Ottkatla had said. "Do you think what Ottkatla said about me is true?"

My father nodded. "As long as you don't let your fears keep you from becoming an excellent leader. And as long as you get that token in Aldinnvollr."

I grinned, letting myself enjoy the idea of being... important. Capable. Responsible. Not just a random, worthless person, like my mother always said.

"I'm going to send you back to the Realm of the Living now. Take care. I will be watching over you."

I blinked, and my orientation changed. When I opened my eyes, I saw wooden beams above me, and some kind of heavy cloth draped over them. I was in a bed. A fancier bed than I could have ever imagined. Heavy, warm fur blankets covered me, and I could hear the low crackling of wood burning across the room from where I lay.

The night before came back to me. After doing the rites for the two young men, I hadn't been able to get up again. Haldrek had fetched one of the night guards to walk with us back to the estate and keep the way lit as he'd carried me back into the hall. Part of me was embarrassed and felt like a burden, but my exhaustion had overwhelmed me to where I couldn't move, much less fuss. Inside the thegn hall, I'd heard people fret until Haldrek told them about the rites.

Then I fell asleep, more tired and empty than I had ever been in my life.

Now I was awake. And more refreshed than I expected. Haldrek—or someone—must have brought me up here. When I sat up, a physical weight around my neck caught my attention. A pendant. And in my right hand, I held another one. Mattie's. As I examined it, I noticed that the front had the Gunvald Gaming Studios logo engraved into it. My conversation with my dad, as well as the revelation that Mattie and Haldrek were siblings, weighed down on me more than either pendant.

A knock at the door pulled me out of my thoughts.

"My lady? Are you awake?"

I groaned as I tried to roll out of the bed, my muscles aching more than I thought possible. "Yes."

The door to my room opened up and a servant girl popped her head in for a second before disappearing again. Then she came in with a curtsy.

"Master Skuti told me to check on you. And Thegn Andrattür told me to wake you up if you were still asleep."

"What time is it?" My skin tingled with nervousness as my stomach grew heavy. The few times I slept late growing up, my mother had punished me—whether or not I had an excuse.

"Near midday." The girl began opening up and browsing through the two wardrobes in the room. "Not to worry, though. Master Skuti and Thegn Andrattür spoke of all you did yesterday. It would exhaust anyone." She sighed, looking at the last wardrobe. "My apologies, my lady. Master Skuti is seeing that some proper attire is made for you. In the meantime, you may wear what clean attire is here, though it be your father's, or I can find you something more feminine if you wish, though it would be of lesser material."

My head spun and my stomach growled as I saw another young woman bring in a tray of food behind the first girl. I was starving. It felt awkward to have someone tend to me, given how I'd grown up. But food was more important right now than clean clothes. "I... uh... can wear whatever attire is here, if it'll fit me."

The girl bobbed her head and gestured to the table where the food sat. "If you would like, you can eat. I will find something for you to wear." She turned back to the wardrobe she'd just been in, and I made my way over to the food on the table.

Dried fruit, bread, and a steaming stew similar smelling to what I had had at the inn sat on some kind of metal plate wear. A spoon and a sharp knife accompanied the meal. With brief hesitation, I ate the stew. It filled me up more than I thought. When I finished, I turned around to see the girl staring at a set of clothes laid out for me on the bed. She glanced up.

"I hope this is pleasing, my lady. I tried to find what I thought would fit you best."

"It looks good to me. Let's see how it fits."

A bit later, I walked downstairs to the main hall in my new attire. Despite what the maid had said, I didn't think it looked too masculine. I still wore pants, a long, woolen undershirt, and the quilted gambeson I'd had ever since I arrived here. But on top of all of that, I now wore an ankle-length, sleeveless tunic with buttons from my neck to groin. The rest of the gown was open, allowing me to walk more like normal than I expected. The maid had also given me a belt and a small leather pouch attached to it. I tucked Mattie's pendant in there for safekeeping until I could give it to her.

As I walked up to where Haldrek, Mattie, and Skuti were talking, Haldrek glanced up at me and smiled wide, as if he was trying to keep himself from laughing.

"You look even more like your father now that you're wearing his clothes."

Skuti turned around and grimaced. "My apologies, my lady. There haven't been too many women of high rank abiding here since your grandmother. I've seen to it that you will have more feminine and better fitting attire made soon." He focused on the maid behind me and waved her away. She hurried off.

"It's not that bad. I can still move around in it, and I'm used to wearing pants where Mattie and I come from."

"Still, it is fitting that you have your own attire. Especially once you become thegn." He continued to look me over, though with a more analytical eye, until he stopped at my pendant. "Hmm... Did you find that in the thegn's quarters? Or have you had that pendant all along?"

"My father gave it to me. Last night." I turned to Haldrek and Mattie. "He pulled me into the Realm of Ghosts again. I got to see him argue with other thegns in front of Ottkatla over who would be a better thegn. Then Ottkatla said that she accepted me. Said something about going to Aldinnvollr." I inspected the pendant more closely. It had an engraving of what I assumed was a swan lifting off into flight. Much like the back of the thegn's chair. The swan itself was inked black. "She told my dad to give this to me."

"More proof that you are the thegn-heir." Haldrek walked over with Mattie trailing behind him. He pulled out his pendant. Both of ours had a button-like knob at the top. I pushed the knob in on mine, making the front metal cover pop open, revealing a smooth glass stone held in place by the back piece of metal.

"What do they do? I got the impression that these are important, but..." I tapped on the glass-like stone, wondering if something would happen.

"Maybe they're like the charms from my dad's ga- stories." Mattie glanced at Haldrek for a second before looking at me.

I realized this was likely the most casual way to give Mattie *her* pendant. "You have one too, you know. My dad said your father would be upset if you didn't get yours." I closed mine up again and fiddled with the pouch on my hip, holding Mattie's pendant, trying to ignore the fact that Haldrek was now staring at me.

"She has one as well?"

I shrugged, trying to be nonchalant about the whole thing. "That's what my dad said." I undid the leather pouch strings and pulled out the pendant, giving it to Mattie.

Both Haldrek and Skuti leaned over as Mattie brushed her thumb over the engraving. After a moment, she turned to me.

"Are you serious?"

"That's what I was told."

Haldrek gripped his own pendant and scowled, his expression darkening as our attention turned to him.

"That *rutting alvjävla!*"

His voice cracked with the last word, and I froze, not knowing whether to stay away or try to placate him. Panic flooded me, but as quick as his anger showed up, it disappeared, replaced by a momentary slackness in his shoulders and jaw. He stared at the pendant; lips still pursed.

"Thegn Andrattür?" Skuti gestured for Mattie to stand behind him. She backed away from Haldrek.

Haldrek shook his head and dropped his pendant, brushing a thumb against each eye, not quite removing the damp shine from under them. "My apologies.

Ina... Mattie... Master Skuti... I..." He turned to me, his voice somber. "May I use your thegn stones again?" I nodded, trying to ignore the anxious pit inside my stomach.

"Yeah. Of course."

He left as I glanced back and forth between Mattie and Skuti.

Skuti turned to some of the books on the table next to him. "This makes things more interesting." He focused on Mattie. "I presume your father wed your mother in your homeland?"

"As far as I know. Why does that matter though?"

"Because you are a legitimate half-sister to Haldrek, and I say that because I do not remember Thegn Svartån mentioning any other traveling companions from Andrattür, other than Haldrek's father. Do you know your father's name, by chance?"

"Svante Gunvald. But I'm pretty sure that Haldrek and I are siblings." She looked in the direction that Haldrek walked off in. "Even if he's not happy with the fact."

"Why do you think so? I mean, other than the pendant?" Skuti cocked his head, gathering up the books.

"Well... Haldrek looks an awful lot like my dad. I noticed it yesterday, but I said nothing because, well... we were all busy with other things and..." She gestured in the direction that Haldrek had left. "Plus, my dad told my mom he had a son from a previous marriage. My mother got the impression that the reason my half-brother didn't come with him was because of immigration difficulties. But now I wonder..."

"The dragon stone?" I asked.

Mattie grimaced. "If it flung the two of us into random places, maybe he feared Haldrek would get flung into some random place or—"

Skuti cleared his throat. "Or it is something far simpler than that. Thegn Andrattür is the only son of your father and his first wife. So, if anything happened... Haldrek would be his heir. If he had taken Haldrek with him, there would have been much contention in Andrattür after your father's departure."

I frowned, glancing back at my pendant and then at Mattie and Skuti. "So now that Mattie's here, how does that affect Haldrek?"

"It shouldn't affect him much." Skuti shook his head. "Haldrek is still thegn for the foreseeable future. But until he marries and has legitimate heirs... Mattie could claim to be the next thegn of Andrattür if something should happen to him." He sighed. "That said, with the most current events—"

"*Master Skuti...*" Haldrek's voice boomed in warning and even I jumped as he entered the hall. "Now is not the time for gossip."

Skuti bobbed his head in deference. "Thegn Andrattür. Of course. My apologies." He looked back at me. "I should return these books to your library. I also need to find that Hethurin man from yesterday..." He turned to me. "You mentioned something about Aldinnvollr? I assume that is to get the thegn armor, correct? You'll need something to wear before then and the Hethurin can help you." His head spun back and forth until he saw someone.

"You there! Come here!"

Llamryl quickened his pace as I glanced over at Haldrek. He still wore a grim, annoyed frown as he glanced at Mattie.

"Master Skuti?" Llamryl bobbed his head with respect.

"When Lady Ina finishes speaking with Thegn Andrattür, please take her and her friend Mattie to the armory. There should be some armor and weapons there fit for them to use for the present time."

Llamryl bobbed his head, and after a quick bow to both me and Haldrek, Skuti hurried off.

Haldrek turned his attention to Mattie, his voice still terse. "Do you know anything about the Annals? In particular, the Mirratoft Annals?"

She pursed her lips thoughtfully. "I want to say they're a record of some kind? I remember my... dad mentioning them. In his stories."

Haldrek nodded. "They're a genealogy. Each of the thegn families has one recording their ancestry back to Bjornulf the Brave and his wife, Freya. In Svartån, it's the Svanunge Annals. In Andrattür, it is the Mirratoft Annals."

"So those descended from Andrattür's thegns would be in the Mirratoft Annals?" Mattie asked, her voice soft.

"Correct. The story goes that there is some kind of magic imbued into each set of Annals. That allows the books to keep a somewhat accurate record of one's relations."

"Somewhat?"

"The Annals have been around for over two thousand years." Haldrek grimaced and sighed. "Bjornulf and Freya had *lots* of descendants, both legitimate and illegitimate, so the magic doesn't always add people to the books as soon as they are born. And people don't often look into the books until there is an issue over inheritance. Like Ina and Hardbein."

Mattie straightened her posture as her expression grew cautious. "So... am I in the Mirratoft Annals?"

Haldrek paused, looking around at our small group. He locked eyes with Llamryl and gestured toward the stairs behind us. "The armory? Would you check on it? See what armor is available for Ina and Mattie?"

Llamryl bobbed his head. "Y-yes. Thegn Andrattür." He hurried off as Haldrek turned back to Mattie and me.

As soon as Llamryl left, Haldrek focused on Mattie. "I had my *husceorl* check. You're in the Mirratoft Annals." His gaze fell to the table between us. "And you're my half-sister."

We were quiet for several minutes as I tried to gauge Haldrek's demeanor. His face carefully guarded his emotions. He didn't seem happy about the fact, but he didn't seem *angry* either.

Finally, he spoke up again. "If my—*our*—father was still alive, I'd have many questions for him. That said, the implications of us being siblings are not as important right now as ensuring Ina takes her rightful place as thegn of Svartån. So as long as you are an ally to her, I have no quarrel with you."

Mattie nodded. "I would never hurt my best friend, so as long as you are nice to her... I have no quarrel either."

An hour later, Mattie, Haldrek, and I returned to the hall from the armory. A long chain mail shirt that Haldrek had called a *hauberk*, and a vest made of dozens of small leathery plates had replaced my masculine 'dress'. On top of it all was a woolen robe with Svartån's insignia on it. Leather gloves covered my hands while more chainmail covered my legs and feet and cinched tight into leather boots. Despite the many layers, I felt more flexible and agile in the armor than I had in the other clothing.

Skuti glanced at me from where he stood speaking to a man with salt and pepper-colored braids in both his hair and beard. They clinked as the stranger shifted to see me.

"I wouldn't worry, if I were you, Modolf." Skuti gestured to me. "While the thegn fell at the Battle of Drattüjert, it seems the dragons haven't forgotten us yet."

Modolf glanced at me and then focused on Skuti, wide-eyed with surprise. "So, *she's* the thegn-heir of Svartån?"

Skuti crossed his arms and raised an eyebrow at the man. Modolf straightened up, turning to me. "City guards saw Isillas ships on the horizon from the Eldingheimr lighthouse early this morning. The gesith of Eldingheimr requests men if you have them."

I looked back and forth between Haldrek and Skuti. The thought of fighting chilled me. I had no training. Plus, that would delay me getting to Aldinnvollr.

That said, I knew that coming to Eldingheimr's aid would help me in the eyes of Eldingheimr's gesith. And I could use all the goodwill I could muster.

"We—I—will send men. And I... will join them." I turned to Skuti, who had an eyebrow raised at me. "How many warriors do you think we can pull away from repairs on the estate?"

"I would advise a *sattar* of men." He turned back to Modolf. "How many ships?"

"Only two, but still..."

"We don't... want to look weak." I said with a soft voice, betraying my attempt to sound more confident than I felt. I didn't want the Isillas to think we were prime for an invasion. Not after the initial attack. "Skuti, will you...?"

He bobbed his head. "I think one of the Hethurin *sattars* would be more than happy to engage the Isillas once again."

"My lady?"

I turned around to see Llamryl walk up behind us. He bowed before me and Haldrek.

"I would like to take my men to fight beside you if need be. Many of them fought against the Isillas when they attacked here, and they would be eager to repay that."

"How long would it take to rally your men?" I focused on Modolf. "I expect the gesith wants warriors as soon as possible?"

"Yes, my lady."

Llamryl walked past us and down a few steps. "My men will be ready within the hour. We will meet you at the northeast gate, if that pleases you."

"It does. We'll meet you there."

Llamryl hurried off, and I turned to Haldrek. "I assume you want to join as well?"

"Of course." He grinned.

I turned to Mattie. "Will you come as well?"

Mattie glanced at Haldrek before focusing on me. "If you want me to. You know my fighting skill."

I laughed. "You can throw a few fireballs at them."

She smiled widely as well, and I turned to Skuti. Before I could say anything, he shook his head.

"I'll keep things running smoothly here at the estate. And make sure those priests don't slack off again."

I took a deep breath and turned to Modolf. "Then let's go to Eldingheimr."

# Chapter Six

Eldingheimr was quieter than I expected. Despite being a good-sized port city and looking similar to what I remembered in the games, the lack of people milling around and quietness as Haldrek and I rode through the city gate unnerved me.

"My lady?"

I stopped my horse. Modolf approached me on foot from behind.

"Something's wrong, isn't it?" I asked.

He grimaced. "There should have been guards at the gate." Putting his hand on the hilt of his sword, he surveyed our surroundings. "I'd ready my weapon if I were you." He then glanced back at Llamryl and his men. Llamryl raised his hand and the men behind him shifted into a defensive position. Even Mattie looked alert, and little flames licked the outside of her right glove.

My stomach squeezed tight as I focused on Modolf and grabbed the hilt of my sword. Was I really going to fight?

We continued into the center of town. As we turned the corner to where the docks were, I could hear the terse sound of people whispering to each other and saw a crowd of villagers staring down a group of soldiers. Isillas soldiers. They stood in front of one of the nicer buildings in the area, blocking anyone from coming near it.

"By the dragons..." Modolf gasped. "Where's the gesith?"

"Probably in his home." Haldrek said in a low voice. "With whoever the Isillas are protecting."

"The gesith would never negotiate—"

"But he'd buy us time." Haldrek got off his horse and turned to me. "Ina. This is your time to show Eldingheimr who you are. I'll have your back should there be a fight, but you need to be the leader."

I slipped off my horse, chest pounding. Looking back at the *sattar* behind me, I got the sense that bringing them into the tension between the Isillas and the townspeople wouldn't help. Instead, it might cause more bloodshed than I wanted.

"Llamryl? Have your men stay alert, but don't have them do anything. Yet."

He bobbed his head once, and the men relaxed a little behind him, filling the street, but keeping out of view of the main crowd.

I waved Mattie over and focused on Haldrek and Modolf. "So... do I announce myself or just try to walk in there?"

Haldrek glanced over at the large group. "They won't let you in unless you demand it."

I grimaced, uncertain of *how* to do that. Making myself the center of attention was terrifying enough, but demanding something?

"Who do I demand to see? The gesith? Or whoever is leading the Isillas?"

"The gesith." Modolf said. "We don't know *who* is actually leading this group."

Haldrek grumbled. "I *think* I know, but... Modolf is right. We don't know for certain. And the gesith was the one who asked for aid."

I turned back toward the crowd. The tension between the townspeople and the Isillas was growing, and I wondered if I could use that to help me. I also tried to imagine what I would do if this was the video game. As I took a deep breath, I walked forward into the crowd. Much to my surprise, they parted for me until I reached Isillas soldiers.

"I demand to see the gesith of Eldingheimr."

The Isillas soldier in front of me glanced down. "No."

Of course, it wouldn't be easy. "As thegn of Svartån, I demand you let me through."

"There is no thegn of Svartån, only Seirye, Prince of Unesari."

I turned to Haldrek and Mattie in disbelief for a moment before turning back to the elf.

"Who?"

The elf's pale skin reddened, making him look less corpse-like. "Unesari is what *your kind* call Svartån, but it was Unesari long before your arrival and it will be

Unesari long after." He placed a hand on the hilt of his sword. "Whoever you think you are, if you wish to see another day, I recommend you leave."

I heard a few sheaths rattle behind me, and I gripped my hilt. Haldrek said he'd have my back, but I was still going to protect myself—or at least try to—if the elves attacked first.

"Fine. As thegn of Svartån, I demand to see Seirye. *Prince of Unesari.*"

"No." The soldier pulled out his blade, and I flinched, pulling my own blade in front of me. Metal rang out as our blades met and I stumbled back. In an instant, all chaos broke loose, and I got pushed into the elf, landing on my knees and his chest. The point of my blade wedged in his throat, making him gasp as someone pulled me up and pushed me forward through the door of the manor house. I skidded to a stop in front of a doorway where I saw two men—rather a man and an elf—in the next room, facing each other.

"Bow before me!" The elf held his sword against the side of the man's exposed neck.

"Never!"

The door slammed shut behind me, blunting the din of the fighting outside. I glanced up to see Haldrek, Mattie, and Modolf in the house with me.

I stumbled to my feet and turned to see the elf swing at the man, who stepped back a second too slow and fell to the ground.

"Gesith Atlisson!" Modolf ran forward into the room along with me. A spell hit him, knocking him back to the doorway. He groaned but stayed put.

"And who are you?" The elf narrowed his eyes at me, making a part of me want to hide. My mouth dried up from the fear that rose inside me, afraid to say the wrong thing.

"I'm... the Thegn of Svartån."

"You don't sound very sure of that." One side of his mouth flicked upward.

"*I am* the Thegn of Svartån." I spat out the words again, hiding my fear with anger.

The elf stepped over the gesith, and toward me before he stopped. "I've fought the so-called Thegn of Svartån. Many of them. You are not any of them." He swung his sword at me, and I stepped back, dropping my sword as I fell on my butt. The tip of his sword just missed the chain mail covering my throat.

"Seirye!" Haldrek jumped over me, sword swinging.

The elf rolled out of the way and cast another spell at Haldrek, knocking him down. Haldrek groaned, and I grabbed for my sword, heart racing, as a spurt of fire shot toward Seirye. It nicked him, leaving a bright red welt on his cheek.

I turned to see Mattie on the other side of the room, wide-eyed in surprise. Flames licked her glove.

"Blunt-eared kythmage!" Seirye spat out behind me, holding a hand to his face.

I scrambled to my feet and swung at him with all my strength. My attack went high, and his helmet tumbled away—along with my sword—revealing ice white hair that blended in with his skin. Seirye's eyes widened with shock for a second and then I flew backwards, my entire body burning like it was frostbitten. Seirye scowled at me, his face marred by Mattie's welt. My chest froze and for a moment I was sure I was dead.

"*You* are not part of my plan." He glared at me before knocking Mattie to the ground with some kind of spell as she ran to my side. "And neither are you." Ice formed on his hand for a split second as I rolled over to block the spell he aimed at her.

Instead of more icy pain, there was a guttural shout and a thud. I turned around to see Haldrek on top of Seirye, dagger raised. As he went in for the kill, Seirye disappeared in a cloud of ice and Haldrek's dagger thudded into the wood floor.

"Bastard son of Ilva!" Haldrek's tone was deep and angry as he sat up. I rolled off of Mattie and surveyed the scene. Modolf was still against the frame of the doorway and clutched his chest just under his armpit as he stumbled to his feet. The gesith lay prone on the other side of the room, but I could see his chest rising—barely. Mattie was still on the ground next to me, and even though she groaned as she sat up, I was happy that she could move.

My body felt numb and cold—as if I'd been submerged in icy water for hours. Haldrek wobbled over to me and gave me his hand.

"Good job for your first fight." He turned at Mattie. "You too."

Haldrek glanced over at the gesith as he pulled me up. Modolf was already by Gesith Atlisson's side, and I could see a pale-yellow glow as he tried to heal him.

"Stop, Modolf. I'm tired." The gesith groaned, swatting at his hands. "Thegn…" He stopped and frowned as I knelt next to him. The same feelings from when I watched my dad die in my dream overwhelmed me again. "Whoever you are, send me to Mirroth."

I wondered if I had enough strength to do the ritual again and looked at Haldrek for support. Haldrek nodded, and I turned back to the gesith. "I'll send you to Mirroth."

He exhaled, and I watched as a blue haze developed above him, turning into a human shape. The gesith's ghost bowed to me.

I inhaled as I raised my hands and tried to remember the words. "Tenelth..." There was a pause as my mind swam, trying to remember the next words.

"*Lohikärras første drage...*" Haldrek's voice was soft next to me.

I repeated the phrase and let Haldrek guide me through the rest of the rite. When I finished, the gesith's ghost faded, disappearing to Mirroth.

After a moment, Mattie asked, "Now what do we do?"

Haldrek turned to Modolf. "Who was the second in command here?"

Modolf closed his eyes. "Me."

Haldrek's sorrowful eyes met mine. "It is the Thegn's right and duty to name a new gesith when one passes. Often, it's the second in command. Unless there is someone else that the Thegn wishes to be the new gesith."

I turned to Modolf, tired and achy and not wanting to go search for the gesith's replacement. "Modolf, do you want to be the next gesith?"

He shrugged, looking worn out. "I will do as you command. I am an old warrior. Devoted to Eldingheimr and its people. How long will I be a useful gesith, I don't know, but I will fight for my city, my people, and my thegn for as long as I can."

"Then you're the new gesith." I turned to Haldrek. "Anything I need to do formally?"

He shook his head. "You will have to say something tonight when you present yourself to the people of Eldingheimr, but otherwise, no."

"Then let's..." My head swam as I struggled to keep my balance. Haldrek knelt next to me and held my arm to keep me from falling over. It was comforting.

"Let's get you somewhere to rest. You'll need more energy for tonight. And for whatever lies ahead."

That night, Haldrek, Mattie and I sat at a round table at the upper level of the tavern, drinking the local mead and watching people celebrate the 'defeat of the Isillas' as the skald in the center of the room called it. He waxed poetic about how fierce I and the people of Eldingheimr had fought. I groaned as he went on, glad to be in the shadows up above. While Haldrek, Mattie, Modolf, and I had been confronting Seirye, the crowd outside and Llamryl's sattar of warriors had thrashed the soldiers who had come with Seirye. With the Isillas eliminated, Eldingheimr was in a mood to celebrate.

"Looks like you have won their admiration, Ina."

I turned to Haldrek and took a large gulp of the celebratory mead, enjoying the sweet flavor and how relaxed I felt. "For now. And I don't know what for. I didn't kill Seirye. That would be worth celebrating." My extremities still tingled from the ice magic he'd cast on me, despite the mead and the healing tonics Haldrek, Mattie, and I had received earlier.

Mattie sat beside me, across from Haldrek, watching the merriment and music below while taking a sip of her drink. She'd declined the mead offered, asking instead if they had something called kavasir. Her mouth turned upward into a grin as Llamryl started dancing barefoot on the coals in the firepit below while drinking from his mug as well. It seemed dancing on coals was a test of one's courage and strength here in Svartån.

"You did well for your first time confronting the Isillas." Haldrek flashed me a smile, making my cheeks heat up. "The Hethurin may not have powers of illusion, but the Isillas do. They are masters of manipulation. Even in our brief encounter, Seirye was trying to manipulate you."

"Really?" I stared at Haldrek in disbelief. "I mean, he made me angry, but he did nothing worse than... well, most other people in my life... before now."

"You've dealt with masters of illusion and manipulation before?"

I shrugged. "Maybe? I've never been witty or strong-willed enough to combat them though." That was the reason I loved the Lohikärra video games so much. I got to be a tough, badass warrior who battled through the land and defeated my foes. Something I couldn't do in my actual life. I took another drink of the mead, which reminded me of summer in Fargo. "I liked to pretend that I was. The stories of Lohikärra let me pretend I was the ultimate warrior. Undefeatable. But then I came to the real Lohikärra and... I'm the same person I was in Fargo."

"Well, you did something that a lot of Lohikärran warriors haven't been able to do. At least that I've heard of or seen. It was as though Seirye's illusion magic didn't affect you." Haldrek tipped his mug to me. "You might not think that is powerful, but it is."

I smiled, the thought of being powerful giving me more of a buzz than even the mead. "You think so?"

A half-smile lit up Haldrek's face, making my insides tingle. "I think you give yourself less respect than you deserve."

I laughed a little into my mug. "And I think you give me too much credit. Honestly, I could kiss you for everything you've done for me these past few days."

"Oh?" Haldrek's grin widened. "I don't think I'd mind that."

My cheeks flushed as I met his gaze. The room grew warmer, and the idea of us touching flooded me with giddiness. I leaned toward him. I wouldn't chase a kiss, but if he wasn't complaining...

He leaned forward, close enough that I could smell the sweetness of the mead on his breath and feel the heat from it.

"Hey, you two... You have a guest."

Mattie's voice pulled me back, and I turned around to see Modolf standing next to her. How long had he been standing there? I took another drink from my mug, hiding my face. I wasn't going to kiss anyone in front of an audience, but my thoughts tugged back to how close Haldrek had been.

"I... had a question. But I can return later if I'm interrupting."

Out of the corner of my eye, Haldrek shook his head and leaned back. I grimaced before pulling the mug away from my face. "Go ahead. What's your question?"

Modolf cocked his head in confusion and then focused on me. "May I ask a favor of you, my thegn?"

I nodded, my brain a little too slow for words.

"If you are traveling to Katla soon, would you take a box for me to the Hethurin orphanage near there?"

"Of course. Do you have it with you?" I shifted to sit up and paused as I wobbled.

Modolf shook his head. "I will bring it to you and Thegn Andrattür tomorrow if you wish."

"That works." I smiled, trying to lighten the serious expression on Modolf's face.

"Thank you, my thegn." He bowed again and as he turned to leave, the skald downstairs stopped singing, bringing a lull to the festivities.

A man, downstairs by the tavern bar, raised a flagon and shouted, "To our thegn, who chased off the Isillas and gave them a sample of Svartån justice. To Askel Atlisson, our noble gesith, who gave his life defending Eldingheimr and will forever enjoy the halls of Mirroth. And to Modolf, our new gesith, may he show our enemies what genuine fear is."

Haldrek tried not to crack a grin as he raised his mug. Modolf's eyes widened in embarrassment. I got the impression that he was not one for seeking attention. Haldrek shouted, "To Modolf!"

I raised my empty tankard, feeling jubilant. "To Modolf! The new gesith of Eldinghammer."

People cheered downstairs, and the music started up again as Modolf shook his head, grinning, and bowed to me once more. I turned to see Haldrek with a big, toothy grin. It made me want to kiss him.

"What?"

He put his tankard down and glanced at Mattie before focusing on me again, his smile softer and less playful. "We should get you to bed."

"Why?" I tried to sound like I was teasing him, just in case he was flirting with me again.

"Because you, Ina, are a lightweight."

Mattie and Haldrek helped me back to our shared room in the tavern that night. I had drunk more mugs of mead than I could count and was ready to sleep.

When I opened my eyes, however, I was back in the blue lighted main hall at Svangendom, and my father was pacing in front of the throne. Had I upset him? Had I not done the right thing with Seirye? Should I have gone to Aldinnvollr instead? I watched him until he noticed me. In an instant, I was in his arms as he squeezed me tight, lifting me off my feet.

"I was wondering how long you'd be until you fell asleep. You did well for your first encounter with Seirye. He's a sneaky bastard."

I smiled as my dad put me back down. "He's the same as the character in the games, isn't he?" There had been a minor elf villain referenced in some of the Lohikärra games named Seirye, and I only connected the two after the altercation with him. "You've dealt with him before?"

My dad laughed. "Yes. He's still pissy that Ottkatla overthrew him and has sworn vengeance on our entire family."

"Great. Am I supposed to defeat him once and for all?"

"That would be nice, but not required. After all, he has his own method of warfare. Attack, retreat, attack, utter destruction. Part of the reason he's so difficult to fight against. That said, you have another threat right now. One that may interfere in your ability to fight Seirye."

"Hardbein?"

He straightened up. "You *need* to get to Aldinnvollr. Hardbein isn't threatening to murder all the people of Svartån, but he will divide the land." My father paused. "Svartån needs to be united if it is to fight off the Isillas."

"How do I get Hardbein to go away then? And don't tell me to get the gesiths to pledge their allegiance to me. Haldrek's already mentioned that."

My dad sat on the edge of the fire pit and gestured for me to join him. "You already know. Ottkatla's token—the thegn armor—will prove that you are the chosen Heir of Svartån."

"So...? Head out for Aldinnvollr?"

"The thegn armor will be in Ottkatla's Barrow. Which is in Aldinnvollr. When you have gained it, Ottkatla will tell you what you need to do to gain the thegn weapon of Svartån—The Destroyer of Illusions. Once you have those, there is little that Hardbein can do to claim the title of thegn."

I grimaced, still not confident that I could do any of this. I wanted to be a thegn, and a powerful hero—but it seemed like a far-off dream. Even more fantastical than Lohikärra. "I'm not a warrior, Dad. Even if I gain Ottkatla's armor and the Destroyer of Illusions... How am I going to be a good thegn? One that people would follow? I know Modolf and the people of Eldingheimr pledged their loyalty to me, but will the others? And even if they do, I don't know the first thing about leading."

He raised an eyebrow at me. "What did you do when you first got to Svangendom?"

"I told Hardbein to leave?"

"You showed leadership. You started doing rites, training. I saw what you did with Llamryl's *sattar* today. You led them and they listened. Your gesiths will do the same. They will also give you advice and if you are wise, you'll listen to some of them."

"Will they follow me on a battlefield?"

"So long as you give wise counsel."

I stared at my hands, trying to focus on all the thoughts swirling around in my head. "How many gesiths do I have? Or should I have?"

My dad grimaced. "Fifteen—one for each major town in Svartån and one for the estate. You need to restore some of those positions, as you did with the gesith of Eldingheimr and as you will have to with the gesith of Svangendom. The rest will—or should—respect you as thegn."

I groaned, my head still swimming.

"You're going to have a miserable headache tomorrow morning, you know that?"

"From the mead?" I thought of how much I had drunk before going to bed. Eldingheimr had brought out some local mead for their celebration. It tasted good and made me more relaxed and less anxious than I had been in a long time, so I didn't refrain.

"You were keeping pace with Haldrek. He's bigger and has built up a higher tolerance to mead than you. Unless..."

I groaned, knowing that I was a lightweight and what that meant. "No, I never drank at home. Mother kept her liquor cabinet shut tight and getting drunk would just mean... yeah, I didn't drink in Fargo."

"Then you'll have a sizable headache when you wake up. Tell Haldrek to pour you a hangover tonic. It'll taste vile, but the headache will go away."

"Good to know..." I raised an eyebrow at him. "So, what else do I need to know? I don't even know what questions to ask right now."

"Know that I have complete faith in your abilities. You will be an amazing thegn and warrior one day."

I leaned forward and groaned again. As glad as I was to hear that, it didn't soothe my anxiety as much as I wish it did. "I still feel like an idiot for getting my butt kicked by Seirye."

My dad laughed. "You want to know a secret? Seirye kicked my butt the first time I met him. Completely fooled me into thinking I could overpower him. I didn't realize how much he relied on magic. Illusion or otherwise."

"I remember the ice magic he sent my way." I rolled my shoulders, as if to release stiffness from my muscles. His attack had given me superficial frostbite on my fingers, but Haldrek made sure I received the proper healing for that after we left the gesith's house. Still... it reinforced my feeling of weakness. "I barely know any magic or fighting skills. How on earth am I going to be strong enough to defeat him when he attacks again?" Mattie and I may not have been part of his original plan, but we were going to be part of whatever was next. If he hadn't stopped trying to invade Svartån since Ottkatla, then why would he stop with me?

"Training and more training, honestly. And *go to Aldinnvollr*." My father grimaced. "As loath as I am to admit it, Seirye was right in one regard. You're not the Thegn of Svartån. Yet. That said, the thegn armor of Svartån will strengthen your claim." He reached out for the pendant around my neck. "By the way, this will help you improve your skills as well."

I frowned at my pendant. I'd forgotten all about it. It didn't help that it reminded me of the awkwardness between Mattie and Haldrek. "How?"

My dad smiled. "The more you train and increase your skills, the faster it will fill up. When it does, you get a boost to either your health, your magical strength, or your stamina. Sometimes two or all three of them."

I grimaced again. "I'll probably be boosting my stamina for a while."

He laughed and stood up, helping me up as well. "You do as you see fit. I'm sending you back now. Sleep well and remember to ask Haldrek for that tonic."

The Realm of Ghosts faded from my view. But instead of waking up, I found myself back in the living room of the Fargo house. My mother stood in front of me, shaking her head, and a sense of unease fell over me.

"I can't believe you would accuse Robert of something like that."

The memory and all the attached emotions came flooding back in an instant. Soon after Robert had arrived, he had begun sneaking into my room. While he never actually touched me, he still creeped me out, and I had finally mustered up the courage to tell my mother.

Only to hear this.

The anger at her disbelief built up inside me. Why would I lie about something like this?

"I'm finally happy for once and you ruin it by accusing Robert of *watching* you? You're making *me* out to be the bad guy by saying this."

In real life, I had stuttered and stumbled over my words at this point. I wasn't trying to make my mom the bad guy. I just wanted Robert to stop. Now, though,

I stared at her, my voice ragged with anger and hurt. "You *bitch*. Why would I lie about something like this? Why wouldn't you believe your own daughter?"

"How dare you try to ruin my life? My happiness. I've done nothing but take care of you and protect you, and now you're telling me I'm not doing good enough? That the man I trust is hurting you? That I'm hurting you? How selfish can you be?"

"I'm not selfish! *I* was never selfish! *I* just wanted to be safe. *I* just wanted someone to protect me. *I* wanted a mother who actually gave a shit about me!" My language surprised me, but it felt good to tell her off finally. The weight of that resentment lightened, but in its place came aching tiredness.

"Go to your room. I don't deserve this abuse from you. You can come out when you're ready to apologize to me. To Hrothbere." Her voice changed from its normal harsh, heavy tone to a sharp lilt with the name.

*Hrothbere?* I had never heard her say that name before.

She walked off, and I closed my eyes, slumping to the floor as emotional exhaustion overwhelmed me.

Then a hand touched my shoulder. *Hrothbere.* The name popped into my mind again as I recoiled from the hand, sensing that it was Robert. I opened my eyes and realized I now sat in my room. It was nighttime, and while I couldn't see anything, I was hyper-aware of Robert's presence behind me.

"You really think your mother would believe you over me?" I could feel his lips by my ear as I tried to pull away. I was frozen, though, and the more I tried to move, the tighter he squeezed my shoulder.

"I wish you'd die, Robert." I said, wondering if I was still in this nightmare.

"She told me she regrets you even being born. That her life would be so much better if you didn't exist." His hand began stroking up and down my arm, tickling me and making me cringe at the same time. "But I know you are valuable. You have something your mother doesn't even know about. I just have to figure out how to... *take it.*" He grabbed my shoulder, harder this time, and I jumped away.

I expected to hit the hardwood floor and hurt myself, but there was nothing. I scrambled to get up and run, but only sensed Robert get closer behind me. He laughed and then shouted, "Who are you to be thegn? I'd be a better ruler than you. Or Hardbein."

I kept running as he got closer, and I got slower, weighed down by what felt like armor tightening around my torso and legs. Once I stopped, he grabbed my shoulder again, but this time I lunged back, scratching his face. As soon as my nails hit flesh, he screamed, and a bright light blinded me.

# Chapter Seven

I jerked away from the brightness and lunged again with my free arm, clawing at the presence as hard and fast as I could.

"Leave me alone, Robert!" My nails made contact with trimmed facial hair, and I recoiled. Robert was clean-shaven.

I opened my eyes to see the blurry outline of a person staggering back. He rubbed his beard roughly as I curled up on my bed against the wall. I sank my head into my pillow, trying to escape the headache that now enveloped it.

"Ow. It's Haldrek. You have sharp nails, you know that?"

I exhaled and closed my eyes as I groaned, shaking. No more mead. Ever. When I opened them, the door of the room was open and Haldrek had left. I wondered if I had pissed him off and he'd stormed away.

When he returned, he was still rubbing his cheek and held what resembled an oversized match. He lit the solitary candle on the small table between his bed and the one that Mattie and I shared. I realized that Mattie had disappeared as well.

"I'm sorry about scratching you," I said. "I…"

"It's fine. I startled you out of what sounded like a nightmare." He shrugged. "At least you weren't in the Realm of Ghosts again."

"I was, though. And then I fell asleep, and my nightmare started."

I figured 'nightmare' was the closest thing to what I experienced. Memories of my mother and Robert. Him chasing me. Even on the nights he hadn't snuck in to watch me, I had sensed his presence in my room, and it terrified me.

"So… who is Robert? You've mentioned him before, haven't you?"

"My mother's live-in boyfriend." I inhaled. "He…" My head throbbed sharply, and I ducked my head into my pillow, curling up into a ball again. "Do you have any kind of tonic that will help? Too much mead."

"Yes." Haldrek got up. "The barkeep will have at least one on hand." He hurried out of the room, leaving me to cope with my headache. The only upside to the pain is that it hurt too much to let me think about Robert or my nightmares.

A moment later, I heard footsteps and miserably looked up to see Mattie enter the room.

"Hangover?"

I groaned, not wanting to nod. "Never again."

She patted my back and pulled my hair out of my face before sitting down on the bed across from me, making it creak. I was too miserable to look up.

"I saw Haldrek heading downstairs as I came up. I guess he's going to get you something?"

I shoved my face into the 'pillow' I had slept on the night before. A mixture of funk and body odor from who knew how many people permeated it. It was disgusting, but the ache in my head faded.

"I talked to Llamryl this morning as well. He wanted to know what he and his *sattar* should do next." She sighed with annoyance. "Some people here were getting *antsy* about them being in the city. They were *allowed* to bed together in the tavern's stable only because you were here."

I twisted my head so I could look at her. "I'll talk to Modolf." Another wave of pain squeezed my head, and I groaned, burying my head in the pillow again.

A moment later, I heard footsteps and turned to see Haldrek put something on the table in the room. He then patted my back gently while sitting down on the edge of the bed. "This tonic doesn't taste good, but it'll take the headache away and help you feel less... miserable."

I sat up, holding onto his shoulder for stability, and squinted at the bright light seeping in through the window. Haldrek handed me the drink and pushed a piss pot in front of me. Not very comforting, to say the least. I pinched my nose and downed the concoction in a couple of gulps. It made my stomach churn as soon as it hit, and I curled back up on the bed, shoving my face in the pillow.

Haldrek rubbed my upper back as I fought the urge to puke up everything. If this was the 'cure' for a hangover, I would never drink mead again. After a few minutes, the queasiness in my stomach subsided, as did the throbbing in my head. I peeked from my pillow, opening one eye to see Haldrek sitting by my side, watching me, and Mattie still on the bed across from me.

"Never. Never again will I drink mead."

He laughed and leaned over as if to kiss my temple. I flinched, and he stopped. Instead, he gently tousled my hair and said, "We should probably get going soon. I have the package from Modolf as well. For the orphanage near Katla."

I eased my way into a sitting position as he got up to put his gear on. "What's our plan from here on out? Are we heading back to Svangendom? Or…"

Haldrek paused. "Or what?"

"My dad mentioned Aldinnvollr again. Something about armor and Seirye."

Haldrek nodded. "The thegn armor. Outward proof that you are the true leader of Svartån. And superb armor." He jiggled his chainmail leggings as he put them on and sat on the bed next to Mattie. "Better than this stuff. Mine should be back in Mirratoft by now."

I frowned, partially from confusion and partially from the hunger pangs that were now coming on.

"A thegn's armor, once he—or she—has claimed it, will always return to the thegn or their estate if it's lost or taken. The only reason it won't return to him—or her—is if they have died." He paused, as if remembering something. "I doubt Hardbein will be able to retrieve the armor from Aldinnvollr. But still… we should get there sooner rather than later."

"What about the package Modolf wanted us to take to Katla? And Llamryl's *sattar*?"

Haldrek grunted as he stood up and began tying his chainmail leggings to a belt around his tunic. "Delegation, Ina." He then wiggled in his own gambeson for a few moments before Mattie tugged on the bottom hem to help him. He glanced at her in surprise and then focused back on me. "It's not a thegn-heir's place to deliver packages. As nice as it was of you to agree, Modolf should know better. But what's done is done. If I were you, I'd have Llamryl and his *sattar* return to Svangendom and have him dispatch a few of his men to deliver the package on your behalf."

My face warmed up with embarrassment. I should have known that. "Meanwhile, we head to Aldinnvollr?" I tried to remember what the place was like in the last Lohikärra game Mattie and I had played. The name *sounded* familiar, but I couldn't picture it.

Haldrek pulled his chain mail shirt over his head. "How much do you know about Aldinnvollr?"

I shrugged and winced. My headache had disappeared for the most part, but my head still twinged if I gestured too quickly. Mattie turned to Haldrek as he put the stiff leather vest over his chain mail and looked at us for help.

Mattie got up and began buckling up the vest behind Haldrek. "How long has it been since Torsten Orrestsson was a thegn of Lansiranikä?"

Haldrek laughed out loud, making me jump. "Centuries. I mean, he's more recent than some other thegns that the epics speak of, but…" Haldrek paused again, as if thinking. "He fought alongside my—our—*ahnfader* Engli the Victorious. So… five hundred years?"

My eyes widened as I turned to Mattie and Haldrek turned around.

"What?"

She shook her head. "Nothing. That was just the last… story… epic… that I read. I thought it was more recent. I guess not." She glanced over at me, and I bobbed my head in agreement.

Haldrek frowned and shook his head. "The most recent was Hallmund the Orator. And that epic has been around a while as well."

Our conversation lulled before being interrupted by my stomach growling once again.

I stood up, expecting to be wobbly. Much to my surprise, I wasn't.

"I—we—should probably get ready." I looked down to see that most of my armor was still on me. The only things that I had to put on were my chain mail shirt, leather vest, and coat/robe-like thing with Svartån's insignia on it. A slight relief after the misery of the hangover and tonic. Though I didn't remember even taking those off.

"Haldrek insisted you'd sleep better with at least the chain mail and leather vest off." Mattie raised her arms as Haldrek helped her with her leather vest. "He said you'd sleep better if we removed the chainmail leggings as well, but I warned him that you kick in your sleep."

Haldrek rubbed his chest. "It still hurts where you kicked me last night."

I grinned a little. I *was* an active sleeper, and Haldrek didn't seem worse for the wear. Grabbing the chain mail shirt, I started looking for the arm and neck holes.

Haldrek stepped forward to help me figure out the shirt and gestured for me to stand up. My neck and chest heated up and emotions rushed over me without warning, as I did. A sudden jittery excitement at Haldrek's closeness, and then fear and shame. What was I going to do if he or Mattie weren't around to help me? I should know how to put my armor on by myself by now. Did he secretly think I was incompetent now? The delegation comment hurt, even though he didn't mean it that way. I should have known that already, though. Maybe I was incompetent? The intense emotions and comments from my mother and Robert in my nightmare came rushing back. I was the problem. Incompetent. An inconvenience to everyone else.

"Ina?"

Mattie's voice brought me back to reality, and I saw Haldrek holding the leather vest in front of me.

"Sorry." I put my arms out and let Haldrek strap me into the vest. "I should know how to do this by now."

Haldrek frowned as he walked behind me to cinch the vest, and Mattie cocked her head.

"How long have we been here? It's not like we grew up with all this stuff."

"She's right. You two have only been here a few days. And putting on armor usually requires another person's help. Which is why I helped Mattie earlier when she was putting on her armor and why I needed one of you two to help me with this leather plate vest."

I grimaced, my mouth feeling too heavy to say anything. When Haldrek finished, I put the last piece of armor on and turned to them.

"Thank you."

Haldrek shrugged. "We should get going. Aldinnvollr's more than a day's ride from here and we need to get there before Hardbein, if we can help it."

It was well after dark by the time we stopped to make camp. An old ramshackle tower—Osvif's Refuge—served as our temporary shelter. Mattie and I knew the tower from the previous Lohikärra game. In it, the chief character fought incursions of mountain trolls alongside the Thegn of Svartån, Osvif the Orc Killer. In the game, it was a high and mighty tower attached to a large stronghold.

Now the stronghold had all but disappeared except for the tower, which loomed high into the night sky. Still, it was useful for us as Haldrek created a campfire on the stone floor. He was also quick to unpack some wolf skins and other necessities from the bag he had somehow gained in Eldingheimr. For how much most Lohikärrans seemed leery of *using* magic, magical items seemed fine. So, it didn't surprise me when Haldrek mentioned that he had an enchanted satchel, allowing him to carry much more than usual.

After we had finished our small meal, Mattie went up to the top of the tower for her portion of guard duty. Haldrek and I rested and after a moment, he looked up from where he sat, tending to the fire. "You did good today."

"Huh?" I frowned in confusion, trying to remember what extraordinary thing I had done.

"Riding the horse and hiking through the deep snow, carving your way up the hill." He grinned. "You're hardier than you look, but it wouldn't surprise me if your pendant lit up soon."

I pulled the pendant from under my gambeson and examined it in the campfire's light. There was nothing unusual about the pendant itself, but as I fiddled with it, I pushed the button to open the front cover and saw that the glass inside looked different from when I had first opened it.

"Huh." The glass had darkened at least three-quarters of the way up and a bright '*2*' was in the middle.

"What?"

"Your pendant. Does it have a number on the glass?" I peered up at Haldrek as he watched me.

He grabbed the chain that his pendant was on and pulled it out to examine it. "On the glass?"

"Yeah. Mine has a two on it and looks like it's almost full of whatever this dark stuff is."

He popped his pendant open. "Mine says twenty-eight. It's almost full as well."

I laughed. These *were* just like the level up bars in the games. They showed you how far along you are until your next advancement.

"What's so funny?" A slight smile made its way to Haldrek's lips, and I tried to ignore how much warmer I felt just then.

"Just a memory. Of some games that Mattie and I played after she arrived in Fargo. One of the few nice memories from growing up."

Haldrek nodded, but said nothing. I watched his expression to see how safe it was for me to bring up something I had wondered about all day—his somewhat calm acceptance of Mattie being his sister. Even with his initial outburst of anger. I had expected more resistance or even complete denial. He didn't seem irritated by my comment, so I pushed forward.

"You and Mattie seem to get along better today."

Haldrek looked up at me. "What do you mean?"

"I mean, you two are acting like siblings, or at least friends. Which I'm glad for. I wasn't expecting it. I know if I'd found out I had a sibling I'd never known about; it'd take me time to wrap my head around it."

"Especially if they had more time with your parent than you did?" He winced and then shook his head. "I shouldn't say that. It sounds like most of Mattie's connection to our father is through whatever he left behind." He paused. "As it is, I had an interesting dream last night. My father visited me and told me not to punish Mattie for any misgivings I might have toward him."

"But..." I got the impression that there was more.

"I may have yelled at him for the misgivings I did... *do* have. I wished for a lot of things over the years, but that doesn't mean I will get them. There's nothing I can do to change the fact that Mattie is my... my half-sister." A grin popped up for a second before disappearing. "She is stubborn enough to be my father's daughter, that's for certain."

"I trust her, if it helps at all. She was the only person I trusted in Fargo."

Haldrek glanced away. "Perhaps."

I paused, trying to find the right words for what I wanted to say. "It's going to take time for you to trust her, isn't it?"

He bowed his head, focusing on the worn stone floor. "We've only known each other a few days and while I take your word—and my father's—that I should trust her..."

"What?"

"Only time will tell if I can trust her in the same capacity that you do."

A thought popped into my head and as uncomfortable as it was, I knew I needed the answer, or it would continue to bother me. "Why do you trust me, then? We've only known each other... four days? Why... Why trust me more than Mattie?"

"Simple. You and I've had a few more conversations like this than I have with Mattie. And... Rhaegos told me I could trust you. Before you even arrived."

I frowned, and he shook his head.

"It's not something to worry about for now. The most important thing is ensuring you become the Thegn of Svartån. All I'm saying is that I've only known Mattie a day or so and time will tell how much of an ally she will be."

Our conversation fell silent to the crackling of the campfire between us. I twisted my pendant around and thought about everything that I had seen and heard in the last few days. Especially compared to what I grew up learning.

Haldrek questioned Mattie's allegiances, and I questioned my reality. As much as I wanted Lohikärra to be real, and to be powerful for once... Who was I to be important? Lohikärra was real. This wasn't just some weird wish fantasy dream. So why wasn't someone like Mattie or Haldrek the hero of the story?

"Ina? Are you alright?" Haldrek's voice drew me out of my thoughts.

I focused my attention on him. "I'm just thinking about everything. It's hard to explain though."

"Try me. I'm sorry if I've come off too harsh. On Mattie, that is. I know you've known her longer than I have."

Taking a deep breath, I tried to organize my thoughts. "I... understand. I trust Mattie, but yeah... we've only been here a few days, if that, and... It's just surprising to me that Mattie isn't the hero of this story or game or whatever we're in. She has more talent, wealth, social ability, smarts, everything."

"Says who?"

"My mother. Robert. Most of the people that Mattie and I both knew. I'm just the idiot friend who likes the same world and stories as her. Growing up, my mother told me over and over that my education was a waste because I was so stupid. That..." My throat tightened as my sight blurred with tears and my cheeks grew warm with embarrassment. I ducked my head to hide my face from Haldrek.

"That what?"

"Nothing. I just... I feel like I... like maybe my mother is right and everyone who is saying I'm capable of these great things, like my dad and you, are overestimating what I can do? What if I'm just putting up a really good facade? What if I'm doomed to failure and I should just let others be in charge? Who am I to be in charge? How do I know if I'm responsible enough to be a thegn?" I rested my head on my knees and let my forehead sink into the chain mail. The discomfort of the metal links felt like some kind of penance.

"Ina... you're not putting up a facade. I've met many people who wear false faces in order to look good, both at my estate and at the palace in Drattüjert. They would never talk like you are right now. As for your mother... from what you and your father have mentioned, she sounds like a witch. One with great skill in the Illusion arts."

I laughed bitterly to choke back a cry. If magic existed on Earth, that would be the most logical solution. "If you can't trust your mother, who else can you trust? I mean... What if I am this oblivious screw up and my mother is right? She's known me my entire life. How do I know she's *not* right? I don't want her to be right, but what if she is? How do I know that people aren't lying to me just to be nice?"

Haldrek stood up and walked over in the tiny space we had made as our camp for the night. He sat next to me and wrapped his arms around me. Given his size versus mine, his arms enveloped me, and it was comforting. I started crying and said, "I don't want to be weak. I can't be weak."

"You're not weak." He sighed, holding me tighter. His hug was more comforting than I expected. "Your mother, it seems, is skilled with illusion magic. Like the Isillas. And you have been the target of her spells for many years." He paused. "This is why I despise illusion magic. Such spells can make you question your own mind. What you see, what you hear, what you think."

I nodded. "So, how do I... how do I undo whatever she's done?"

Haldrek sat up and stared at me. I noticed the color of his eyes for the first time. Blue like mine, but deeper somehow. Staring at them made me uncomfortable. Vulnerable. I turned away.

"If you have spent years having illusion spells cast at you, it will take time to undo the magic. Perhaps in the future, we can visit my estate. I know there are books there which talk about the reversal of illusion spells and how to ward against them. Until then, just remember that your mother's words are just spells. They are not real, and she used her magic to twist reality."

I kept staring at the wood burning in the fire as his right hand covered mine. It was comforting. How long had it been since I arrived in Lohikärra? Only a few days and yet... it felt like ages, and I felt like Haldrek and I were much closer than if we had met in Fargo. We were more than just peers and I sensed that Haldrek was helping me less out of a duty and more out of... something else.

I turned back and saw him watching me. He leaned forward and kissed the top of my head, near the hairline. My nerves lit up like electricity had zapped me, but in a good way. I froze, not knowing what to do. How to react.

We heard steps coming down from the tower and he took his hand off of mine.

"Your turn to stand guard, Haldrek." Mattie walked over to where we sat and raised an eyebrow at him.

Haldrek cleared his throat as he stood up and scooted around us.

"I'll be back."

"Haldrek." He stopped at the bottom of the stairs as I turned to him. "Thank you."

A warm half-smile crossed his face before he headed upstairs.

After a moment, I turned to Mattie. "How was it up there?"

"Cold." Her mouth twisted up. "It should cool Haldrek down a bit."

My cheeks warmed up more than they already were. "What do you think of him?"

She shrugged. "He looks like our friend Henry from back home, but his personality is different. He's not a bad person, I guess." She paused. "You like him?"

I held my breath for a moment. The sensation of his hug and the kiss on my forehead still lingered, and it made me feel good. Part of me wished for more. Like the kiss we'd almost had the night before. Still… "Only as a friend. I've only known him for a few days. Probably isn't smart for me to like him as more than that."

"It could be, given the circumstances."

I popped up in surprise. "What?"

"You both are or will be thegns, and Haldrek is the Thegn of Andrattür. Andrattür has always been one of the more powerful thegn-lands in the games. He seems well respected here in Svartån as well."

"What are you saying I should do?"

"Do what *you* want to do. If you're interested in him, don't hide from it. As long as he treats you well, see where it goes. And…" Mattie sighed. "If we're here for the long term, having Haldrek as an ally isn't the worst thing in the world."

I smiled, tossing a few sticks into the fire. "I do like him. It's just… every time I've liked a guy, he's either been into boys or into girls, not like me." My grin faded as I remembered a few of the guys I had had crushes on when I was younger. "For all I know, Haldrek's betrothed to some other woman here and… he's just doing me a favor, because of my dad—"

"He's not." Mattie laughed and looked up at me. "Betrothed, that is. At least that's what my dad said."

"What?" As soon as I opened my mouth, though, it made sense. Their dad had visited Haldrek, so why not Mattie?

"We've both been having funky dreams since we got here. My dad visited me once. First night after I arrived in Lohikärra. Since we'd been playing the game and then got thrown into this world, I thought it was all my imagination. Given everything that's happened while awake though... Anyway, he told me a bunch of stuff, including info on Haldrek and both his and my destinies."

"Which is? Are?"

"Haldrek won't be the Thegn of Andrattür for much longer." Mattie sighed and said, "He's... got bigger duties, so to speak. I guess he's in line to become the High King now? If the people of Lohikärra can kick the Blodnar out. If that happens, my father said I would need to take his place as thegn. Which I'm not sure I'm too keen on."

"Why not?" I frowned. "You'd be great ruling a thegn-land. You always did that well in the games. Plus, you've always been good at group projects and teams and... just people in general."

Mattie laughed. "Doesn't mean I enjoyed it." Her expression sobered up. "It'd mean being in charge and being the center of attention. *Always.* With the games at least, I could stop and do something else or go on some quest, and nothing would change until I returned. But I can't do that here. Plus, let's be honest, how well do you think the people of Andrattür would handle having a black thegn?" She poked at the sticks in the fire. "You like the games because you can be powerful in them. I like them because I can be anonymous."

"We can both be someone we're not," I said.

Mattie sighed. "At least here, you can act like your character. You did that pretty well in Eldingheimr. With Seirye and all."

My stomach twisted as I remembered yesterday's events. "I didn't feel powerful. Seirye almost killed me, and then I got drunk and did stupid things."

"Like what?" Mattie asked as she cocked her head at me. "You named a new gesith so Eldingheimr would stay safe, and you'd continue to have allies against your cousin Hardbein? You did what you needed to do. Seirye may have gotten the best of us this time, but you tried, and it showed that you're willing to protect your people. Both Seirye and Hardbein are trying to take your title from you. So, you need to prove that you're the one who deserves to be the Thegn of Svartån."

"Do you think I can do that?"

Mattie smiled. "You're strong. I've seen it. I've heard it. You just can't be afraid to let that strength out." She laid down on the wolf skins that Haldrek had made into a bed. "I'm tired. Unless you plan to go up top, I'll be back on guard duty soon."

I laid down on my pile of skins, listening to the crackling of the wood and embers. Tomorrow we'd be in Aldinnvollr, and I'd once again have to convince people I was my father's daughter and thegn-heir. I had done it in Eldingheimr, but as I fell asleep, I wondered if it would be that easy in Aldinnvollr.

"Ina! Wake up!"

Mattie shook me awake as I heard footsteps clambering down the stairs.

"What's going on?"

She threw my chain mail shirt over me as I saw Haldrek block the doorway and knock someone back.

"We're being attacked! C'mon!"

I pulled the chain mail over me as quickly as I could and grabbed a nearby sword and shield, my heart racing as I followed Mattie outside. One man was already on the ground as Haldrek cut another down.

"There she is!"

I spun around to see a man swing his sword at me. Without thinking, I put my shield between me and it. The blow knocked me to the ground, and I rolled away, my left arm aching as I swung at whatever moved near me in the dim light. I stumbled to my feet as my sword hit something solid, and I staggered. I tumbled over a large stone, hitting my back into the nearby rock wall and gasping as it knocked my breath out of me.

"Ina!" Mattie swung her shield above my head, another attacker backing off as I got to my feet again. She lobbed a fireball at him as another shout made me turn around. I swung at the man running at me and was rewarded with a grunt as my sword pushed through his armor. His eyes widened for a second as I pulled back, my sword pulling out of his torso with ease. Stunned, I stared at him, limp and bleeding on the ground. He curled to his side, and I screamed, jabbing my sword through him until he stopped moving.

Then I sensed someone's presence behind me. I jerked away and twisted back to see Haldrek behind me.

"Easy, Ina. We got them."

I realized I was shaking as he put his hand on my shoulder and I dropped my sword and shield to the ground. Mattie's tired groan made me look past him.

"Mattie?" Haldrek took a step toward the sound.

"I'm fine. I think. Waiting for the adrenaline to go away. Be careful, I'm next to a ledge. Guy slipped off of it before he could do anything."

She cast a small orb of light, showing us where the ledge was. Haldrek stepped gingerly toward her and put his hand out to help her. In a moment, he pulled her back to solid ground.

"No injuries?" Haldrek examined us as we returned to the tower.

Mattie sat down on the wolf skin pelts as soon as we got inside. "None that I can feel yet. I'll probably have bruises in the morning though."

"Same here." I shuddered and sat down on my wolf pelts, putting the sword and shield back where I'd found them. I noticed my helmet sitting on the ground next to them and groaned. Another reminder of how much I didn't know.

Haldrek exhaled. "Thank the dragons. You two stay here. I'm going to check and make sure there aren't any more surprises." He took a torch stump from near the doorway and lit it on the embers between Mattie and me before heading out again.

Once he left, Mattie leaned her head against the wall. "That was terrifying."

I sighed. "At least you could defend yourself."

Mattie shook her head. "I might have injured one or two, but the only reason that one guy is dead is because he didn't watch his footing."

The thought of Ottkatla's Barrow came to mind, and I groaned. "We're—I'm going to have to do that again when we get to Aldinnvollr." The thought of doing it alone made me sick, and the thought of not doing it made me feel worse. Either way, my chest squeezed tight with anxiety, and I gasped as tears started rolling down my cheeks.

"Ina?" Mattie crawled over to me and gave me a tight hug as I started sobbing, my body shaking as I tried to control my breathing. "Ina..." She squeezed me tighter as I tried to match her breathing and calm down despite my rising panic.

"I..."

"What's going on?" Haldrek's voice made me look up. Even through my tears, I could tell he was holding something in his hand.

"Panic attack. I think." Mattie said, her voice low. She squeezed me tighter and as comforting as it was, it embarrassed me that Haldrek was seeing me this way.

He sat down next to us and stoked the embers in our campfire, lightening up the small shelter. After a few minutes, he said, "Your first ambush is always terrifying, no matter how much you train beforehand."

"I'm... I'm supposed to do this... *this*...in the barrow, though. Alone. And... And I don't know how to fight." My heart had stopped racing, but my throat squeezed tight again as I ducked my head into Mattie's arm.

"You don't have to do it alone. At least not the first part."

I turned to Haldrek in confusion.

"If it's anything like Wiglaf's Barrow, there are two parts. The main barrow where your honorable ancestors are buried and the inner barrow where Wiglaf—or Ottkatla—is buried. I could enter with a few trusted individuals and make my way through with them. The inner room was the only place I had to fight by myself."

"What happened there?" My heart and nerves had calmed down, so I sat up.

Haldrek exhaled. "I fought some of Wiglaf's undead guard. Then approached his tomb where he bestowed my thegn armor upon me." He shuddered. "Worst part wasn't so much the fighting. It was the undead. They weren't the fastest or hardest warriors to fight. Just... undead. I hate anything undead."

If there were undead in Ottkatla's barrow, I could handle that. Maybe. But I still felt sick about fighting by myself. "Is there any way we—I—can train before going to Ottkatla's Barrow?"

Haldrek focused on the item in his hand. It was a blood-soaked piece of paper with scribbled runes splattered across it. "We should get to the barrow sooner rather than later. The men who attacked us are loyal to Hardbein."

"What?" Mattie and I spoke at the same time.

He gave the paper to Mattie and me. "Read it."

Mattie examined it for a few moments before cursing under her breath. She turned to me. "He's right. This is a note from Hardbein. It says to delay us one way or another until he gets to Aldinnvollr."

"How did they know we were heading up this path?"

He shrugged. "Hardbein likely had some of his men stay in a few of the towns nearby to Svangendom and just wait. It wouldn't have been hard for those in Eldingheimr to slip away in the chaos and aftermath of the Isillas attack." He stared into the still inky, dark night outside. "Let me check something."

After he disappeared, Mattie continued looking at the note. After a moment, she said, "The ink's a bit smudged by the blood, but... it says something about the new moon of Deepfrost. I think he's planning to be in Aldinnvollr by then."

"When's Deepfrost?"

"Right now? It's one of the winter months in the Lohikärran calendar. I can't remember if it's the second or third month after the winter solstice, but something like that."

I focused on the expanse outside the doorway. It was pretty dark now, but the moon had been out earlier. At least a sliver. I just had no idea if the new moon was coming up or already passed.

Haldrek walked back through the doorway, pulling me out of my thoughts.

"It's just as I figured. I checked the leather armor plating that one of the men wore. It had the insignia of Elheimsted on it."

"Elheimsted?" I frowned in confusion.

"The Lansiranikän thegn's estate." Mattie said. "Or at least it was in the time of Torsten. Is it still?"

Haldrek nodded. "Which makes me wonder how much Bjorn—the Thegn of Lansiranikä—is involved."

"Didn't Hardbein say that the thegn sent him after the Battle of Drattüjert?"

"He did, but that couldn't have happened. Bjorn was beaten and tied up with the rest of us after the battle. He was in no state to be sending any messages. Which is why I didn't believe Hardbein at Svangendom. There wasn't enough time for him to know or tell Hardbein of Ingmar's death." Haldrek turned to me. "Only one of two things could have happened—either he sent Hardbein ahead to claim the title as his own, believing that your father was going to die or Hardbein did so without Bjorn's knowledge. Either of which would be a foolish idea."

"How close were my dad and Bjorn—the thegn? Were they enemies? Allies?"

Haldrek shook his head. "They weren't close. But they weren't enemies, either. An uneasy peace made worse by Drattüjert politics and squabbling border villages. I think the only thing they agreed on was their hatred of the Blodnar."

"So, Bjorn could see Ina's dad's death as a boon if Hardbein became the next thegn." Mattie began poking the embers again and added a couple of twigs to rekindle the fire.

"He could. However, I'd caution against pointing any fingers just yet. Now is not the time for the thegns to be at each other's throats and without sufficient proof of Bjorn's action, Ina risks losing valuable support from many of the others." Haldrek plucked a few errant briars from his armor with a grimace and tossed them in the fire. "Plus, we've subdued the men for tonight. We'll be in Aldinnvollr by tomorrow and once Ina has retrieved Ottkatla's armor from the barrow, it will be difficult for Hardbein to claim thegnship."

I leaned back against the wall. The adrenaline from my abrupt wake up was fading, leaving me more tired than before. Mattie returned to the skins across from me as Haldrek began prodding the fire.

"You two can go back to sleep if you wish. I'll keep watch until we leave for Aldinnvollr."

"Don't you need to sleep at some point?" I tried to stifle a yawn, but failed.

He grinned and stretched toward me, grabbing his bag. "Any warrior worth his armor keeps a few tonics on him to stay alert. As long as I get some decent sleep in the next day or two, I'll be fine." He rummaged through the bag and pulled out a small glass cylinder. As soon as he opened it, he gulped the contents and grimaced. "By Tenelth's mercy, that... There are those who swear by these tonics, but I can't have more than one at a time."

Mattie laughed and curled up on her pelts. "I guess energy drinks aren't a new thing. Or something unique to our world."

Haldrek turned to her. "You've drunk something like this before?"

She laughed, bobbing her head up and down. I laid down, my exhaustion making it hard for me to keep my eyes open. Their conversation continued softly as I fell back to sleep.

# Chapter Eight

"So where is it?" I surveyed the area around us as we stood within eyesight of a stone gate that told us we'd arrived at Aldinnvollr. Despite leaving at daybreak, we had only just arrived, and the sun had already sunk behind the mountains.

Haldrek pointed to a narrow path where footprints had stamped down the snow. "Here. It looks like someone—or something's—taken this path recently though." He shifted his weight from foot to foot and played with his sword hilt. Something uncharacteristic for him. Then I realized, as nervous as I was about fighting, the idea of dealing with dead things probably didn't appeal to *him*.

"You don't have to come with us if you don't want to, Haldrek. I know you're afraid of ghosts. Just show me the entrance and I'll deal with the rest. This is my ancestor I have to go find."

He stopped fidgeting and turned to me and Mattie. "I'm no coward. Plus..." He hesitated. "I've helped you this far. I won't leave now. If I can survive the *ruumii* in Wiglaf's barrow, I can survive whatever is in Ottkatla's."

Haldrek tied our horses' reins to a nearby tree branch, and we began walking up the hill. Mattie conjured up an orb of fiery light in her right hand to light the way.

"Tell me about these *ruumii*. I think I know what they are, but I could be wrong."

"Ottkatla, much like Wiglaf, had a band of warriors who pledged themselves to her. Their lives, their deaths, everything. After death, they were interred here and became her *ruumii* or ghost warriors."

"So, we'll be fighting ghosts? Like the ones I saw at the estate?"

"No. When awoken, the *ruumii* invoke their bodies to fight. These are warriors of only skin and bone, but they fight as they did when they were alive."

"How do you kill them then?" Mattie turned to us with a frown. "If they're animated through magic, will normal weapons take them down?"

Haldrek grimaced. "We'll see." He grabbed the hilt of his sword on his back and turned to me. "A silver infused weapon can take down the *ruumii*. Both of you should have one, and I borrowed one from the armory at Svangendom to use until I can retrieve the Sword of Wiglaf. Once I get my weapon back, I'll return the borrowed one."

I shrugged. "I trust you. It surprises me that they'd leave anything silver infused just lying around in the armory."

"There are a few pieces, reserved for gesiths and other high-ranking warriors. I spoke to Skuti about it the first night we were there. It's not unheard of for thegns to have weapons in reserve for situations like this."

"Losing your sword and not having time to go get it?" Mattie said, as she stopped to look at him. "I mean... Anything made with silver isn't your run-of-the-mill weaponry. And thegn weaponry has to be more valuable."

"*Yes.*" Haldrek grimaced. "But sometimes an allied thegn or a gesith may lose their weapon and need a spare for a short time. And I didn't lose my weapon. The Blodnar took it from me when they captured me." He glanced back at Mattie in annoyance.

"What else—" I paused as we turned the corner around a ridge and saw a cave opening with a half-dozen men standing in front of it. Mattie's light disappeared as Haldrek pushed me down into a crouch behind a nearby rock. Between the men standing guard and the piles of bones lit up by their lanterns, I took it to mean we had found Ottkatla's Barrow.

"More of Hardbein's men?" Haldrek's voice and breath next to my ear made me stiffen up. "Does that mean—"

"Hey!"

One warrior wandered close to us, and before I could react, Haldrek was up, his sword unsheathed. The warrior staggered back, a hand to his face as Haldrek drove his sword across the man's exposed neck.

In a moment, everyone froze, and the air shimmered, forming into spirits, aware of us.

One of Hardbein's men turned his attention to me and scowled.

"The false thegn. Men, attack!"

By the edge of the cave, a pile of bones began rattling, and I pulled out my sword as one of Hardbein's men ran at me. Our blades hit, and I stumbled out of the way, swinging as much as I could to keep him at bay.

*Hail Svartån.*

I swung again at the man attacking me and turned around at the voice to see a skeleton enveloped in a ghostly haze skewer one of Hardbein's men. I gaped as I watched the creature. The haze that wrapped around the skeleton's bones acted as both skin and joints. While the haze was translucent, I could still make out facial features, and the shape of muscles and armor formed from it.

"Ina!"

My attention turned back to the man I'd been fighting just as his sword slammed against my helmet. I stumbled back and down with a cry, my head ringing. As he raised his sword again, the ghostly skeleton slashed across his chest as if he wore no armor.

"What the—"

The man collapsed to the ground with a groan as the skeleton stabbed him in the chest. The spirit looked down at me, shaking his head. Then he turned away and strode away, out of eyesight. Embarrassment replaced my fear as I realized what had just happened.

"Ina!"

I turned, my head still throbbing, to see Haldrek trot toward me. Around us, Hardbein's men lay dead on the ground, lit up only by the dim light of a few lanterns that survived the fight. The ghostly skeletons had also disappeared, their bones scattered across the ground once more.

"I don't know if I can do this," I said, dropping my sword and bending over to keep my balance.

"Are you all right? Are you injured?" Haldrek knelt down in front of me, looking around at the dead bodies and bones.

"*No.* My head hurts. I don't know how to fight. How can I do this?" I glanced at the barrow entrance. "What if Hardbein's already in there?"

"We fight him." Haldrek brushed his hand across where my helmet got hit and said, "Never take your eyes off your enemy. Thank the dragons, you had a good helmet."

I groaned. "There were ghosts fighting them too."

"I saw. They pulled up the bones to fight." Haldrek shuddered. "This is why I hate the undead."

"Would this be necromancy?"

Haldrek shook his head. "No. Very high-level *ruumii* magic, I'm guessing. These aren't normal *ruumii*. It's almost like any warrior who died here is magically bound to protect this area."

"Why did they start fighting when we arrived?"

Haldrek shrugged. "Maybe they recognized you? So, when the men attacked—"

Mattie groaned near us, and both Haldrek and I turned to her. She sat on the ground, leaning against a tree. As she held her right arm, she grimaced.

"Mattie!" I stumbled over to her as she looked up.

"Getting your arm cut open hurts a lot more than I expected."

Haldrek knelt next to her as she created a small orb of light with her free hand. Across her upper arm, the chain mail had broken and a cut in her gambeson was dark with blood.

"Not the worst injury I've seen." Haldrek turned to me. "Stay here, I'm going to grab something from my pack."

He disappeared into the darkness, and I turned to Mattie.

"Do you... How are you about fighting? In the barrow?"

Mattie shook her head. "Unless Haldrek brings back something to heal me..."

I grimaced, my worries increasing with the darkness. I stared in the opening's direction, wondering what awaited me inside. Honestly, this all scared me. This wasn't a game. It wasn't like I was going to respawn if I died. There were no cheat codes. Just me and Haldrek. Facing actual creatures, both dead and alive.

"You and Haldrek will be fine without me." Mattie hesitated. "I can head to Aldinnvollr. Maybe get a sense for the place." She winced.

"Any... any advice, then?"

"Keep your eyes on who you're fighting," she said. "Like Haldrek said. And try shooting some fireballs." A brief grin lit up her face. "Haldrek will keep you safe, I'm sure. At least until you get to the inner sanctum. After that, it's on you. But..."

"But...?"

"You're the thegn-heir. Unless there's some reason Ottkatla doesn't want you taking whatever item is in there... I think you'll be able to defeat whatever is waiting."

My dream from Eldingheimr rushed back to me. Ottkatla *had* accepted me. My fighting experience might not be the greatest, but... I needed to prove that I was thegn. Not Hardbein. Not anyone else. And if I didn't go in there, it'd be even more difficult in the long run.

"I can do this." I took a deep breath and said, "I just have to treat it like a dungeon run, right?"

Mattie smiled for a split second. "Yup. Just a dungeon run. Fight the *ruumii*, confront the boss. Just think the same thoughts as when you're fighting bad guys in the game."

I laughed. If only it'd be that easy.

Footsteps and hoofbeats in the snow crunched behind us. I turned around to see Haldrek leading our horses toward us, the two of them tied together.

"I have bandages and a healing tonic for you, Mattie." He grabbed them and made quick work of an ad hoc bandage covering her injury through the slashed chain mail and fabric as she drank the tonic.

"Unless you feel fit enough to fight, I think it's best if you stayed here. Once Ina gets the armor, we'll return to this spot before going into town."

Mattie groaned as she stood up and leaned against a horse.

"I think I might stay near the main road. I don't want to be here alone if the spirits pop up again."

Haldrek grimaced. "That's... a better idea."

"I'll see you two back at the main road then." She headed out, leaving Haldrek standing next to me.

"You ready?" He held his hand out to help me up.

"Ready as I'll ever be, I guess." I stood up and facing the cave, we made our way into the entrance.

Inside, the cave was damper and darker than I expected. An eerie blue glow lay before us, but it was still too dark to determine whether whatever created it was down a slope or straight ahead.

"Part of me wishes we had a flashlight. Or a torch." I mumbled.

"A torch would be handy. The undead don't exactly like fire."

I tried to remember the simple fire spell Mattie had shown me back at the thegn estate. As I stuck my left hand out, palm up, I said, "Too-Weli."

A fiery orb burst from my glove and hovered above it.

"Impressive."

I turned to Haldrek. "Now I just have to figure out how to throw it." The fire tingled my skin as it pulled tiny bits of energy out.

He was quiet for a moment before answering. "Try it. Just don't light me on fire."

I laughed softly and flicked my wrist as I said the words. "Too-Weli-Ballo." Instantly, the globe of fire shot from my hand, briefly warming the leather and my fingers before flowing straight and then down towards the bluish light. The craggy screams of some creature followed, and I gripped my sword hilt.

"Shit." I heard the scrambling of feet and swords below us.

"Still handy, I guess. Try it again." Haldrek urged me on.

"Too-Weli-Ballo!" Another fireball burst forward and lit up the hall, as well as a few *ruumii* who were climbing up from below. I gasped as the fireball hit and then consumed the skin that stretched tightly around their bones and muscles. The red glow from their eye sockets disappeared, and they fell back into a pit.

Haldrek charged forward and yelled, "Try not to hit me!"

I ran after him and released another fireball at the ruumii, climbing up after their fallen comrades. As I entered the room with the pit, I pulled out my sword as I turned to my right and swung at the closest skeleton. Its skull toppled down into the pit, where more skeletons scurried around. In an instant, I was pushed forward as Haldrek knocked into me. My left foot slipped on the edge of the pit, and I toppled into it.

"Ina!"

I hit the floor hard on my shield and rolled to my back, just in time to see Haldrek leap down next to me with half a dozen skeletons after him.

"TOO-WELI-BALLO!" I dropped my sword and threw both hands forward as a much larger fireball shot out of them. The recoil pushed me back a bit as the skeletons incinerated.

Then it was silent. Haldrek looked down at me as I tried to catch my breath and ignore the burning pain in my arms and chest.

I expected wielding magic to be less exhausting. My left arm throbbed painfully now. I moved it a bit. *Not broken.* It was definitely going to have a bruise in the morning.

"Are you all right?" Haldrek knelt next to me.

I nodded and put my hand on my chest to calm my racing heart. There was a click as the pendant pressed into my collarbone. I gasped as the floor dropped out from beneath me and everything blacked out. The Lohikärran runes for magic and stamina appeared in front of my eyes. They brightened and grew larger before disappearing. The room inside the barrow returned, and I saw Haldrek observing me. My heart still raced inside my chest, but otherwise, I was less nervous than I had when I entered the barrow.

I sat up, grabbed my sword, and shook my head. "Did I just... level up?" I pushed the pendant against my chest again as Haldrek helped me off the ground. No more clicking.

"I think so? Did everything go black?"

"Yeah. I saw the symbols—runes?—for magic and stamina."

Haldrek grinned. "Then things might get a bit easier for you. It's a strange experience the first time. I usually see fortitude and stamina."

"I wish I'd gotten that; I need more health." I touched my helmet to stabilize myself and felt the dent from earlier. Energy coursed through my body, and I didn't know if it was the leveling up or my excitement over what had happened. It was essentially the same as the game, but in real life.

I focused on Haldrek. "Should we continue?"

He gestured towards the staircase out of the pit. "After you."

As I made my way up, my excitement faded a bit, and I had the uneasy feeling there was a lot more to go through before reaching the center.

I had no idea how long it took us to make it through the barrow or how detailed it was. The only sign of time passing was my fatigue, and even that was sketchy as we battled our way through waves of the *ruumii*. Despite the fighting and how late I *thought* it should be, I still didn't feel tired. And with each fight, I was a little more comfortable wielding my sword and shield.

Upon reaching the most ornate door I had seen in the barrow, relief flooded over me. We had to be close to the end.

"That looks like a puzzle lock. What—" I stepped forward and felt a stone press under my foot. Haldrek pulled me back and down to the ground in one move as I heard the whistle of arrows pinging across the hall. I stiffened as his body pressed up against mine. His warm breath hit my cheek, and I closed my eyes, trying to focus on the fact that he was keeping me safe. Rather than anything else.

When the arrows stopped buzzing, Haldrek jumped up and then gave me his hand. It was too dim to see whether his cheeks were red, and I hoped he couldn't tell if mine were or not. My face and neck were warm enough that I was certain I was blushing.

"There's... there is always at least one arrow trap in every barrow I know of. I... um, I'm surprised we made it this far without setting another one off." He pointed to the raised stones at our feet, and I got the impression that he was avoiding eye contact with me.

I groaned, trying to push my feelings away and focus on the task at hand. "I always forget about that."

He frowned and then shook his head. "If this is anything like Wiglaf's Barrow, we need to figure the puzzle out before the door will open."

"Yeah." I tried to think of something witty or insightful, but my mind went blank as the thought of him on top of me popped back into my head. I shook it away.

I made my way slowly towards the door, making sure not to step on any more raised stones. In front of the door, two raised stone squares of the same size were carved out, one in front of the other. They were about as high as my ankles, and the block closest to the door had a round cutout in the center, while the other had a set of footprints on it.

Haldrek grumbled as I examined the two blocks. "What?" I turned back to him as I raised my foot over the block with footprints on it.

"I have a feeling I know what kind of lock this is. This won't be fun. For either of us."

"Why?" I stepped back from the block, wondering if it would set off another batch of arrows.

"It looks like a two-person puzzle lock." Haldrek started looking around at the carvings on the walls for clues. "One person steps on the block with feet. The other solves the puzzle and enters the next room alone."

I grimaced. "And fights whatever's in there?"

Haldrek returned his focus to me. "That's the idea. I'll step on the first stone. That way you'll be free to go into the inner chamber when you solve the puzzle."

He stepped onto the footprints stone. The other raised stone pushed up and to the side, revealing some kind of dial on a pedestal.

"There's the puzzle."

On it was an ornate stone and metal lock containing three rings and icons, just like in the games. As soon as I figured out the puzzle, I expected the door would pop open, and I'd have to face whatever was in the next room. My chest tightened as panic grew inside me.

I stepped away from the pedestal.

"You think... I can handle it? Whatever's in that room?" I glanced at that door once more.

"I know you can." Haldrek's voice was calm. "You've destroyed plenty of *ruumii* so far."

I stepped back to the lock, glancing over at him for support. I remembered these puzzles from the game. You had to line up the symbols in the correct order or risk being injured.

There were three rings, one inside of each other. Each ring had all three symbols, but the largest ring had a bird emblem similar to the one on my pendant at the top. The middle ring had some kind of long snake-like dragon twisted into a corkscrew shape. And the smallest ring had the logo for Gunvald Gaming Studios—a pair of mountains with a sun rising behind them.

Haldrek cleared his throat. "What symbols are on the lock?"

"A dragon, a bird, and two mountains with the sun behind them."

"Huh. Is the dragon twisted, like it is flying up into the sky?"

"Yes..."

"So, the symbol of Bjornulf, the crest of Svartån, and the crest of Andrattür. Interesting. I guess it makes sense that Ottkatla's Barrow would have the same symbols as Wiglaf's."

"Why?" I turned around to face Haldrek for a moment before looking back at the puzzle.

"Wiglaf and Ottkatla were twins. Firstborn of Bjornulf and Freya."

"So... Which order? Dragon, Mountains, Bird? Dragon, Bird, Mountains? Or all of one symbol?"

"Try 'Dragon, Swan, Mountains'. Ottkatla was born first with Wiglaf's hand tight around her ankle."

I moved the largest circle on the podium to show a dragon, then followed the middle ring with the swan emblem. The room shook, and Haldrek grunted in pain. I spun around to see metal spikes around him like a tiny prison cell while he held his arm.

"Go! You did it! I'll be fine! It just scratched me."

I turned back around to see the door spin open. I only had a few seconds before it shut again. The groans of *ruumii* made me shudder.

"Hurry! Before it closes!"

I ran, slipping through the opening just as it sealed up again, cutting me off from Haldrek. The nerves in my hands tingled as I gripped my sword and moved toward the sound of *ruumii*.

It was time to be the badass warrior I was in the games.

I entered the new area and, in an instant, torches around the room blazed into being, illuminating it with an eerie blue light. Two large, ornate coffins sat in the middle of the room. A couple of stone bridges crossed a moat-like area, one close to me, but swarming with *ruumii* and the other on the opposite side, with few creatures between me and it.

Two *ruumii* near me staggered up and growled. I gripped my sword tighter as my panic turned into something different. A strange sense of excitement. Just like in the games. A grin tugged at the corner of my mouth. A couple *ruumii* charged me, and I stepped up, cutting one across the midsection before hooking the other's ax with my sword. I held on tight as it grunted, trying to pull my weapon away from me. It was strong for an undead creature.

"Arrgh!" I pulled away, freeing my sword. As I stumbled back, I angled myself away from the attack just as one of the *ruumii* slammed his sword against my shield. I held it above my head as I stabbed him from below. He fell, and I tried to ignore the ache growing in my left hand.

I made quick work of the next few *ruumii*, inching my way toward the far stone bridge. It was double arched, linking the two sides of the channel with a smaller stone island in the middle. And it was now crawling with *ruumii*, making their way across and toward me. As I knocked one of the *ruumii* into the channel, there was a cracking sound from the coffin island in the middle of the room. I glanced over to see one coffin opening.

"What the—"

"Grah!" A *ruumii* swung at me from my left. I swung around in just enough time to block the blow and stab him. More pushed toward me and knocked me back a few paces. I pushed back, knocking one into the channel and hearing him scream. The *ruumii* paused for a second, and I pushed forward onto the bridge, hoping I could outrun most, if not all, of them.

Then I stopped. As I got to the middle of the bridge, I saw a heavily armored *ruumii* standing on the opposite side. It held a large, bearded ax in one hand and a large teardrop shaped shield in the other, its beady red eyes staring me down as it grinned maniacally. I stepped back over the bodies of the other fallen *ruumii* as he charged. Blocking his attack with my shield, I swung my sword across his neck and chest, dodging the top of his shield, just as I had seen Haldrek do a few times earlier. He backed off before swinging at me again.

"*Hul! Rah!*"

I dodged the blow and tried to balance on the bridge as he did an overhead attack. As I slammed my shield into the path of his ax, I shoved my sword into his torso, and pushed him into the water below. The sword ripped from my glove, stuck in the creature. Only as he fell and screamed, did I realize the liquid was some kind of toxic material. Something that oozed and hissed around the fallen *ruumii*, eating at their corpses.

I shuddered and ran for the center of the coffin island. When I looked up, I gasped.

Ottkatla herself, in elegant red and purple robes, hovering a few inches above the ground with her arms raised as if in victory and a sword in her right hand. An odd sort of whitish glow emanated from her, giving her an almost angelic aura.

My eyes widened, and the ache in my left arm intensified from the weight of the shield as I took in the situation's gravity.

*This is it. She's the dungeon boss.*

I patted my armor, expecting to find another weapon, but there was nothing.

*Shit.*

She turned to me and smiled, relaxing her arms.

"Welcome, Ina. And well done. *You* will be my thegn-heir." She lowered to the ground and there was a compulsion to walk over to her.

I followed it.

"You're not the dungeon boss?"

She frowned at me in confusion and then laughed. "I don't understand what you speak of, but if you wish to fight, I can."

"No... I'm good." I shook my head, hoping this wasn't some kind of strange ploy or trap.

"You have already passed your first trial. I had this barrow created to not only house my remains, but to refine my heirs and separate those who would lead Svartån with strength from those who would not. Your father's cousin came seeking my rewards, but they are not his to take."

"Hardbein?"

Ottkatla nodded once.

I stared at her as she sheathed her sword in a belt around her waist. She grabbed my shoulders, and we lifted off the ground. I gasped in fear as I clamped my eyes shut. Cold air rushed past me as we hurtled somewhere far above where we had been.

"Open your eyes, Ina."

I peeked one eye open and saw that we were high above the mountain that the barrow was inside. Light flooded the air, and I could see mountains and valleys beneath me, as well as the shimmer of water out the corner of my right eye.

"What is this?" I blurted out, not thinking other than I was high up.

Ottkatla laughed again. "This is Lohikärra. If you stay here, you will be a powerful thegn of Svartån, second only to me in sagas and epics. But more importantly... you will deliver Lohikärra from its enemies and reform it into the powerful nation it needs to be."

"I'm a nobody. I don't know how to rule."

Without warning, we dropped through the ice-cold air, and I braced for impact and pain. Instead, my body stopped, hovering just over the stone floor as my armor and clothing got pulled away from me. I gasped for a second at my nakedness and then warmer clothing bound around me, followed by heavier armor. My feet rested on the stones and the weight of everything lightened.

Ottkatla stood in front of me, smiling. "Do not let that illusion blind you. You will be the future thegn of Svartån and as my heir, you are worthy to wear my armor.

If you were not, it would not bind to you as it does." In that moment, a strange, comforting feeling about her overwhelmed me. I wanted to both hug her and cry at the same time. "Go forth, Ina, and bring yourself before Rhaegos's shrine. She awaits you there with a final token so that all will know who you truly are. Then show the world the power of Svartån, of Lohikärra, and its women."

There was a bright flash of light, and I covered my eyes as Ottkatla disappeared.

When I opened them, I noticed that a warmer yellow glow replaced the blue light from before. Much to my surprise, the door I had come through was still shut. I needed to find a way out and back to Haldrek.

I examined the area for an exit, as I brushed my hands across the metal plates that covered my shoulders and glanced at my chest plate. Even though it resembled my former armor, everything was shinier and newer looking. My leather and metal armor vest had disappeared, and in its place was a fitted plate metal version carved with the Svartån insignia. Along with the new metal breastplate, there were plate metal coverings for my elbows and knees. Full metal gloves covered my hands, cinching in below my wrists.

Now I felt like a badass.

I walked toward the back of the coffin island and began feeling around on the wall for a crack or something that might signify a door or a trigger. A raised stone on the ground next to the wall stuck out. It resembled the other 'triggers' in the barrow.

"I guess there's only one way to find out..."

I raised my shield to cover myself and stepped on the stone. The sound of rocks moving made me jump back. In front of me, bright stars popped out of the darkness.

I grinned. "There's the back door."

As I surveyed the valley below, in the dim moon and starlight, the beauty of the area struck me. The silence of the snowpack made the scene serene. Even peaceful. A place I wouldn't mind staying in. Or call home.

With that, I headed down the path around the mountain. It was time to rescue Haldrek and visit Aldinnvollr.

# Chapter Nine

As the path darkened under the surrounding trees, I cast a fireball above my hand to light the way. When I'd received the new armor, I'd regained a sword, but I still felt more comfortable with something lighting the way.

I wondered, as I walked, if I had to loop around to the front of the barrow to find Haldrek again. Or if he was still in the barrow and I hadn't hit the right trigger? I hadn't thought of that as I left the barrow.

"So... *you're* the true Thegn of Svartån now? I'll be damned."

I stopped, looking around for the source of the ominous voice. Then I was down, face first on the ground, head throbbing. I spun around to my back as something cold and sharp slashed my left cheek and past my chain mail.

"Too-Weli-Ballo!"

A fireball pushed the person back, illuminating them briefly. They wore all black with a mask that covered everything except their eyes.

"I won't fail like my brother *Hrothbere*."

"*Who's Hrothbere?*" My voice exploded with anger as I grabbed for a dagger on my waist to defend myself.

The fireball extinguished as the person jumped into the air. They landed on me with another jab at my throat. Again, on my left side. I tucked my chin into my chest, stabbing at them with my dagger as something hard bit into my new helmet with a thud. My dagger dug through leather and into something harder. It rewarded me with a grunt as I struggled to push the person away.

"Too-Weli-Ballo!" Haldrek's voice came out of the darkness along with a fireball.

The fireball hit my attacker, singeing me as they rolled off. Footsteps thudded toward us as the assailant stumbled to his feet and disappeared into the darkness.

"Ina?" Haldrek knelt next to me, hoisting a globe of light above us. His eyes were wide and frantic as he examined me. Pulling my chain mail away from my neck, he exhaled. "It's just a graze."

"It doesn't feel like a graze." My neck stung and burned as I focused on the light above us. "I thought…"

"I know a few simple spells. But I'm no mage. Let's get you to Aldinnvollr. Don't move your neck too much." He gently helped me up, keeping my neck as still as possible.

I held my neck as we walked down the path, hoping that I wasn't bleeding too much.

"How did you get out of the barrow?" I leaned into Haldrek as he guided me, keeping me from stumbling off the edge of the path.

"As soon as the door shut behind you, the cage I was in, released. I figured there'd be a back door to the barrow, so I ran back the way we came. I was wandering around the side of it when I heard you cast that spell. Figured something was up if you were throwing a fireball at someone."

I laughed a little as my voice shook, making my injury burn. "I'm glad you were nearby."

"I'm glad too. I suppose if he sent men of his to hinder you from getting to Aldinnvollr, it shouldn't be surprising that he sent an assassin as well." Haldrek paused, and I got the sense that he was trying to control his emotions. "Next time I see that coward of a cousin of yours, I'll…"

I thought back to the attack. My attacker *was* an assassin, but…

"I don't think Hardbein hired that assassin."

"Why not?"

"He—it sounded like a man, anyway—made a remark like it surprised him that I was the true thegn of Svartån. And then something about a person named Hrothbere. His brother. How he failed or something."

"Hrothbere?"

"That's what I heard. I don't know anyone by that name though." The strange memory dream from a few nights earlier came back, and I shuddered. That name seemed to pop up everywhere all of a sudden. "Did my father have any gesiths or know anyone by that name?"

"Hrothbere is a common name here. He probably did. But why does that make you think that it wasn't Hardbein?"

"Hardbein's only known about me for, like, a few days? There's no way he could arrange to both have men prevent us from getting to Aldinnvollr and then a backup assassin in case they failed. Right? And if the assassin was referring to one of the other soldiers... from Osvif's Refuge... Who is this Hrothbere person? Was he one of those soldiers?" I groaned, my head throbbing almost as bad as when I'd been hungover.

Haldrek shook his head. "Who else would try to kill you, Ina?"

"Seirye? Did my dad have any other enemies?"

"I doubt an elf like Seirye would use human assassins to kill someone. That's just... Whenever I've fought him, that wasn't how he fought. It's always been about illusion and magic for him." Haldrek paused as we got to the main road. "As for your father's enemies... There were a few thegns who were not on friendly terms with him, but... it'd be dishonorable for a thegn to send an assassin after another thegn. Or their family."

I groaned. "You're telling me all the thegns of Lohikärra are honorable?"

Haldrek shook his head as we reached Aldinnvollr's gates. "No. But I can't see any of the other thegns sending an assassin after you."

"Even... Lansiranikä?" I wobbled, and Haldrek steadied me.

"Even Lansiranikä." He hesitated and then said, "We're almost to the road. Let's see if Mattie is there. We can patch you up quick and then find a healer in Aldinnvollr."

I was lightheaded as we entered the tavern. A nearby maid turned her attention to the three of us and gasped as she tugged at her headscarf. Haldrek growled, "Have you never seen an injured warrior? Go find a healer."

The maid scurried off as Haldrek sat me down at a nearby table, and Mattie sat down across from me. Mattie had been silent during the quick walk into town, but I wondered if that had more to do with fear or fatigue. "What... what happened at the barrow?"

"I got the armor." I grinned weakly, trying to keep my head upright as Haldrek helped get my helmet off and pull my chain mail and leather cap away from my head. Mattie fidgeted with her own injury, pulling her chain mail away from it.

"Then an assassin tried to kill her outside the barrow." Haldrek kept his voice low. He gently took my chin and examined my injuries again.

"*What?* Do you think? Someone Hardbein hired?"

Haldrek turned back to Mattie. "I think so, but Ina doesn't. I guess the man mentioned something about a man named Hrothbere."

I closed my eyes and leaned on Haldrek's shoulder to keep the lightheadedness from overwhelming me. "It sounded like Hrothbere was supposed to do something to me, but he failed, so the assassin had to finish the job."

"It looks like he almost succeeded. There's blood all over your neck and you look paler than normal."

Haldrek wrapped his arm around me and shifted me into a more comfortable position against him. "She'll be fine as soon as a healer gets here. She lost blood, but her injuries won't be fatal."

The maid came back with a dark pot of something and bowed to us. "I have something for the injury."

"Injuries." Haldrek gestured to Mattie's arm, and the maid bobbed her head.

As much as I wanted to stay cuddled under Haldrek's arm, I leaned back up into an upright position and let her dab at the cuts as Mattie inspected the salve.

"It's a mixture of wine and herbs. It allows minor injuries to heal quickly." The maid commented. "A family recipe."

"Hmm... do you have that recipe?" Mattie turned to her as the maid finished covering the cuts with the salve and fiddled with some cloth, wrapping it tightly across my neck and lower jaw.

"Not here. I learned it from my mother. But I know there is a book with the recipe in it. Back at Svangendom."

I turned to her in surprise, wincing as my injuries stung. "Are you from Svangendom?"

She adjusted my head and finished with the cloth. "I am. I was born there and lived there until this past summer. Then I set off for adventure... and ended up here."

Mattie frowned. "Are you happy here?"

The maid shook her head. "Not really, but—"

"Meri! What's going on over there?"

Meri adjusted her headscarf over her ears again as she turned back to face a man on the other side of the room. "They needed a healer. I'm just finishing up." She began tending to Mattie's arm, gently removing the bloodied cloth that Haldrek had used as a bandage.

I noticed a few people stare at me and I hid my head, trying not to focus on the attention. Meri focused on Mattie's arm as she asked, "Do you need any food or drink?" She gestured to Haldrek. "I remember you from Svangendom. Thoreg will be pleased to have a thegn here."

"Thank you. Food for the three of us." He glanced at me. "And kavasir as well."

Meri bowed her head in acknowledgement and upon finishing Mattie's re-bandaging, hurried off.

Haldrek surveyed the tavern before focusing on Mattie. "How are you feeling?"

She raised her injured arm. "All right. I'll feel better once we have some food and a place to sleep."

A heavyset man walked over and scrutinized us for a moment. "Meri said a thegn had graced us." He focused on Haldrek. "Thegn Andrattür?"

Haldrek turned to him. "I am. You have two thegns gracing you, though. Or rather soon enough."

The man smiled for a split second. "I heard. The other one is with the gesith tonight. Arrived this morning."

"That man's not a thegn or a thegn-heir." Haldrek nudged me to sit up. I did so, and the man's eyes went wide as he stared at me. "*This* is whom I am speaking about."

"Well... this should be interesting." The man started laughing. "The gesith won't be pleased to learn he's hosting the wrong person."

Haldrek opened his mouth to respond as a hearty, meaty smell hit our noses and I turned to see Meri and another girl return with food and tankards.

"You three will have to visit him tomorrow. And clear up this confusion." The man studied my new armor. "Haven't had this much excitement in a while." He turned to Meri. "Go prepare a room for these three. Now."

The man gestured to us as she hurried away. "Enjoy your food and if you need anything, just ask." He walked back over to where some other patrons were being boisterous. Haldrek and Mattie began devouring their food as I surveyed the tavern. The eating area was larger than either the first place I'd visited with Haldrek or the tavern in Eldingheimr. Someone was strumming an instrument, and the chatter was louder, but people still stared at me, which made me nervous.

If Hardbein was in Aldinnvollr and the gesith here was already entertaining him…
I had a feeling the next few days were going to be eventful.

That night I fell asleep in an instant. I only woke up when I sensed a presence
staring me down. Opening my eyes, I was in some foggy, grayish realm. A dream?
Wherever I was, this was nothing like I'd experienced before. My anxiety rose, and
I tried to move. Nothing. Frozen in place, I saw Hardbein watching me.

"You are not fit to rule. In any realm. You can barely fight to protect yourself,
much less others." He pulled his sword from his sheath and began examining it.
A smirk crossed his face, and I tensed, trying to imagine a weapon in my hand.
Nothing appeared.

"And what have you done, Hardbein?" Another voice popped out of the mist,
and Robert walked out with *his* typical swagger and smirk. He eyed me with a
grin, making me feel naked all over again. His appearance confused me as well. My
dreams had always been of home or here, but they had never come together like
this.

Hardbein scrutinized Robert in disgust and surprise. "Who are you?"

"The only one fit to rule. I have more battle expertise than either of you
combined." Robert turned to me as I cocked my head at him. He sounded…
different. I'd never heard him use the word 'expertise' before. And the crisp lilt
that he spoke with was uncomfortably familiar, but not from him. He took a step
toward me. "I want just one thing from you, Ina. And if you don't give it willingly,
I'll take it by force."

My skin crawled at the comment as he continued toward me, and I sensed
another presence behind me.

"Who in the dragons do you think you are?" Hardbein took a step toward
Robert and in a flash, Hardbein was on the ground, bleeding and a blade stuck
in his gut.

Hardbein faded into nothingness as Robert stepped toward me, his lecherous
grin growing. "I promise if you give me what I want *willingly*, it won't be so
painful."

Still frozen in place, my entire body flooded with terror, and I did the only thing
I could think of. I scowled at Robert with the most dangerous look I could muster.

"Go away. You *don't* belong here."

He smirked, stopping to look at himself, and then back at me. "Neither of us belongs here, but here we are."

He touched my cheek, his palm and fingers ice cold, leaving the sensation of frostbite in their wake. I flinched, closing my eyes as he got nose to nose with me.

Then a grunt, and his presence disappeared.

"Pretentious *elf*. Learn to imitate a Lohikärran better before you try to intimidate one."

I opened my eyes to see a dark haze form into a man in front of me.

*What on earth?*

"Even a Svanunge is better as thegn than you." The new person, robed in dark leather apparel, *felt* like the assassin from earlier in the evening. He stood beside Seirye and shook his head as the elf glared at him. "Don't think you're the only one who knows how to intrude on and manipulate people's dreams." Seirye disappeared, just as Hardbein had. The deathly pale assassin then focused on me and smirked like someone who'd just caught his prey. "*I'm* the only person who gets to kill you."

He jumped at me, dagger ready, as I collapsed into the darkness with a scream.

# Chapter Ten

I didn't sleep well after the nightmare, not knowing what to make of it. My neck burned with an intensity I hadn't felt in a while until Meri came up to tend to my injuries in the morning. As I ate with Haldrek and Mattie afterwards, I mulled over what I'd do next.

"Ina..." Haldrek's voice pulled me out of my reverie.

"Huh?"

"Are you not hungry?"

I focused on my food again, which I'd been playing with. "I didn't sleep well last night. And I'm worried about Hardbein. If he's been with the gesith here..."

"Once the gesith sees you wearing the Thegn armor, he'll know who Ottkatla has accepted as her heir." Haldrek tapped the piece of brand-new armor covering my shoulder before taking another bite of his porridge. "You need to eat to heal. And to train."

I continued to stir mine, reluctantly taking a bite. Even though the food was delicious, and Meri had fixed my bandages, just chewing still made my neck and face hurt.

"My injuries aren't helping either." I wished I had some headache medicine to dull the ache in my jaw. Back home, I could sneak some aspirin or something, but here, I had no idea what they had, beyond what Meri had given me.

"Meri said the balm she put on your cuts should help. Is it not?" Mattie looked up from her breakfast.

"A little, but—"

The tavern door opened and the sound of a large crowd outside caught our attention. Haldrek stood up in an instant, and Mattie followed as I finished another bit of food, hurrying after them.

There was a tug on my chainmail sleeve, and I turned to see Meri next to me. "You know what's going on outside?"

She pursed her lips thoughtfully. "The gesith is out there with the man who's been calling himself thegn. I have a feeling... be careful out there. I mean..." She ducked her head as if too nervous to continue. "Something's off. With the gesith and the other man."

I nodded and followed Haldrek and Mattie outside. Despite being in my thegn armor and feeling like I stuck out, no one paid attention to me. Instead, everyone's attention was on Hardbein.

Hardbein stood in front of the crowd with another man who I assumed was the gesith. After surveying the crowd, he spoke, "My fellow Lohikärrans, last night I received a vision from your great predecessor, Ottkatla. She visited me with a message. A message both promising and daunting..."

I surveyed the crowd, trying to get a feel for their mood. Some listened to Hardbein intently, while a few had confused expressions. In the corner of my eye, I saw a few people along the edge of the crowd slip their caps or headscarves over their ears.

"... Ottkatla told me that Svartån must be *cleansed* before she will accept her new heir. Too long my cousins have allowed elves to live and mingle with our kind. Such actions have left Svartån *weak*. No longer. We fight the Blodnar to the south and are on the brink of invasion from the north." He paused for effect. "*Tell me*, when the northern elves attack, who do you think the Hethurin will fight alongside? Us or their elven kin?"

Grumblings of agreement flowed from the crowd, and my stomach tightened. The Hethurin along the edge of the crowd stepped back and despite my desire to stay invisible, the emotions bubbling up inside of me were a repeat of my first night in Svartån. I knew what *cleansing* meant, and there was no way I was going to stand idly by.

"Lies!" I pushed my way forward as the crowd split in front of me. "Ottkatla said nothing about 'cleansing Svartån' and every Hethurin I've met has been devoted to Svartån. They have just as much to lose from the Isillas as anyone else here."

Hardbein's eyes widened for a second, and then he smirked. "The False Thegn. I'm surprised you're here." He leaned over to the gesith and whispered something in his ear. The gesith bobbed his head, and my stomach churned with anxiety.

"You say Ottkatla has spoken to you. When?" The gesith scrutinized me, his arms crossed, and his mouth down turned into a grimace.

"Once after I arrived at Svangendom. Then yesterday. When I went through her barrow." I gestured to the armor that I wore. There was *no* way that either Hardbein or the gesith could question the armor.

The gesith scratched his chin. Like he was calculating something. "I see you wear the thegn's armor. If you survived the barrow and spoke to Ottkatla, then..." He grimaced and turned away from my stare.

Out of the corner of my eye, I saw Hardbein glance at one of his men. I got the sinking feeling that he'd try to take the armor one way or another.

Haldrek stepped next to me, staring down the gesith. "Why do you hesitate? I can vouch for her as well. I fought by her side inside the barrow and saw her after she left—wearing the armor."

The gesith stiffened up and bobbed his head in irritated deference. "Thegn Andrattür."

Hardbein glared at me. "Why would Ottkatla give an *outsider* the Thegn armor?"

"I could say the same for you." My voice sharper than I expected.

"I may have been born outside of Svartån, but I'm no outsider. I'm still a Lohikärran and I've fought alongside many of these warriors. Can you say that?"

I hesitated. I wasn't a Lohikärran. At least, I wasn't born here. But that didn't seem to matter to Ottkatla.

Hardbein said, "Even if Ottkatla gave you the armor, are you even capable of *using* it? You have no fighting skill. How are you supposed to lead the people of Svartån if you can't even fight for them?"

"I *can* fight. How else do you think I got through Ottkatla's Barrow?" I paused as a smile crept to my lips. "You'd know that if you'd gone through it. Did you even get to the inner room and talk to her?"

"Of course, I did. She told me..." Hardbein's expression turned to a scowl. "It doesn't matter what she told me there. I know what she told me last night, and that was that Svartån must be cleansed of all elven kind. *Especially* before the northern elves attack. If you truly cared about the people of Svartån, you would cease your attempts at becoming thegn. Allow them to have a thegn who could *truly* protect it."

He regarded the crowd, and cheers rose behind me. My neck heated up and a voice inside my head told me I would never gain Aldinnvollr's allegiance. I pushed it aside despite its persistence.

"See? The people want a thegn who can protect them. *Me.*"

I squeezed my hands into fists to toughen my resolve. "Last time I checked, Ottkatla chose the thegn of Svartån. And she chose *me.*"

Hardbein scowled but said nothing. Instead, the gesith of Aldinnvollr spoke.

"Enough." He looked between Hardbein and me. "Are the rumors of Isillas invading true, then?"

Both Hardbein and I nodded. I spoke up before he could say anything. "They've attacked some of the eastern villages, the Hethurin village at Svangendom, and took a swing at Eldingheimr. I confronted Seirye there."

"What about the two other times?"

"I wasn't yet in Svartån."

The gesith scratched his chin again. "I've lived in Aldinnvollr my entire life and devoted myself to Ottkatla's choice of heirs. I cannot deny that you wear the Thegn armor. And yet..." He turned to Hardbein for a brief second before focusing on me. "I've fought with Hardbein during the few times when Svartån and Lansiranikä have fought together. So, I know that he could defend Svartån. As for you... I have yet to see or hear of your feats in battle. I trust Ottkatla, but I don't trust you."

He paused again and regarded the crowd for a second. "If you made your way through the barrow, then you know you need to gain Rhaegos's blessing and Ottkatla's. So, it has been for prior thegns. Prove yourself worthy of Rhaegos and I will set my stave with you, despite my better instincts. But if you do not, I will assume you dead and follow one who can protect my people and Svartån." He eyed Hardbein for a split second. Then he waved to the people, and I heard the crowd disperse behind me.

Turning back to Hardbein, he asked, "What needs to be done to keep Aldinnvollr safe? Other than the Hethurin?"

I took a step toward them, not yet ready for him to dismiss me. "Svartån doesn't need to be cleansed of *anything*. Hardbein has done nothing to prove that you should—"

The gesith ignored me, but gestured to a guard behind him, who moved toward me. I turned to see Haldrek's expression darkened in a way that would make me pause if I were the gesith. He turned to the guard, making the warrior stop in his tracks. Haldrek then turned back to the gesith and Hardbein.

"Gesith Aldinnvollr, I would *not* dismiss Ina so readily if I were you."

The gesith turned to Haldrek and took a deep breath as if dealing with a kid. I realized in that moment that the gesith was likely at least twice Haldrek's age. "With all due respect, Thegn Andrattür, shouldn't you be more concerned with Andrattür's well-being than Svartån?"

"I am." Haldrek kept his eyes locked on the gesith. "Svartån's well-being is intertwined with Andrattür's. But it will be difficult for Svartån to stand if they don't have a thegn who neither Ottkatla nor the dragons have chosen."

"I agree. That's why I have neither set my stave with Hardbein nor your shield maiden yet. She can prove to me that she has both Ottkatla and the dragons' blessings. But in the meantime, I have a town and a shrine to protect." He paused, glancing at me. "She may keep your bedroll warm at night, but it doesn't mean she'll keep Aldinnvollr or Svartån safe."

I stood there frozen, my chest tightening in anger as Hardbein barely suppressed a laugh.

"You have shown much foolishness today, gesith. In word and action. Be grateful you are not one of mine." Still staring at the gesith, Haldrek shook his head. "Let's go Ina, even if the gesith has been blinded by his own pride, Svartån still needs its true thegn."

When Haldrek and I returned to the tavern, Mattie was waiting for us down in the eating area and Meri was tending to the various guests.

"It upset Thoreg that Meri was hiding in our room." Mattie took a sip from her tankard as she focused on us. "Made her come back down a few minutes after you left. I figured I'd come back down as well. The *kavasir* they have here is better than I expected."

I sat down, still tired from Hardbein's actions and still aching from the assassin's attempt. Anger joined in at an intensity I hadn't experienced before, and the only thing keeping me from fighting Hardbein or the gesith was knowing that I *wasn't* as skilled at combat as either of them. Haldrek sat down next to me and patted my back as I leaned forward. "Apparently getting the armor wasn't good enough proof for Hardbein or the gesith here."

"That doesn't surprise me. What... exactly went on out there?" Mattie put her tankard down, expression grim.

I kept my voice low. "Hardbein told people that Ottkatla wants Svartån *cleansed* of anyone with elven blood. Which is *not* what she said at all."

Mattie took another sip of her drink. "I wonder if that's because she only fought against certain elven races? And knows that elven 'blood' technically flows in all her descendants' veins."

"What?" Haldrek furrowed his brows at her. "Where did you hear that?"

"In one of the stories that my—our—dad left behind. A short tale about Ottkatla's arrival in Svartån. There's lore that her partner/lover/consort... whatever was an elf. Not Isillas elf, mind you, but another race. If I remember correctly, the Isillas had enslaved this individual and when Ottkatla began fighting them, he joined her. The rest was... history? Maybe?"

"Hmm..." Haldrek glanced around at the people in the tavern. "True or not, it probably isn't the best if Ina started talking about that. At least not right now."

"I agree. I'm curious if there's a physical copy of that story somewhere, though. It'd be interesting to read." She paused and turned to where Meri was serving drinks to others in the tavern. "What's going to happen with the Hethurin in town? If Hardbein is... wanting to cleanse Svartån of them and the gesith is inclined to follow him..." She turned back at me. "I'm afraid of what will happen if we don't nip this in the bud."

"They're safe. For now, I think." I paused as Meri brought tankards over for both Haldrek and me. "I need to go to the Shrine of Rhaegos. The sooner the better. Both Ottkatla and the gesith mentioned gaining a token or blessing from Rhaegos. The armor might convince a few people here that I'm the rightful thegn, but... proof from a dragon..." I thought back to when my dad visited me after I confronted Seirye. He'd mentioned going to the shrine as well. The more I thought about it, the more I realized that the shrine was the key.

"If you have Ottkatla's armor and whatever Rhaegos is supposed to give you, only a fool would question whether or not you were a thegn."

I looked over at Haldrek. "How am I supposed to get it, though? Ottkatla mentioned the second token at the shrine, but am I supposed to offer something there or is it another dungeon?" I tried to remember what the shrine had been like in the video games, but nothing striking came to mind.

"An offering, I believe." He tugged at his beard thoughtfully. "I don't remember your father mentioning any kind of dungeon there, and the one time I visited I only saw the shrine and a small cave behind it."

"Any ideas on what to offer?" I focused on the inside of my mug, hoping some kind of idea would pop up.

"Some kind of token? Food? Mead?" Mattie offered.

Haldrek shook his head. "Dragons don't accept mead, or any kind of man-made drink." He took a sip. "When I had to climb to the shrine above Mirratoft, I brought an offering of hunted meat, including the blood of the creature."

I groaned. I'd never hunted in my life.

"You don't have to do that, though. Other thegns have brought jewels, weapons, and other items in the past. It just needs to be of value to you."

I laughed in frustration. "I have little on me that is of value to me. There's my pendant and the armor, but I doubt I'm supposed to offer those."

Mattie twisted her mouth thoughtfully. "What about that book from the library at Svangendom?"

"The language primer with the stories of Bjornulf and Freya?"

She nodded. "Not that I'd recommend you destroying any book, but maybe Rhaegos wouldn't destroy it." She turned to Haldrek. "Is the offering always literal? Could it be metaphorical? I mean... how much do dragons need jewels, weapons, or other items like that?"

"They don't, but they have their hordes too." Haldrek scratched his beard thoughtfully. "Rhaegos may take the book as an offering, if it is an item of value to Ina." He tapped my chest where my pendant hung under my gambeson. "When we have some privacy, you can technically use your pendant as a thegn stone. At least that's what your father did often after returning from your world. I never figured out how to use my pendant to connect with other thegns or my *husceorl*. That said, you could send word to Skuti that you need that book."

"How long would it take for someone to get here from the estate?" I pulled the pendant from under my gambeson. "I don't know if we have that much time."

"It's still early. If you contacted him soon... someone could be here by tomorrow or the next morning."

I stood up to return to the room we shared. As I did, Meri hurried over, grabbing my arm and tugging at her headscarf again.

"My thegn..." She whispered. "I... heard you defend the Hethurin outside. I... just wanted to say thank you."

I furrowed my brow in confusion for a moment before it hit me. Meri had mentioned growing up at Svangendom. *She* was a Hethurin.

"I know what it's like to be an outsider. It's not like I'm *not* still an outsider in some ways. So, I won't treat other outsiders like I was treated. Plus, I was being honest. I haven't met a lot of Hethurin, but the few I have, have been loyal and hard-working."

Meri smiled. "Thank you." Someone shouted for her, and she hurried away.

I touched the pendant under my gambeson again and took a deep breath. The sooner I could get Rhaegos's token, the sooner I could confirm to everyone that I *was* the true thegn and the sooner I could help everyone in Svartån, both Hethurin and non-Hethurin alike.

Skuti seemed unfazed by me contacting him through the pendant. He told me he would retrieve the book and send it out with the estate's fastest rider before dark. After Meri re-wrapped my bandages, Haldrek and Mattie and I left the tavern again. Haldrek advised that we spend more time outside of the tavern, not only to show more people of Aldinnvollr that I was the true thegn, but to prepare for any conflicts or mayhem that may arise from Hardbein and his men.

We made our way to a nearby blacksmith shop on the edge of town closest to the barrow. Haldrek noted that it was best for us to keep our weapons sharp—just in case—and I was inclined to agree with him. As we walked through town, people stopped and stared, and I tried not to think too much of it. I *wanted* them to know I wore Ottkatla's armor, and that I was the thegn-heir, but being the center of attention still unnerved me.

"Here's a group I wasn't expecting today."

I looked up to see the blacksmith standing in front of his forge, tools in hand, and looking at us.

"A thegn, a thegn-heir, and an... Ixafean warrior woman?" He studied our group carefully. "How can I help you three today?"

"We need to get our weapons sharpened." Haldrek patted the hilt of his weapon. "They've grown dull from fighting Isillas and *ruumii*."

The blacksmith gestured over to a stone grinding wheel. Haldrek unsheathed his weapon and handed it to the man as he sat down.

The sound of metal against wet stone grated against my ears, but the blacksmith and Haldrek were unfazed by the shrill sound.

"You… expect to be using your weapons soon?"

"Hopefully not, but it's always good to be prepared. I've never been comfortable with a dull blade."

The blacksmith said nothing, but made quick work of the blade sharpening. After a moment, he stopped, cleaned off the blade, and handed it back to Haldrek with a respectful bow. I gave him mine and as he started on it, he said, "It's good that you came now. With the gesith's new order, I'm afraid I'll have to close up the forge early or have my apprentice work on some of the bigger requests. She's good, but I prefer to be around, just in case."

"What new order?" I knew that the gesith had still been making plans with Hardbein, but I'd hoped his promise of giving me time to 'prove' myself would keep the Hethurin in town from any harm. Now I wondered how much his words were worth.

"Did you not hear?" He paused, taking my blade away from the grindstone. "After the 'announcement' this morning, the gesith sent some of his guards to tell us Hethurin that we need to double our offerings at the Shrine of Rhaegos if we're to stay *welcome* here." He shook his head, pressing my blade to the grinder again. "I don't mind giving offerings to Rhaegos. I've felt her blessings in my family and my wife and I keep a household shrine, but… we're already paid less for our work than our non-Hethurin neighbors and now we're supposed to give more?" A spark flew from the grindstone and he paused, lightening up his touch. "I pay my coin to the gesith every year and I've fought *loyally* under him. I've no love for the Isillas and no attachment to whatever breed of elf the thegn's mage—Pep—Pef—Pefannyus—or whatever his name was." He sighed. "I mean no disrespect, but… we've done nothing to deserve this." He wiped down the sword and handed it back to me with a bow as well. "Worst part is… the offerings don't 'count' unless one of the Aldinnvollr guards acknowledges it."

"*What?* So, if a guard isn't happy with someone…" My mind immediately arrived at the worst-case scenario.

The blacksmith took Mattie's barely used sword and examined it, his forehead creases deepening briefly. Then, with a shrug, he began sharpening it. "Wouldn't be the first time an Aldinnvollr guard demanded extra coin from his Hethurin neighbor to do his job."

"That's not right. Either the gesith's order or the guards taking extra coin." I shook my head. "Have the Hethurin in town started taking these extra offerings to the shrine yet?"

The blacksmith snorted in derision. "The gesith demanded a few of the better-off Hethurin in town to 'be an example'. *Or else.* Thankfully, I'm not one of them. I can make the extra offering, but..." He gestured to his shop. "I'm the one who does most of the work here. Even with my apprentice, I'm working before the sun rises and after the sun sets."

Haldrek crossed his arms and furrowed his brow thoughtfully. "Can you send someone else from your household to give the offering?"

The blacksmith sighed. "I could. But I don't want to endanger my wife or anyone else. I don't know if any of you have been to the shrine, but the path up there is narrow, and parts are along an edge. And I don't trust the guards not to cause an accident."

"You're not afraid for yourself?" Mattie asked, as he handed her the blade.

He shook his head. "I've lived in Aldinnvollr for more years than the gesith has been alive." He stood up and turned to face the mountains outside the far side of town, beyond the tavern. "I know these mountains and ridges like my own family. And I know how to keep myself safe." Turning back to us, he continued. "Not that I don't trust my wife or children, I just... I'd rather not worry about them."

I glanced back and forth between Haldrek and Mattie, before focusing on the blacksmith. "Try to delay going up there for the next few days. I... I plan to make my offering soon and after that, the gesith should know exactly who I am."

The blacksmith smiled. "Thank you. For your advice. I hope you are right about the gesith. He is a powerful warrior and has kept us safe for many years, but... he's stubborn to a fault sometimes."

I nodded and walked away with Haldrek and Mattie, mulling over what the blacksmith had said and still agitated from before. A new thought popped into my head as well. As we reached the inn, I said, "I think we should head up there. Today. At least check out the route and make sure the Hethurin are being treated fairly."

Both Mattie and Haldrek stared at me in surprise.

"You don't have your offering yet." Haldrek gestured toward the mountains. "It wouldn't be wise to go to the shrine without one."

"I wasn't planning on going to the shrine itself. I just wanted to see the path. And see if what the blacksmith said is true."

He gestured for me to lead the way. "Let's go up there then."

The path was just as perilous as the blacksmith had made it out to be. Despite the actual path being clear of any ice or snow, it was narrow at many parts and hemmed along the edge of a mountain nestled against Aldinnvollr. Every so often there were metal poles to hold on to, but beyond that, there was little to keep a person from tumbling off the side if they weren't careful. Still, the day was cloudless and, in the distance, I could see an enormous dragon shaped statue.

There were plenty of people who traveled the route from Aldinnvollr to the shrine with us. The people were quiet and the mood somber as the path zigzagged up and toward another landmark. A massive arching bridge that connected the path—and Aldinnvollr—to the shrine and the decorated grove that surrounded it. I didn't remember the bridge from any of the games.

As we got in sight of it again, I turned to Haldrek and asked, "When was that built? And who built it?"

He shrugged. "Ages ago, I think. I'm sure there's a book or something about Svangendom about it. I would assume it's been here as long as the shrine has. This path is the only way to it. As far as I know."

A woman in a bright blue knotted headscarf in front of us turned around with her young child and said, "Ottkatla, blessed be her name, created the shrine. To celebrate her final victory over the Isillas. It's said that through Rhaegos, she caused the dragons to build this bridge so that all might bring offerings." She paused to look at the shrine in the distance before returning her attention to us. "Dunno how true it is, but it's been here since before the town was even a town."

"Sounds like you know a lot about this place." Mattie grunted as a Lansiranikän warrior barged past us without so much as a word. I gripped a metal pole sticking out of the rock wall for balance as Haldrek grabbed the woman and her daughter, keeping them from stepping too close to the edge of the path.

"Thank you." The woman smiled at Haldrek. She glanced in the direction of the passing warrior before turning to Mattie. "I've lived in Aldinnvollr my entire life. Most people here have. My mother's family's been harvesting stone and ore here since as far back as I could tell you."

Mattie looked back at the direction we had come from. The walls of Aldinnvollr were only just visible from where we were. "And you never wanted to leave?"

"Oh. I did. When I was younger, I wanted to serve the dragons. Be a priestess. But... my kind aren't allowed that privilege." She tugged at her headscarf, much like Meri did. "So, I stayed here, married, had my daughter and have worshipped the dragons the best I can." Her expression grew grim. "That's why we're here now." She clasped her pendant. "I've come to offer Rhaegos my necklace. It's one of the few treasures I have left."

We arrived at the middle of the bridge and Haldrek bobbed his head as he stopped. "I'm sure Rhaegos will accept the token. I can tell you from personal knowledge that the dragons honor devotion."

The woman bobbed her head, her expression still showing doubt before she continued on. I peered over the edge of the bridge and down to the river below. The bridge was a long arch, so we stood at the highest point. I shuddered, less from the cold and more from the height.

"This is the Shrine of Rhaegos." Haldrek's voice made me turn to face him. "Once you get your book, we'll come back up here, and you can offer it to Rhaegos. For now, this is as far as we should go respectfully."

"Is there some kind of magic force field keeping us from crossing the bridge?" Mattie asked with a frown.

Haldrek shook his head. "Knowing Rhaegos, I don't think she would care one way or the other if people came up here without some kind of offering. As long as we take care of their shrines, most dragons don't care. But the priests of Tenelth would mind."

"What would they do if we crossed without an offering?" I asked, wondering if they had built the shrine in this uninviting place for a reason.

"At best, chase us from the shrine and cause a scene. At worst, curse you and report back to the gesith what happened... which..."

"Is the last thing I want to happen. At least right now."

Haldrek studied the crowd around us. "But we can stand here and watch. Know what to expect when we return." He tapped my armor. "You standing here in the Thegn's armor where everyone can see you isn't a terrible thing—"

The sound of thunder in the distance interrupted Haldrek as his eyes went wide, and he started looking around in concern. I looked up at the sky to see if some kind of storm was nearby. Instead, there were blue skies as far as I could tell.

More thunder rumbled as people ran back across the bridge. A few Aldinnvollr warriors stood across the far end of the bridge to keep those already at the shrine from fleeing. Screams mixed with the increasing thunder, and I heard the word *avalanche* shouted behind us.

"Move! Back to the other side of the bridge!" Haldrek grabbed my arm as Mattie started hurrying back to where we'd come from.

"Why aren't they letting people get on the bridge?" I pulled my arm out of Haldrek's grip, adrenaline pumping as I ran forward.

"They haven't given their offering yet!" He grabbed my arm again in an attempt to hold me back. "Ina!"

"They'll die if they stay over there!" I yanked my arm away from Haldrek and started running toward the warriors blocking the way, pulling my sword out as a threat.

"Move! Let them on the bridge!"

The thundering intensified as I ran into one of the soldiers, knocking him down and creating a gap for people to move past. The wave of people knocked me back onto my butt as I glanced up to see a white wall blanket the shrine from above. Fear flooded me as I saw how close it was. The sound of snow crashing down drowned out all but the nearest screams.

Then another crack and thundering. I watched as the shrine statue bent over and shattered under the weight of the snow, causing a smaller, quicker flood of snow to course toward us along with rock shards.

"Ina!" Haldrek grabbed me and pulled me up as even the Aldinnvollr guards fled back across the bridge.

A young, panicked scream nearby snapped me back to reality, and I grabbed a child's hand as Haldrek dragged us back across the bridge. Huddled groups of people tucked themselves under rock outcroppings on the other side, their eyes wide in horror.

As soon as we stepped under the rock outcroppings and off the bridge, I turned back, clasping the girl to my armor. The noise became deafening as I watched snow pour into the river valley below on either side of the bridge. The sharp upward curve of the bridge kept the snow that fell there from reaching us. Every so often I'd see something dark pop out of the snow falling off the far cliff and pray that it was something inanimate, like a rock or a tree.

Then, as quick as the avalanche had started, it slowed, leaving a deathly silence and snow covering everything that had been on the other side of the bridge.

Haldrek turned back to me, and I saw absolute fear in his eyes. Then anger as his jaw muscles clenched tight.

"What were you thinking, Ina? That... that was *insanely* stupid. *Careless.* You could have gotten yourself killed! Both of us!"

My chest tightened with overwhelming shame. And then anger. A strange sense of fury flooded over me. "What the hell was I *supposed* to do? Leave people to die because the nimrods who guard Aldinnvollr and the shrine wouldn't let them through? *No!* I was going to protect these people! I'm their thegn. *Aren't I?*"

"You're a better thegn alive than dead. If..." He shook his head. "Never mind. I... Never mind."

He started looking around. A rising din of crying and hysteria surrounded us. After a moment, I saw him gesture toward someone, and Mattie popped out from behind another outcropping.

"Thank the dragons you're safe as well." He stared at the bridge and then back at Mattie. "You did the smart thing."

"I didn't have people to protect. Though..." Mattie squeezed in next to me and gave me a tight side hug, making room for the little girl still clinging to my right hip. "We're not exactly going to respawn here if we get killed."

I groaned. "Yeah, I know. I just—"

"My baby!" The woman with the bright blue headscarf hurried over to where we stood, and the girl let go of me to hug her. Both mother and child began bawling as they held each other, and my throat tightened as I tried not to tear up myself.

Haldrek sighed and turned to me. "It was good you did what you did, I suppose. I just... don't scare me like that again."

I smiled. Then a new sound arose. On the other side of the bridge, an unearthly howl started, and I looked over to see strange icy ghost snakes writhing around in the air.

"That's not good." Haldrek stared at the creatures and then turned to me. "We need to get back to Aldinnvollr. We need a new plan quick."

# Chapter Eleven

"What were those things, Haldrek?" I sat at a table inside Thoreg's tavern with him and Mattie that night, replaying the events of the day in my mind and trying to figure out what we'd do now that the avalanche had destroyed the shrine. Even if I returned up there with the book, it was going to take time for things to be cleaned up and repaired. And time was something that none of us had.

"They're ice drakes. Not quite dragons, but related." He took a sip of his mead and surveyed the tavern. Haldrek and Mattie had their backs to the wall, but behind me I could hear people talking in subdued voices. The avalanche and destruction of the shrine had increased tensions in town. "I've dealt with them sometimes in Andrattür. They only arise when someone has offended a dragon or an area that is special to the dragons."

My chest squeezed tight as I wondered if my running across the bridge had caused them to pop up. If Rhaegos *really* wanted an offering from me and I had done something more stupid than I thought. Haldrek had apologized for yelling at me at the shrine and I understood why he had yelled, but it left me with this unsettled sense that I had made things worse.

"Are you thinking they popped up because of the shrine's destruction or... something else?" Mattie asked, equally subdued.

"They popped up because—"

"My thegn!"

I turned to see Meri rush over to us from the main door, popping in from whatever errand Thoreg had sent her on.

"My thegn... you have to help. Please." Meri looked ashen, and a few people stared at her for a moment before going back to their own business.

"What's going on?"

"The gesith. And the Lansiranikän man. There are rumors that Rhaegos' anger caused the avalanche. And that the gesith is acting on those rumors. The Lansiranikän warriors are already convinced that this is proof that the dragons favor their gesith." She lowered her voice. "A few have already begun harassing the Hethurin in town. And the town warriors ignore it." Meri dug her nails into the wooden table as Haldrek and I stood up. Mattie shifted over to comfort her as Haldrek put his hand on my shoulder.

I followed him out of the tavern and across the main snow rutted road to a well-lit wood and stone building that stood out from many of the other buildings. Walking up to the door, I ignored the memories of dealing with the priests of Tenelth and knocked as hard as I could.

The door cracked open, and a woman peered out at me. She gasped and then shut the door in my face.

"What the—"

The door opened again, this time with an older man staring down at me.

"What do you want? The gesith is *busy*."

"I'm here to speak with him. About an urgent concern."

The man stared at me and then at Haldrek. "The gesith is trying to fix the chaos you and your *beloved* half-breeds caused." He slammed the door in my face once again, and I turned to Haldrek. I wanted to knock again, but I didn't want to agitate an already tense situation.

"Don't leave until you see the gesith. He needs to know that he can't just dismiss you."

I nodded and knocked on the door, louder this time. The man from before opened the door again.

"I said—"

"I am *not* leaving until I see the gesith. Neither I nor any of the Hethurin did anything to cause this chaos. It was an avalanche!"

The man went to shut the door on me again and I jammed my foot in the door without thinking. A satisfying thud resulted as it hit the chain mail covering my foot. I bit back a grimace as pain shot up from the sides of my foot and continued to stare at the man.

"Very well." The man opened the door slightly away from my foot and walked away.

"How's your foot?" Haldrek asked, and I turned to him.

"It hurts, but nothing I can't ignore. It's not broken if that's what you're wondering." I turned back to see the old man open the door.

"The gesith will see you for a few minutes. But if you think you're going to change his mind, you're a bigger fool than you look."

I ignored the man and walked in with Haldrek behind me. The hall was narrow, with the walls covered in wooden slats. Every so often there would be a door, more often closed than not, but heat from small fire or coal pits escaped from the ones that were open. Another door stood at the end of the hallway. The old man opened it and gestured for us to head in. I straightened up and entered to find the gesith and Hardbein bent over a table in the center of the room. Braziers surrounded the room, giving it both enough heat and light to keep everyone comfortable.

Before the gesith could say anything, Hardbein focused on me. "You *demand* to see Leiknir, even though you have no right. It's a good thing he's not in a foul mood. What do you want?"

There was a slight flash of annoyance on the gesith—Leiknir's—face as he glanced at Hardbein. He turned to me. "Yes? What?"

"I heard... that you believe the destruction caused today was because of Rhaegos's anger. And that you're punishing the Hethurin because of that."

The gesith glanced over at Hardbein, who didn't even try to conceal his smirk. "I see no other reason. That shrine has been here since the days of Ottkatla, and as soon as you arrive, it's destroyed by a strange avalanche. What else am I to think, but that this is an omen of their displeasure and you do *not* have the dragons' blessing? Do you have any proof that I am wrong in this?" He glanced up at Haldrek and raised an eyebrow as if daring him to speak.

"Avalanches happen all the time in the mountains. And if you think that the dragons are angry with me, why punish the Hethurin? They were giving offerings to Rhaegos and the other dragons. They did as you ask. Why would Rhaegos punish them for that?"

"You admit you were there then?" Hardbein said in surprise, and the thegn shot him a tense glance.

I hesitated, remembering what Haldrek had mentioned on the bridge. "I was, but I stayed on the bridge. Last I heard that wasn't offensive to the dragons."

"Are you so sure?" Hardbein said. This time I glared at him.

"You have guards who watch over the bridge and shrine," Haldrek said behind me. "Do they give offerings every time they are at the shrine?"

The gesith grimaced. "That is a different story. The men who guard the shrine are a small group already accepted by the priests of Tenelth to guard the shrine and bridge. They do not need to give more offerings than normal."

He waved his hand in the air, dismissing Haldrek's question, and turned back to me. "I told you this morning that I would follow you if you received the dragons' blessing, but it seems we've received the dragons' curse for even entertaining the thought. So, I'm setting my stave with the true thegn-heir of Svartån: Hardbein. You have the thegn armor, but... now I wonder if you cast some kind of magic to gain that armor. Perhaps that is why Rhaegos shows her displeasure. And perhaps why Ottkatla visited Hardbein last night."

"*What?*" I gaped at the gesith. "It was an avalanche! You are a fool if you think that's an omen of the dragons' pleasure or displeasure. You—"

"Enough! I've made my decision. If you love these half-breeds so much, tell them they have until dawn light to leave Aldinnvollr."

I took a step toward the gesith in anger, but Haldrek grabbed my shoulder.

"Let's go, Ina. It seems the gesith has already made his decision."

I turned back to him in surprise, but before I could say anything, he gestured to the door and nudged me out.

I flipped between anger and fear as we arrived back at the tavern. The gesith's absolute refusal to listen still made me rage inside, but I also feared that I had made things worse for the Hethurin.

Opening the door to the tavern, I saw Mattie still sitting at a nearby table. Meri was hurrying around the tavern but glanced up as we entered.

"How'd it go?" Mattie took a sip from her mug, watching me.

"It didn't. He refused to listen and decided that Hardbein was the real thegn, despite me having the armor. He also decided that the Hethurin have until morning to leave Aldinnvollr."

"What?" Mattie's eyes widened in horror. "Where are they going to go?"

"Somewhere. Anywhere. I will not let them get slaughtered." I shook my head and then focused on Haldrek and Mattie. "Svangendom. They can go there. Help rebuild the village and once I've settled this with Hardbein, they can choose to live there if they wish. Or go elsewhere."

Haldrek gestured to Meri as if he was requesting a drink, and I saw her weave her way back to where Thoreg filled drinks. "He probably thinks that they won't leave in time." Haldrek said. "This is his way of following Hardbein without decreeing wholesale slaughter."

"I'm surprised he's being that delicate." Mattie said, sarcasm dripping from her voice as she took another drink from her mug. "From what Meri's told me, it doesn't seem like many of the people here would miss the Hethurin if they disappeared."

Haldrek sat down next to her as Meri brought over two mugs for him and me. I turned to her. "How... how would you feel about returning to Svangendom for a time?"

She widened her eyes, saying nothing as she took a rag from her apron and began scrubbing at something on the table. "What happened with the gesith?"

"He's decided that Hardbein is the true thegn. And that the avalanche was Rhaegos showing her disapproval. He told me that the Hethurin have until dawn break to leave Aldinnvollr."

Meri stopped scrubbing the table. "*What*?" She straightened up and started looking around before turning back to me. "When were you going to tell people? After a good night's sleep?"

"Hey!" Haldrek's voice boomed in warning. Meri stood back, fear in her eyes. He continued in a quieter tone. "We were figuring out a way to keep you all safe. The gesith just now decided this. How many of... How many Hethurin live here?"

"Maybe fifty. Men, women, and children combined. Most live on the edge of town, but some are in families with non-Hethurin."

My heart twisted with guilt over the whole situation. "Do you know anyone who could alert the Hethurin, so they are ready to leave as soon as day breaks?"

Meri grimaced. "Of course." She glanced up at the people in the tavern and then tossed her rag on the table and hurried out the front door.

As soon as she left, I groaned and knelt my forehead to the table, letting the nose plate rivets of my helmet thunk against the wood.

"What have I done? I came here to get the armor and whatever Rhaegos' token was and... now the Hethurin here are being run out of town."

"It's not your fault, Ina." Mattie grabbed my hand and squeezed it to comfort me. "The avalanche, the gesith, even Hardbein. All of that—outside of your control. But you're doing what you can to protect the Hethurin, even if the gesith and Hardbein are being assholes."

I looked up at her, embarrassed by the tears rolling down my face.

"She's right." Haldrek said. "It's been a long day for all of us. I'm surprised you're not more exhausted. How is your neck feeling?"

I touched it, realizing I'd been too busy doing other things to focus on it. The muscles in my neck were still sore, but the injury didn't sting at all.

"Better. I don't know if it's Meri's doing or just being focused on everything else, but it doesn't hurt as bad." I focused on my mug, not feeling thirsty. "We need to figure out how to get the Hethurin to safety. How long is a trip from here to the estate again?"

"On horseback, it would be a day to a day and a half. But they'll be walking. So, it could take up to a week, depending on how slow they are."

I nodded, exhaustion finally making itself known. "There will be warriors among them, right? So, they'll be safe. Hopefully. Do we know if there is anyone other than Meri who would know how to get back to Svangendom?"

Haldrek and Mattie regarded each other for a moment, until Haldrek turned to me and said, "The rider coming from Svangendom will know. But I doubt he'll be here until after the Hethurin have to leave."

"Perhaps they could shelter at Osvif's Refuge until he has given me the book and returns to Svangendom? That's far enough away from Aldinnvollr to keep them safe, right?"

Haldrek scratched his chin thoughtfully. "They could. We need to talk to Meri once she returns."

Our conversation lulled as Haldrek returned to his drink. I smelled mine. *Kavasir.* Probably better for healing than alcohol, anyway. I took a small sip, hoping it would help me feel better.

"Ina?"

I looked up again to see Mattie playing with her mug.

"Yeah?"

"How would you feel if I headed back to Svangendom with the Hethurin?"

My eyes widened and I sat back. "I... Why do you want to go back?"

"I think I could help you more back there. And in case Hardbein tries again for the estate, I could let you know." She tugged at the leather strap holding her pendant. "The pendants seem to work like mini thegn stones, and I think I can figure out how to improve on that aspect." She paused. "I've definitely felt as welcome here as the Hethurin and I... yeah, I think I could help you more back at Svangendom."

"You can go back if you'd like, then. I'm sorry... I'm sorry people haven't been more welcoming." My head got woozy again, as if I'd had drunk more mead, and I groaned. I'd messed up things for the Hethurin and now I feared that in the craziness of everything, I hadn't noticed that Mattie wasn't being treated well and I had done nothing to fix that.

"Don't be sorry. This isn't your fault. You've been busy with everything thegn related—rightfully so—and it's not your responsibility to stand up for me all the time. I'm not going back to Svangendom because of anything *you've* done. I'm *not* mad at you."

Still feeling awful, but knowing that Mattie was right, I exhaled, my body relaxing a bit. If I'd done something terrible, she would've let me know.

"Another thing we need to figure out—once the Hethurin are safe—is how to get Rhaegos' token." Haldrek tapped his finger on the rim of his mug. "We're going to have to figure another way to the shrine."

"You said that the only path to the shrine is over that bridge, right?" I turned to him.

He nodded. "So, we need to figure out how to deal with the ice drakes. They won't let anyone near the shrine until... I don't know, maybe until it's repaired?"

"But how can we repair it if the ice drakes are keeping everyone away?"

Haldrek shrugged. "I don't know. But we need to find a way."

The next morning, as the sky lightened, I stood at the edge of town with a small group of men and women who were less inclined to leave than some of their fellow Hethurin. They stood in the blacksmith's forge yard with him as one of their number. He stood in front of his forge, the reddish light from it giving him an ominous glow.

"I sent my wife and children on with the group to Svangendom, but I'm not leaving. I've spent my life working this forge and I'm not about to leave it because the damned gesith thinks the dragons and Ottkatla despise my kind." He shook his head. "I believe you to be the true thegn, but that doesn't mean I'll flee at the first hint of trouble. I'm as much Lohikärran as I am anything else."

"What happens to your family if the gesith makes an example of you?" Haldrek asked. He had been pacing behind me as I tried to reason with the blacksmith.

"They'll be fine without me. My wife is a strong woman. She doesn't need me to survive. Same with my children. We all die one day, Thegn Andrattür. I don't want to, but if today is it, so be it. I won't run away just because the gesith has lost his mind."

Haldrek stopped. "A good warrior knows when to stand and when to retreat. This is *not* the time to stand. In a few days, Ina will have Rhaegos's blessing, and this entire mess will be over. Don't prepare to die when you don't have to."

"I've made my decision, Thegn Andrattür. There's nothing you can do to change my mind." Light from the sun made the blacksmith's face more visible, and I saw that he wore a stubborn grin.

Haldrek grumbled behind me, and I focused on the blacksmith, hoping I could talk some sense into him.

"Are you loyal to Svartån? If my father came here and asked you to do something, would you do it for him?"

The blacksmith laughed. "I would. Your father would understand that there are some things worth standing and dying for, however."

I looked back at Haldrek, and he shook his head.

As I followed Haldrek out of the forge yard, I turned to him, still sick at the idea of these people dying because of me. "What are we going to do?"

"Nothing. The chances of changing these people's minds are about as likely as changing the gesith's mind. I *hope* that there won't be bloodshed, but I wouldn't bet on that for a second."

"Do we just stand here and let people get slaughtered, then?"

Haldrek shook his head. "I have a plan. It may not work, but it's worth a shot. If it works, it may buy us some time."

I took a deep breath to calm myself, still uncertain as I saw the gesith and Hardbein walk toward us. Behind them gathered a small crowd of both villagers and warriors bearing the Lansiranikän crest.

"Your kind are no longer welcome here. Nor is the false thegn. Hardbein has made it known to me that neither the dragons nor Ottkatla welcome you—any of you—in this land blessed by Rhaegos." The gesith gestured at the buildings behind us. "As those cast off from the dragons, all you have is forfeit. If you try to protect it, your lives will also be forfeit. But if you leave now, I will be merciful."

"Are you serious?" I turned back to see the blacksmith walk forward behind me. "We've lived and died for Aldinnvollr. We've given our best for the dragons. For Svartån and Lohikärra. And on a whim, you expect us to leave? No!"

The others cheered around him, and I heard the rattle of weapons being readied. I glanced over at Haldrek, wondering when his 'plan' was going to happen. He kept a grim focus on the gesith.

"Very well. You've made your choice." The gesith gestured with his fingers and in an instant the crowd behind him surged forward.

Haldrek and I unsheathed our weapons, and before I could think, a villager came at me. I knocked him to the ground with my shield.

"Stop!" I said, taking a swing at another villager and nicking him. "If you touch any of these people, I will *fight* you!" I felt stupid saying those words, barely knowing how to fight, but there was little else I could do.

Hardbein laughed as the villager pushed me back. He charged me as the villager darted off after another Hethurin soldier, knocking me to the ground. "Go ahead and try. The sooner you die, the sooner I get my rightful armor."

He slammed his ax down on my shield. My arm burned as the shield took the blow, but didn't break. Hardbein grunted as he got tossed to the side and I saw Haldrek's shield bear down on him, knocking his ax from his hand and sending it flying to the ground.

"Enough!" Haldrek's voice boomed, and the surrounding people froze. The fighting ceased as Hardbein stared in surprise and anger at him. Haldrek pointed his sword at Hardbein's throat. "If you or *anyone* harms her, I will smite you myself."

Hardbein grabbed for his ax without a word, and Haldrek kicked it away.

From outside my view, the gesith said, "You have no power here, Thegn Andrattür! These are not your thegn lands."

"No, but the dragons do, and Ina does. She's called on Rhaegos before to save our lives. Do you wish for her to call upon Rhaegos and her kin again?"

The gesith hesitated, then said, "They would never aid her in her selfish desires! They've already made their will known!"

"No, but they would aid her in fulfilling *their* desires. Do you wish for Ina to call on them again? You shouldn't be afraid, if you think Hardbein has their blessing and Ina doesn't."

The gesith stood silent, and Haldrek turned his head to me.

"Rhaegos! Help me!" I called out, trying to sound as convincing as I could.

The sky darkened as something flew above us, circling a few times over the town as it made its way in the shrine's direction. A few people screamed and covered their ears, but there was no sound from the dragon except for the thump of its wings against the air, and as soon as it arrived, it was off. I shuddered.

The silence continued for a few moments before the gesith said, "Fine. However, those Hethurin who stay are outside the protection of the village. And you, Thegn Andrattür, you and that shield wench of yours, are no longer welcome here."

# Chapter Twelve

I shook out my left arm, still throbbing from where Hardbein had hit my shield. The gesith had allowed a short truce, allowing the Hethurin, as well as Haldrek and me, to leave Aldinnvollr. The Hethurin had left through the gate near the barrow and Haldrek and I defiantly crossed through town and left through the gate leading to the shrine.

As sore as my arm was, my heart hurt worse. I couldn't overcome the feeling that I had already failed. *I wanted* to give an offering at the shrine, but now it was destroyed. *I wanted* to prove that I was the true thegn, but instead the gesith had doubled down on his belief that Hardbein was the true thegn. *I wanted* to protect the Hethurin in Aldinnvollr, but now the gesith had cast them out because of me.

"Ina?"

Haldrek's voice pulled me out of my thoughts. We were on the path up to the shrine—having no idea of where else to go—but he had stopped.

"What?"

"You've been quiet since we left Aldinnvollr." He hesitated. "Are you... We're going to get Rhaegos's blessing. She hasn't cursed you—or anyone. If she didn't believe you belonged here, she wouldn't have saved us all when we were prisoners." He smiled, as if trying to lighten my spirits.

"I... I'm just trying to figure out how I messed things up so badly in Aldinnvollr." Tears started rolling down my cheeks as I took a deep breath to calm myself. "Even if I get Rhaegos's blessing, even if I have all the proof in the world that I am the true thegn, are the people of Aldinnvollr ever going to accept me? Are the people of Svartån ever going to accept me?"

Haldrek walked up to me, locking his arm in mine and grabbing a metal pole in the rock face with his other hand as we moved past a particularly narrow part of the path. "You didn't mess things up in Aldinnvollr. Hardbein is just... he's a warrior. The gesith has fought with him, so it's no wonder that he supports and believes him. But that doesn't mean that Hardbein is the one the dragons have chosen." He stopped again, this time at a spot that gave us a perfect vantage point over what the avalanche had left of the shrine. "As for whether they will accept you... they may or may not. Not all the people of Andrattür accept me. But that doesn't matter. Because Andrattür is my home, and I am its thegn."

I sighed as we continued up the path. "Is Svartån my home, then? I don't know if I've been here long enough to call it home." Or even if 'home' was a good word to use for what Svartån was. I'd never thought of 'home' as being a place that I wanted to be. Home was never 'safe'. I always dreamt of going somewhere else. Someplace like Lohikärra.

"Svartån is your home if you choose it to be. Home is... home is where you feel you belong. Even if it's not the place you grew up." He hesitated again. "Rhaegos spoke to me about you. Not too long ago."

"What?" I stopped and turned to him as we reached the top of the bridge. The ice drakes shrieked at the bottom where the bridge met the cliff. "When?"

"Before you arrived. The evening before Drattüjert... before Drattüjert fell. That was an interesting night, but Rhaegos bid me come see her at the Mound of Tenelth."

"The place where Tenelth was supposedly buried?"

Haldrek shrugged. "I guess you could say that. Most dragons aren't considered 'buried' because their spirit lives on alongside the human they've bonded with. Bjornulf himself placed Tenelth's bones in the mound. That mound is now a massive shrine where people take offerings and where... when there is a new High King or Queen, the dragons accept them. The shrine is also a place where nearly every person recorded in an Epic was called by the dragons at that shrine."

"Did Rhaegos call you there?" The games had referenced the Mound of Tenelth, but it was never actually a spot that the character could visit.

"She did. I had questions, and she answered them in the only way that dragons do—vaguely." Haldrek laughed and then said, "She told me you belonged here in Lohikärra. That I needed to keep you safe."

My eyes widened as he turned to me with a grin. I asked, "That's why you've been so adamant about helping me?"

Haldrek sighed, and his grin turned serious. "One reason, of many. But... I like you as well now. I like your fire. I like... how determined you are. How strong you are. You are going to be a good... thegn. Ally. Friend."

I tugged at the chain mail on my arm to soothe myself as I stared down at the other side of the bridge and at the ice drakes that flew around in a frenzy. Haldrek's words both made me happy and nervous inside. I didn't feel strong. More like a liability. The idea of someone—other than Mattie—liking me, even as a friend, made my head spin. "Thank you. I... I like you too. Your company. Your support. I'm guessing you'll probably have to go back to Andrattür at some point. I think... I think I'll miss you when that happens."

We were silent for a few moments, and then Haldrek laughed out loud, making me jump. "You think?"

I turned to see him grinning playfully. I grinned myself. "Yeah, I think so. If these ice drakes don't kill me first."

The ice drakes had kept their distance, but as soon as I spoke, one shrieked louder than the others and made a beeline for me up the bridge. I unsheathed my sword as I began stumbling backwards. The ice drake sped up and as I tripped over a loose stone, it slammed into my shield, sending me airborne. My shield arm went numb from the impact and intense cold. A moment later, I hit the ground, my head snapping back with a crack onto the cobblestone path. My vision blurred, then faded out as I tried to remain conscious.

"Ina!" Haldrek's voice sounded far away as he knelt next to me. His words turned into mumbling as I passed out.

Everything was pale, like I was in the middle of a cloud or some kind of fog when I came to. It reminded me of whiteouts from snowstorms back home, and my heart sank at the idea of being back in Fargo. Haldrek was gone, and I didn't feel cold anymore. I just felt neutral.

The fog faded from where I sat, and I sensed an enormous structure both in front of me and behind me. Looking back, I saw the bridge I had just been on, arching up into the cloud that surrounded me. My father—or rather a *much* younger looking man who I sensed was my father—walked out of the cloud with an ornate box in his hands. He wore the thegn armor, though it differed slightly from what Ottkatla had given me. More chain mail, less plate armor, and a simpler cone shaped helmet with a strip of metal over his nose is what struck me the most. Most of his face and neck—or rather his beard—were exposed.

As he passed me, I scrambled to my feet and grabbed for him. My hand passed through him, and he seemed oblivious to my presence.

"Dad?"

Nothing. I followed him, the fog parting for the two of us until we reached the other structure that I had sensed. A massive statue of a dragon with its wings extended as if frozen—or petrified—in mid-flight. A woman whose shoulders were taller than my father walked out from behind the shrine. Other than her height, there was something peculiar—and familiar—about her presence. She looked young and yet her hair was bright white, blending in with the snow and standing out from her earthy green and brown attire. It was braided from the back of her head and down to the ground, where it pooled in a tight coil. The tip of it twitched every so often, not from any kind of air movement, but almost of its own accord.

"Ingmar Svanunge. Thegn-heir of Svartån. What brings you here this day?"

"Mighty Rhaegos..." He stared at her in awe as he knelt to both knees. "I have retrieved fair Ottkatla's armor and blessing. Now I come before you with an offering. The thing that is dearest to me now." He bowed his head and offered her the ornate box.

Without speaking, she took the box and opened it. A smile graced her mouth as she pulled some papers out of the box. "Your research, Ingmar." With a laugh, she said, "Many know the mighty warrior. Few know the intuitive scholar." She paused as she neatly put the rolled-up papers back in the box. "Have you any intention of continuing your study?"

My father was silent for what seemed like eternities before he gazed up at her. "If it pleases you, I would be a thegn to serve and protect the people of Svartån. That is my duty, and I accept it. If being a thegn of Svartån means I must put aside the studies of my youth, so be it."

Rhaegos laughed again. "So formal. And dramatic." She placed the box in front of my father and then turned, disappearing back into the snowy fog. My father's face fell, and I sensed despair as he watched the fog. I wanted to run into the fog and tell Rhaegos to give him her blessing, but I stayed frozen where I stood.

Then she returned, holding a gleaming blade. Its hilt was toward me, and I noticed runes on each side. I had no idea what they said but knew that they held some importance.

"Rise and stand, Ingmar Svanunge, Thegn of Svartån. Take the sword of your forebears and with it, my blessing."

My father stumbled to his feet and bowed again before taking it and placing it in the empty sheath at his side. "Thank you, mighty Rhaegos."

"Before you go, understand this—only those who use this weapon to protect *all* of Svartån may use it. All others are unworthy, and the hilt shall fall from their grasp as if made of the driest snow. If *you* become unworthy, so shall it be." She then knelt to take my father's offering. As she stood up, she handed it back to him. "You gave me what was dearest to you, and I accept your offering. However, it takes more than just a mighty warrior to protect people. It takes knowledge, curiosity, and perseverance. Continue seeking knowledge and use it to protect all of Svartån *and* all of Lohikärra as if it were your sword."

My father bowed more deeply this time. "As... as you wish, mighty Rhaegos."

The snowy fog seeped in around them until they disappeared. A bitter cold wrapped itself around me, and I gasped as my knees buckled and I blacked out again.

"Ina..." Someone stroked my face desperately, as if trying to get me to react. I groaned with exhaustion. I felt like I'd been sleeping for ages but hadn't rested. All I wanted to do now was sleep.

"Ina..." Haldrek's voice became more urgent, and I remember where we had been. My eyes flew open, and I saw that we were in a different place, with the bridge nowhere in sight. Instead, there was the sound of churning water nearby, and we were in a covered spot. As cold as I was, I sensed that we were out of the elements.

"Where are we?" I groaned, trying to sit up. My muscles throbbed and my skin prickled like it had been numb.

"A cave. A traveler's refuge, to be exact. Something carved them out centuries ago. People visiting the shrine, but not wanting to travel from Aldinnvollr, often stayed here." Haldrek exhaled with relief and leaned his forehead against the side of my head. Despite being so cold, nerves all over my body tingled as I enjoyed

Haldrek's closeness. The idea of shifting my head to kiss him came to mind, but my muscles were still too weak and numb to do much of anything.

"What happened?"

"An ice drake attacked you. I don't know why, but it was screaming something about… it made little sense. Though drakes don't often make sense."

"Why not?" I noticed that Haldrek had made a small fire. He moved me closer to it, its heat slowly warming me up. My skin tingled more and grew less frozen, but I wanted to continue resting in Haldrek's arms.

"Drakes are creatures *like* dragons, but still more connected to the elements. They're more impulsive, erratic, and dangerous in some ways. They can speak like dragons, but they sound more like madmen, ranting and raging, never coherent." He shook his head. "I've always been able to understand dragons, not so much with drakes."

"What was the drake saying?"

"Something about us leaving. It wanted us to leave, that's for sure, but the part that confused me is how it spoke of us being unworthy. That makes little sense."

My chest squeezed tight. "It said unworthy? What if…?"

Haldrek shook his head. "It kept chanting the word *Kelvodeg*. Which means unworthy, but it's also used to mean 'was once worthy' and 'not yet worthy'. It doesn't mean you—or I—aren't worthy forever. It just might mean that there is something you still need to do before you can go to the shrine."

"Or it means I've angered the dragons somehow. That I 'was once worthy'." Tears blurred my eyes. "What if I did something I wasn't supposed to? Or didn't do something I was supposed to?"

"I doubt it. I was talking to Teminth while you were passed out, and he would have told me if the dragons deemed you unworthy."

"Teminth?" I frowned at Haldrek.

"The dragon who bound himself with me. Do… do you know anything about *haldragas*?"

I shook my head. It hadn't been a term used in the games, but I vaguely remembered hearing it when I'd first arrived in Lohikärra.

"Haldragas are people that the dragons choose to bind with in order to aid them. I'm a haldraga, as are all the other thegns, and as was your father. Being a haldraga… allows the person to commune with their dragon. Not everyone can become a haldraga, but most rulers, whether they be thegns or the High King himself, will be a haldraga."

"Will I become a haldraga one day? Or…" I wondered if I'd done something to—at the very least irritate the dragons—that I'd given up my ability to become a haldraga.

"I would bet my lands on it. It may take time. You can become a thegn before becoming a haldraga. So, you don't need to worry about that."

"How long? Do you think? Are there things I have to do before becoming a haldraga? Like visiting barrows and shrines?"

Haldrek laughed and shook his head. "The dragons choose when they will bind. Which has caused some anxiety among those expecting to become haldragas."

I exhaled, feeling a little better and my mind less fuzzy. Haldrek gently leaned my head into his shoulder, and I didn't resist. He smelled of wood smoke and honey, which comforted me. I thought back to the vision or memory I'd seen after getting hit by the ice drake and wondered if it had anything to do with being a haldraga.

"When you became a thegn, did you meet a dragon at the shrine you went to?" The words sounded ridiculous as soon as they popped out of my mouth. Of course, he would have seen a dragon, why wouldn't he?

"I didn't, actually. I mean… dragons don't usually visit a shrine when the thegn-heir gives their offering. It's rare for someone to not be a haldraga before becoming a thegn. Most thegn-heirs find out whether their offering is accepted from the dragon who bound with them. Why?"

"I saw something. After the ice drake attacked me. I guess it was a vision or memory? Of my father asking for Rhaegos's blessing. She talked to him directly, and in a human form."

Haldrek laughed and said, "That wouldn't surprise me, knowing Rhaegos. As one of the eldest dragons that still interacts with humans, she does what she wishes. I think there may be only one or two dragons that are older and more respected than her." He paused and tossed a few more twigs into the fire. "What did she say in the vision?"

"My father offered her a box of scrolls. I guess he was a scholar of some sort before becoming thegn. Not that it surprised me. That seems more in line with the little I knew about him. He offered his research to Rhaegos and said that he'd forsake it, if it meant being a good thegn. Rhaegos then laughed at him and told him he was overdramatic."

Haldrek's chest rumbled with another laugh. "That too, is very much like my experience with Rhaegos."

"Then she disappeared and returned with a sword. She said two things that stood out to me. First, that he was to use the weapon given him, for the good of all the people of Svartån, and that if it wasn't, it would fall through the wielder's hands like dry snow. Second, she gave him back his box of scrolls and told him it takes more than just being a mighty warrior to be a good thegn. That he needed to continue seeking knowledge, and that knowledge would help both Svartån and Lohikärra."

"That's probably why when he wasn't training for battle, he was in his library or asking questions."

"Asking questions? Just in general?"

Haldrek nodded. "He never took things at face value, always wanted to know why. Perhaps part of that was because of what Rhaegos told him."

"Maybe." I stared at the twigs being consumed by the fire and wondered if Rhaegos would make herself known to me. If she did, what would she say? Ottkatla had mentioned overcoming my fears, but that was a lot more vague than 'be an excellent warrior and study a lot'. As I watched the fire consume a twig, my fears consumed me. It wouldn't matter what Rhaegos had to say to me if I couldn't restore the shrine.

"What are we going to do now?" I knew investigating the shrine or even rebuilding it would be easy, but now it seemed impossible.

"We need to find a way around the ice drakes. Teminth said they're hurting, and that's why, he thinks, they're raging so much. If we rebuild the shrine, that may calm them. Until then…"

"What?" I cocked my head in confusion. I still didn't have the energy to think critically.

"Fireballs." Haldrek grinned, tossing another small stick in the fire in front of us.

Haldrek's plan wasn't complicated, despite the fact that the ice drakes were unkillable. Their ice form was just a physical presence. One they didn't like, it seemed. Haldrek explained that once they were rid of that physical form, they were less dangerous. Just more of a nuisance. One of us would cast fireballs at them anytime they came at us, while the other… figured out how to rebuild the shrine. Or figure out how to sedate the drakes long enough to allow us to rebuild the shrine. We hadn't fleshed out that part of the plan yet.

My pendant warmed up as Haldrek explained what he knew about ice drakes and how to defend myself from them. I pulled it out from under my layers and let it hang loose as I tried to focus on the scribbles in the dirt that Haldrek had written. My knowledge of Lohikärran runes was still pathetic, and Haldrek had admitted to not having the best handwriting.

After a moment, he stopped, frowned, and pulled his pendant from under his armor. He popped it open and cocked his head as Mattie's voice came out of it.

"At least one of you answers their pendant. Where's Ina?"

I squeezed in next to Haldrek as he showed me the pendant. "I'm here, what's going on? Are the Hethurin okay?"

"They're fine. We're all fine. But there were *two* messengers from Svangendom. The first had your book and said he was told the gesith kicked you and Haldrek out of Aldinnvollr?"

"Yeah... There was a bit of a scuffle after you all left... and it was better for us to leave than to stay. At least for the time being. I think Haldrek and I have a plan for restoring the shrine though, or at least starting that process."

"Let's hope sooner than later. That's why I tried to contact you through the pendant. Another messenger from Svangendom came. He..." Mattie hesitated, as if trying to find the right words. "He was nervous. Jittery, almost. He said Eldingheimr sent word of Isillas ships patrolling in the open ocean just outside the harbor there and that Skuti wants to know what you wished to do, so now I'm wondering if it's safe to return to Svangendom."

"I..." My head swam, and I thought back to the vision or memory of my father and Rhaegos. She had said that only those who protected all the people of Svartån were worthy to wield the blade she had given him. Was Svangendom the right choice for keeping the Hethurin safe? Would they be protected there? I thought they would, but... "I'm guessing there aren't any other places that would welcome fifty or so Hethurin in the dead of winter."

"No. I asked, and both messengers said even the few towns sympathetic to the Hethurin would chafe at such a large number on brief notice. Plus, most of those with me only packed or had enough food on hand to get to Svangendom. If we began wandering from town to town, that would make this journey more difficult than it already is."

I nodded, though I doubted Mattie could see it. "Keep going to Svangendom then. Send both messengers back with word that... that Skuti needs to have defenses up." I turned to Haldrek for guidance. I knew Svangendom needed to prepare, just in case, but I had no idea to what level.

"Tell Skuti to make sure there are guards at the walls both day and night, and they need to be vigilant for anything *different*. Not ready to arms yet but be alert." Haldrek turned to me for a moment before focusing on his pendant. "No lone messengers traveling between Eldingheimr and Svangendom. If the Isillas attack Eldingheimr, they'll be able to put up a good defense, but the estate needs to ensure that word will make it back to them, so they can prepare and rebuff any attacks."

"I'll do that. Thanks, you two." The glass in Haldrek's pendant went dark, and I assumed that meant Mattie had finished the 'call'.

I groaned, thinking about other places that we might need to warn. Other towns along the coast and even...

Despite being unwelcome there now, I knew someone should warn Aldinnvollr as well. Especially if they were a place the Isillas might go after. I turned back to Haldrek. "How long would it take an Isillas invasion force to reach Aldinnvollr?"

"A week from the coast, unimpeded. Unless they were to wipe out all the coastal towns though, that would never happen." He was quiet for a few minutes. "You're thinking of warning the gesith and Aldinnvollr, aren't you?"

"I... maybe? I want to protect all the people of Svartån. Not just the ones who like me." Tiredness and hunger overwhelmed me as I leaned into Haldrek. "That's the right thing to do. Right?"

"It's what a good thegn would do, so yes. But... the Isillas haven't made landfall yet. As far as we know." Haldrek wrapped his arm around my shoulders, comforting me. "It is getting dark, too. Even if we were welcome in Aldinnvollr, it wouldn't be wise to travel back right now."

"Are we going to be safe in this cave overnight?" With everything else swirling around in my head, I hadn't thought about food, shelter, or safety.

"We'll be fine." He nudged his bag with his foot. It seemed a lot emptier than when we had arrived in Aldinnvollr. "Thoreg gave us plenty of provisions last night. Almost as if he knew we'd need them."

I bobbed my head up and down, feeling sleepier than I wanted. Haldrek shifted to lie on his back, pulling me next to him so I could lie on his chest. I relished it.

The thought of kissing him again crossing my mind, as I took in as much of his warmth and scent as I could.

"Let's rest." Haldrek's voice was deep and soft above me, his chest rumbling with every word. "In the morning, if you still wish to warn the gesith, we'll head back to Aldinnvollr."

# Chapter Thirteen

The next morning, we quickly packed up our camp and made our way back to Aldinnvollr. Part of me wondered if it was a fool's errand, but I also knew it was the right thing to do. Even if the Isillas weren't here yet, I should warn Aldinnvollr in case Seirye and his elves made their way up to the town. And... I hoped it would make the gesith more amenable to me. Even if it didn't—as Haldrek expected—I needed to show the dragons I was willing to protect *all* of Svartån, not just the people who accepted me as thegn.

As we arrived at the point where our path joined the main path back from the shrine, we saw a group of men being led by a large, familiar man, decked out in armor.

Haldrek stopped me. "What in Tenelth's name is Hardbein doing up here?"

"You think he's trying to res—" I stopped as I thought of how ridiculous my thought was. Of course, he wouldn't be here to restore the shrine. He was up here for another reason.

"Be ready to unsheathe your weapon, but don't do it yet."

I put my hand on my hilt and took a deep breath to calm myself. There was nothing up here now that would call for Hardbein bringing a group of his men. I counted the warriors behind him—five. Enough to give us a good fight if they chose to.

"I would take your hand off your sword if you don't want a fight, shield-wench."

"What are you doing up here, Hardbein?" I paused. "I doubt you came up here with your soldiers to give any offerings."

He laughed. "No. I'm here to take what is rightfully mine." He gestured to my armor.

"If it was rightfully yours, Ottkatla would have given it to you and not me."

"The only reason you have the armor is because you magicked it away from Ottkatla in the Barrow." He shook his head. "No, that armor belongs to someone who can protect *all* of Svartån—not leave it defenseless when the ice elves come." He tightened his hand around the hilt of his sword. "Now hand over the armor and we can keep this snow as blood-free as it is now."

I shook my head and as I was about to speak, Haldrek grabbed my shoulder and leaned in close to my ear.

"Give him the armor."

I spun my head around and stared at Haldrek. "*What?*"

"Give him the armor." Haldrek's voice was soft enough that I doubted Hardbein or any of his men could hear us. "You're a better thegn alive than dead."

"I'm *not* giving him the armor." I hissed through my teeth, feeling the first pricks of anger and betrayal stab at me under my armor and clothes. "Ottkatla gave me this armor and I'm not about to give it up, just because—"

"We're outnumbered right now."

"We've *always* been outnumbered. Why give up now?"

Before Haldrek could respond, Hardbein shouted, "What's your decision, wench? Do I take the armor in peace or off your mangled corpse?"

I ignored him and focused on Haldrek. "Are you going to help me or not?"

"Always, but—"

I turned around to Hardbein and said, "The only way you're getting this armor is if I'm dead."

"Very well."

Hardbein's sword came out in a flash as he charged me. I blocked it with my shield and stabbed at him with my sword. He blocked it at the last second with his own shield and knocked me down into the snow. Haldrek shoved him back and crouched next to me as a few arrows thudded into and off of his shield. One embedded itself just inches from my foot.

Haldrek jumped up and slammed a soldier back as I scrambled to my feet. Hardbein launched himself at me again, but this time I swung my sword at his kneecap, digging it into some flesh as my shield impacted his face. Hardbein bellowed in pain. He buckled underneath me, and I stumbled forward, my shield and Hardbein's shield keeping me from falling on him completely. Instead, I tumbled off and into the path of one of the Lansiranikän warriors. Hardbein screamed again, but I ignored him as the warrior stabbed at me and I blocked him narrowly. His blade punctured through my chain mail and sliced through my right arm.

"Kill her! Take the armor! Kill *her!*"

Before I could react, multiple bodies toppled onto me as the warriors ripped my shield from my arm and yanked my helmet from my head. Haldrek screamed as he pushed a couple of men off of me and dragged me out of the pile. One man jumped for me, grabbing for my chest plate. With one hand he gripped part of the armhole and with the other he jabbed at the seams of the plates, severing the leather straps and making my chest plate fall loose on one side.

Haldrek stabbed the man and yanked me back in one swift move. The soldier recoiled back, but not before Haldrek pulled the chest plate off completely and they left me in little more than chain mail. He threw it at the soldier, hitting him in the head and knocking him back into the snow.

I surveyed the scene. There were only a few men left who had fought. Hardbein lay curled up on the pathway, holding a hand over his right eye, and something dark dripping between his fingers. A couple of soldiers groaned in the snow as Haldrek stood defensively in front of me. The one soldier who cut my chest plate away from me piled it alongside the rest of my armor and sword.

"We got the armor, my gesith!"

Hardbein gestured at his men, who began gathering the armor and helping him up. As he stood up, he glared at me with his one good eye. "Dragon blighted wench. Go keep Andrattür's bedroll warm and leave Svartån to those who can protect it." He paused, grimacing in pain. "As the true thegn-heir, I banish you from Svartån. If I see your face in these lands again, I'll have your head as a prize."

I scrambled up to face him again, but Haldrek pushed me back without a word.

Hardbein laughed. "Looks like even your allies grow tired of you."

I moved again, this time to grab my armor, but immediately the soldiers who remained readied their weapons and Haldrek put his arm in front of me. I turned to him angrily as he shook his head.

"A good warrior knows when to fight and when to retreat. Now is not the time to fight. Let's go."

I stared at him while the soldiers and Hardbein left. With *my* armor. As soon as they were out of earshot, I turned on Haldrek. "Ottkatla *gave* that armor to me. And *you* let them have it." My throat tightened in anger, pain, and with the growing sense of betrayal.

He shook his head and put his arm down. "It's not worth fighting them over right now. You can still deal with the shrine without it."

"What the hell does that even mean?" My anger rose further at Haldrek's sudden change in behavior. "If I didn't need the armor for the shrine, why get it in the first place?"

"Let's go back to the cave. You're a better thegn alive than dead." He gestured back in the direction that we'd come from and put his hand around my right shoulder. Instead of letting him, I shoved him away with all my strength, making the injury on my right arm burn. He only took a few steps back, but his eyes widened in surprise.

"Don't touch me! I..." My mind blanked as I tried to express my feelings. "Go away!" I couldn't think of anything else to say, and the urge to be alone overwhelmed me, so without another word, I stormed off.

I ran as fast as I could back up the path to the cave where we had been. Our footprints made it easy to find again. Despite telling him to go away, I could hear Haldrek keeping up behind me, and he didn't sound as winded as I felt. Which pissed me off even more. My chest burned and tightened, but I didn't know if that was from running or the overwhelming anger and hurt inside of me.

Once we reached the cave, I ran to the opposite side of the fire that we'd made earlier, red embers glowing.

"Too-Welli-Ballo!" I threw my hand toward the campfire and imagined a fireball engulfing the wood. Fire shot from my hand and latched on to the wood without hesitation.

"Ina. Please—" Haldrek paused near the entrance of the cave, hands raised to placate me.

"I told you to go away! I can't trust you. I can't trust *anyone* here. Leave me alone!"

"Ina... I was trying to protect you back there! Hardbein has no issue with trying to kill you. If he had known—"

"So, letting him have the armor was the solution?" I said, sarcasm dripping with every word. "If that was the case, why not give it to him in Aldinnvollr, huh? Why even trek here in the first place?" My pendant weighed heavy against my chest, and I pulled it out. "What about this? Should I have given him my pendant, too?"

Haldrek pursed his lips as his face flushed with frustration. Anger was bubbling up inside him, too. "Ina... Get a hold of yourself. If Hardbein knew the truth, he would have killed you and then taken the armor. And then he *would* have been the real thegn of Svartån."

"What truth? I thought whoever had the armor was thegn?"

"*No*. You think he's going to fit into that armor? It's not going to all of a sudden fit him because he took it. I promise you; you will have the armor back in your hands soon. Because that's how it works."

I stared at him, still angry. Still hurting. Still cold and tired and hungry. Still miserable. "Then why the hell didn't you tell me that earlier? You just enjoy seeing me make a fool of myself?" The volume of my voice frightened me, but the release of anger was more intoxicating.

"Ina..." This time his voice was more of a growl. "You know why. I *don't* enjoy seeing you make a fool of yourself. If I didn't want to help you, I wouldn't be here. I have *plenty* of work waiting for me in Andrattür. Before you ask, I'm not just doing this because of your father. I'm helping you because you are the true thegn of Svartån, and you are going to be an amazing one. But you can't act this way over one defeat."

*One defeat*? My anger had been fading until that one comment. My mother's voice crept into my mind, reminding me of how incompetent I was. How I would never do anything right and eventually everyone would grow tired of me. That I ruined everything, and people were happier when I wasn't around. The people of Aldinnvollr had shown me that. I kicked a half-burnt stick out of the fire as hard as I could, releasing more of my frustration.

Haldrek's eyes widened. He stepped back as it fell to the ground between us and got smothered by the snow I'd tracked in.

"I haven't had only 'one defeat' since I've been here." My voice trembled with anger. "I've had multiple setbacks, and every single plan I've made up has failed. *I've failed.* Get the gesith to accept me as thegn? Failed. Protect the Hethurin? Failed. Give an offering at the shrine? Failed. Not only that—but the whole freaking town also thinks I blew up their beloved shrine. Even if I could protect them from whatever's out there, they wouldn't let me! I'm a failure, Haldrek. Who knows, maybe this is Ottkatla's and Rhaegos's way of showing that I'm not worthy anymore. Maybe that's what the ice drakes were screaming about. I'm not worthy anymore."

"Ina... That's not—"

"What if it is? How do you know they weren't screaming that? Maybe I'm *not* worthy? Maybe Rhaegos is flying around thinking 'geez, how can I get this stupid girl to go away? She's making things worse for everyone.' Maybe I'm not this super badass warrior that I'm supposed to be. Maybe—"

"Would you just shut up for a moment and listen?" The anger in Haldrek's voice made me jump back. "Stop being so difficult!" He growled in frustration, his fists tightening. "You are impossible sometimes. You think you're a failure, but you're not. You've made a few mistakes, but we all have. *I've* made plenty of mistakes. I've been trying to help you this whole time, but I'm getting sick and tired of you thinking you're worthless. I'm sick and tired of trying to encourage you when... when... do you even *care*?"

"Of course, I care!"

"Act like it, then. Act like a thegn for once!"

His words cut into me as if he'd swung his sword. My lungs squeezed tight as I tried to hold my pain in, a pain worse than anything I'd yet experienced in Lohikärra. It bubbled up inside of me, making me want to scream and lash out. "*I hate you!* You *know* I'm trying my hardest. I'm trying to act like a thegn, but that's not good enough, is it?" My chest felt like it was about to burst from anger. "I *never* should have trusted you. I regret ever meeting you! Go away! Just *go* away!"

His jaw tightened as he clenched his fists and stared at the cave roof. His shoulders sagged as he looked back at me and shook his head. "Very well." Without another word, he turned around and walked out of the cave.

I dropped to the floor and tucked my head in between my chest and legs, wrapping my arms around them as tight as I could. Though my arm hurt more doing that, I didn't want anyone or anything to hear me as I broke down sobbing.

My heart sank as my anger at Haldrek faded into more of a dull ache in my chest. I hadn't expected him to leave. I hadn't expected him to listen. No, I'd expected him to... I'd expected him to get angry at me like my mother always did. Yell at me. Hit me or scratch me or tell me I was a loser and a failure. But now... I was alone. And that felt worse.

"I'm so stupid." Tears began welling up in my eyes as I went over our fight in my mind. I'd said some of the same things my mother had said to me over and over again. Things I swore I'd never say to anyone else. Not only was I a terrible thegn-heir, but I was a terrible person in general. As much as it hurt when Haldrek had told me to give Hardbein the armor, I knew I couldn't do anything in Lohikärra without him.

My head sank further between my knees and my chest as I let myself just cry. I'd tried to be brave and strong and do what I was supposed to do, and where had that gotten me? Nowhere. Anger, bitterness, and self-pity swirled around inside me, leaving me exhausted.

"Ina?"

I glanced up, hoping to see Haldrek, but instead there was a bluish glow over the whole cave. My father sat at my side, a somber expression on his face. He poked at a ghost replica of my campfire, though his was more robust.

"What... Am I dead?" I peeked at my arm, wondering if the damage had been worse than I thought.

He shook his head but said nothing. A sense of disappointment flooded me, and I failed at choking back a sob.

"I'm sorry. I'm... I'm... worthless. I tried everything, but I... I don't know what to do now. I've failed you; I've failed Ottkatla, I've failed Haldrek." Another sob made its way out.

He turned to me with an expression that was both kind and chastising. "You definitely came to blows with him. Verbally, that is. Not the best thing you could have done."

"Yeah, I know. What do I do now?" My chest burned again with frustration and anger. "How do I fix all this? The shrine? Haldrek? Am I supposed to fight someone? Get the armor? Throw myself off the ledge of the shrine in the name of Tenelth and hope that's a good enough offering?"

My father laughed. "Don't throw yourself off that ledge quite yet." His grin disappeared, but his expression stayed thoughtful. "No, just listen."

I groaned. "Listen? What does that even mean?"

"Exactly what I said. Listen." The edge of his mouth twisted back into a slight grin.

"I *have* been listening. I've listened to many people and voices. Some even that I shouldn't have."

"Like?" He cocked his head and held my gaze until I looked away in discomfort.

I shrugged. "I dunno. The voices in my head, mostly."

"The ones that sound like your mother?"

"Yes…"

"Those voices haunted me as well. To my dying day." He paused. "Don't listen to *those* voices."

I spun around to face him. "But you just told me to listen!"

"Yes. But you need to choose who you're going to listen to. And when you do, *listen*."

I huffed. "I thought you came here to help me."

"I came here to comfort you and keep you from giving up." He paused. "Hardbein's actions have greatly angered the other thegns—your *ahnfaders*. It wouldn't surprise me if he received visits from them. That said, I think he's too stubborn to be frightened off by spirits."

"Do they still hate me?" Hardbein may have pissed them off, but I had done little to gain their approval.

"They… when you gained the armor from Ottkatla, you took on the mantle of being thegn—regardless of who acknowledges it—and you still need to uphold the title you've accepted. If you just gave up, then you would risk their condemnation and Ottkatla's."

"I never wanted to give up, and I still don't. I'm just not sure how to go forward. With everything going the way it went here."

"You will. Just listen and you'll know what to do." He wrapped his arm around my shoulders and gave me a squeeze, kissing me on the side of my head. It felt like a cold, dry breeze against my head and shoulders. Despite feeling comforted, I shuddered. "I need to go now and tend to some things. But I'll be watching. And supporting you." His presence faded, and with it, the bluish tinge in the cave faded back to normal daylight colors.

The nearby howl of an ice drake made me perk up, pulling me out of my thoughts. It sounded… different. The sound wasn't angry anymore; it was more… in pain? Like it was hurting. My heart raced and my chest ached again, but not with anger this time. The shrill sound made my insides curl as I listened to it. I *knew* that sound—or at least the emotion that caused it. Was I hearing this because *I* was hurting? Or because something had changed?

The urge to figure out why the ice drakes were howling in pain grew, and I stood up as best I could. I needed to go to the shrine—broken or not—and do *something*. Kicking some snow that had blown into the cave over the fire, it doused quickly, and I glanced around for something to take that could help me. Unfortunately, the little that Haldrek and I had left Aldinnvollr with was in his sack and now with him.

Another ice drake howled, and I shook my head, leaving the cave. I needed to find out what was causing the ice drakes to howl with such pain, and how to fix it. I thought back to my dad's words. *Listen*. Maybe that's what I needed to do to figure everything out. Just listen.

My curiosity made me more careful as I headed up the path to the bridge, but still I slipped a few times. The cries of the ice drakes grew louder, but that fueled me further. I needed to know why the ice drakes were making this new sound. It still just sounded like shrill cries, but every so often, I thought I heard the world *help* in their howls.

I stopped to catch my breath at the top of the bridge. Some debris had settled nearby, and I squatted down to watch the ice drakes for a few minutes and listen. They wove back and forth, but there were a few moments when none of the ice drakes were near the edge of the bridge. After listening to them for a moment, I wondered if they were reacting to something from the avalanche, or the destruction of the shrine itself. I tried to think back to any lore from the games—and wished Mattie was here. She would know.

I pulled my pendant out from under my gambeson and chainmail and popped it open, and stared at the glassy interior, wondering how I could 'call' her using it. With no better ideas, I held it up to my mouth and said, "Mattie Gunvald."

Nothing.

I sighed and put it away. Even if I got a hold of her, what would I say? *'Hey, do you know any lore about the Shrine of Tenelth from the games? By the way, I had a massive fight with Haldrek, so we don't have his help anymore.'*

I put the pendant away and shook my head. This was something I had to figure out by myself. If I did... maybe, then I'd consider myself worthy of being thegn.

I stopped. The thought had never occurred to me before. *I* didn't consider myself worthy. I... what if that was what Haldrek had heard from the ice drakes? What if part of being worthy included *me* thinking I was worthy? I closed my eyes and listened to the howling in the air. I didn't expect to understand anything, but...

*Help Ottkatla heir.*

My eyes snapped open, and I watched them writhe around. I needed to help them. They hadn't popped up until after the avalanche had broken the shrine, so maybe that was how I could help them? I didn't know how to restore the shrine now, but... if I could make it to the base in one piece...

Just then I noticed that the edge of the bridge was empty. The ice drakes raged along the edges and back of the shrine area. If I could run off the bridge and hide somewhere while they weren't looking, I might sneak my way to the shrine and figure out how to fix it. If one of them saw me and chased me, though....

I imagined a blazing inferno coming out of my hand and felt it tingle. A smile crept to my mouth as I put my hand down and waited, watching them churn back to the edge of the bridge.

A few moments passed until there was a gap, and I bolted for a chunk of rock big enough to hide me. The shrieks intensified behind me, and I dove behind the rock, fluffy snow covering me. I spun onto my back and waited for an ice drake to pop out from behind and attack. I clutched at my injured arm as my nerves screamed in pain from my quick movements. My palm tingled with warmth as I stayed quiet, ready to cast a fireball. A few seconds passed and... nothing. The shrieking faded, and I crawled around the corner to see the ice drakes swarming around the shrine side of the bridge. I sighed in relief.

I took a moment to look around and noticed something strange about the rock I hid behind. The way the rock had broken, I knew I was looking at the interior, but it had plant-like roots and veins plastered across it. Most of the veins were dead and brown, but in a few areas, the veins were still greenish gray, standing out from the dark gray color of the stone. Out of curiosity, I touched one of the greenish-gray spots and one of the ice drakes shrieked with pain. Enough to make my chest freeze. The injury on my arm seared with pain. I gasped and recoiled. The spot faded into a brown color, and I shuddered. These veins proved a connection between the ice drakes and the shrine. Perhaps restoring the shrine meant healing whatever was inside these stones?

If so, the shrine base would have more answers. I turned around and searched for what could be the base of the shrine. Snow might still cover it, but given the size of the statue, I guessed the base would be sizable as well. I surveyed the far edge of the shrine area and saw a large squarish lump with pointy shards of rock jutting out from it. What caught my attention, however, was something completely different.

Stuck in the snow, a stiff corpse wearing Lansiranikän armor leaned against the squarish lump. After ensuring there weren't any ice drakes around, I hurried over to the frozen man and examined him for anything of importance or that could help me.

His head was cracked in on the side with dark blood matting his hair and discoloring his face, making his expression with eyes wide open even more unsettling. His spirit floated nearby, glaring at me. I avoided looking at the corpse's face, trying to remind myself that he was in fact dead, *and* that he would have been among those trying to kill me earlier, if he hadn't been here. His left hand lay on top of his chest, tight-fisted and frozen around something that he'd been holding at the time of his death.

I swallowed some bile and tried to ignore the fact that his ghost was staring at me as I tried to pull the item from his hand. Anger emanated from the spirit, but it stood still, as if unable to move.

"Not so tough now, huh?" I said, the sound of my voice calming me a little. "I wonder if you're the one who caused all this chaos?" As far as I had experienced, spirits couldn't hurt those still in the realm of the living, only when some kind of magic melded them with a body.

I peeled back the soldier's fingers and eased the piece of paper out of his hands, uncrumpling it. The note contained a variety of runes that made little sense to me. The only ones that looked familiar were the runes for what I thought was 'Svartån'. I cursed my foolishness once again, wishing Haldrek or Mattie were here to read this. But I'd have to deal with that later. After tucking the note into an opening in my leather glove, I shifted my attention to the shrine's base. As I dusted some snow off of the base, the ice drakes howled in pain once more and my arm burned as if my injury was being ripped apart. I pulled my arm back to my chest, revealing brown dots within the stone.

Once my arm stopped aching, I went to touch the shrine base again. In an instant, a shriek and stinging in my ear made me stumble back. I glanced up, catching sight of the dragon from yesterday circling around above me. The overwhelming sense of being caught where I wasn't supposed to be, flooded me.

*Foolish little one... why do you meddle here? Do not provoke me. You are not yet worthy of my shrine.*

"Rhaegos?" My chest tightened in fear. I thought I'd pissed her off before, but now...

A shrill scream rent the air, and I plugged my ears tight. Waves of pain washed over my body, and the urge to throw up made me gag. When the scream stopped, every nerve in my body burned. I saw Rhaegos fly around once more and then zoom off into the clouds.

Without another glance, I bolted for the bridge. Ice drakes or no ice drakes, I wouldn't stay where I wasn't welcome. Despite the pain Rhaegos had caused, this was only a warning. If I was still at the shrine when she returned... that would be more dangerous than anything Hardbein could throw at me.

# Chapter Fourteen

The next morning, I woke to the sound of footsteps crunching in the snow outside the cave. After fleeing the shrine, I'd returned to the cave with barely enough energy to stoke a campfire before passing out. But now, as soon as I realized where I was, I tried to sit, only to find my body stiff and almost frozen. My arm throbbed with pain, and the ashes of the campfire in front of me were dusted with snow.

"Ina!" Haldrek's voice made me look up. Behind him, Mattie and Meri entered the cave. My eyes widened, and I blinked a few times to make sure I wasn't just dreaming. But the cave seemed normal, and I was just as cold and achy as I had been when I fell asleep. No, this was real. I smiled as wide as I could, and the strange sound of both laughter and crying came out of my mouth at the same time.

Pulling myself up, I leaned on my left elbow and checked my pendant. I hadn't called them. Why were they here? And how did they get here so fast?

"We got to ride on a dragon, my thegn!" Meri knelt down next to me and began inspecting my injury. I winced as a sharp pain bolted up my arm.

Haldrek helped me sit up and pulled a bottle from his traveling bag, handing it to Meri. She pulled the broken chain mail and layers of cloth away before cleaning the skin beneath. Whatever was in the bottle soothed the pain in my arm.

Mattie looked up from the fire she'd rekindled and said, "Screams woke me up this morning. A dragon named Sivath landed near the camp and transformed into a human in plain sight of everyone." She laughed. "He walked up to me and said that Svangendom was safe for the moment, but you weren't, so one of the Hethurin and I needed to come with him to help you. Meri was the first to volunteer."

Meri beamed as she finished cleaning my arm. "I was the *only* one to volunteer. I always wanted to go on an adventure." She closed her eyes, and I felt my skin stretch and tingle where the wound had been. I pulled back, but she held my arm firm. "Just a moment. I'm healing your injury as quick as I can." As soon as she finished, she opened her eyes and smiled at me. "There you go."

I focused on the place where Hardbein's warrior had stabbed me, and even though my chain mail and clothing still showed damage and dried blood, the skin underneath was clean, as if there had been no injury at all.

Haldrek knelt down on the other side of me. "I'm sorry I left yesterday Ina. I... I shouldn't have."

I turned to Haldrek in surprise. "And I'm sorry for what I said. Everything. I told you to go away, but that was stupid. I should be... I'm sorry. I lost control of my temper."

"You were tired, hungry, and hurt. We both were. I would have been more surprised if you didn't lash out. But I still shouldn't have left. That was me failing to do what Rhaegos asked me to do. Which is why she was in a grouchy mood yesterday..." He shrugged.

"Don't forget, Sivath chewed you out a little when we arrived at your campsite this morning." Mattie said with a little laugh.

Haldrek sighed. "I deserved that too. I was still angry about our fight yesterday. But Sivath corrected me. As he often has."

We were quiet as I let the fire—and Haldrek's nearness—warm me up. I ached for him to be close and to return to the previous affection he'd shown. Even if just a kiss on the head. Instead, I focused on what we needed to do.

"My dad spoke to me. After you left." I focused on Haldrek. "Rhaegos was mad at me yesterday, too. I went to the shrine to figure out why the ice drakes were howling and found a couple of interesting things, but Rhaegos caught me and shrieked. That hurt."

Haldrek laughed softly. "So that's what I heard. I thought it sounded more like a warning. But I thought she was yelling at me."

"Yeah... I was being stupid. But I realized that the ice drakes connect with the shrine somehow. There was something inside of it that... when I touched it, the ice drakes reacted."

Meri bobbed her head up and down. "Local lore spoke about that when I got here. The shrine is a living thing, imbued with all the elements and dragon essence as well."

"That would make sense. The shrine's destruction was like a wound. So, restoring it..." A sudden bolt of energy surged within me, "Meri, do you think you could heal it using your healing magic?"

"Would be like healing an injury." Meri stared at my arm. "I could try. I just don't know if I have enough energy. Mending takes energy out of the healer."

Haldrek scrambled for something in his bag and handed Meri some bread he'd received in Aldinnvollr. I remembered eating some of it at Thoreg's tavern and knew that it had meat, cheese, and some kind of vegetable or herbs in it as well. "Have you eaten yet today?"

She shook her head and grabbed the bread, scarfing it down. Haldrek grabbed a few more of the palm sized loaves and handed them to Mattie and me before grabbing his own.

"All of us will need strength to help restore the shrine." He took a bite of his own bread and asked, "What else did you find interesting at the shrine yesterday?"

"A man in Lansiranikän armor next to the base. He was half buried in snow, head bashed in, so I assume the avalanche killed him, but he had a note in his hand. And his spirit was not happy that I was trying to remove it." I patted my right hand to figure out where the note had slipped to after I'd tucked it into my glove. Fishing it out, I handed it to Haldrek. "I think it says the name Svartån in it, but beyond that..."

"We need to teach you more of the runes." Haldrek grinned as he opened the note. After reading it for a few moments, his grin disappeared. "That *alvjävla*..." He turned to me. "This note is directions from Hardbein on how to cause chaos at the shrine among the Hethurin. He planned on one of his men cutting down some Hethurin and making it look like they had started the fight. Which would have brought the wrath of the shrine guards and the priests down upon them."

"But the avalanche..." Everything connected in my head. As horrible as the avalanche was, it may have prevented something much worse.

Haldrek grimaced. "Who or whatever started the avalanche kept that warrior from doing what Hardbein sent him to do."

I finished the bread that Haldrek had given me and looked around at the three of them. There was still a little voice in my head telling me I was a loser who had screwed up so many things, but now... I ignored it. I had a plan I was confident in, and I knew that Haldrek, Mattie, and Meri could help me.

Rising to my feet, I said, "We should start for the shrine if we're going to fix it today."

The four of us hiked back up the mountain to the bridge and the snow flooded cove where the ice drakes still howled. Even before I could see anything from the top of the bridge, the sound of roaring and screeching welcomed us. As did the spirits of the few dead people whose remains hadn't washed into the valley below, including the Lansiranikän soldier who continued to glare at me. I tried not to think about their half frozen, mangled bodies under the snow ahead of us.

These people had died because of the gesith's stubbornness and Hardbein's general assholery. But I wasn't about to let their deaths be for nothing.

Haldrek cocked his head as we stood there, listening to something. "That doesn't sound... the ice drakes here sound more in pain now than angry."

Mattie raised an eyebrow at him. "You know the difference?"

Haldrek pointed to the top of the mountain that towered above us and behind the shrine. "Andrattür is on the other side of these mountains. I've had to fight my fair share of angered ice drakes when defending my people. These cries are not vengeful like those."

"I thought you said they only attack people who are unworthy of... being somewhere?" I asked, trying not to think about what Rhaegos had said yesterday or what might happen if we failed at restoring the shrine.

"That's the lore. And that's what these drakes seemed to be screaming when the shrine was first destroyed. And it would explain their initial anger. But I don't know if it's always true. Sometimes they came down because someone did something that angered them. Sometimes not."

"Did they speak to you?" Mattie raised an eyebrow at Haldrek.

"Yes, but not like most dragons, though. When the ice drakes speak, it's more like a madman—incoherent." He paused, listening to the screeches above us. Then he turned to Mattie. "Do you understand these creatures?"

She furrowed her brow in concentration. "I understand certain words they're saying—*us, help, Rhaegos*- but not all of it. The intonation and rhythm are familiar, though. Why?"

"Nothing. Just more proof, I guess." He shook his head and readied his sword. "What's the plan, Ina?"

I grabbed the hilt of Mattie's sword, pulling it out of my scabbard. After leaving the cave, we had loosely figured out our respective parts. Haldrek, Mattie, and I would deal with any ice drakes while Meri made her way to the shrine and mended its wounds. Since Mattie preferred magic and had barely used her sword, she had given it to me, leaving both of her hands open to cast fireballs. "Yesterday I noticed that there's a short amount of time when there aren't any ice drakes near the bottom of the bridge. If we can run fast enough while they're away from the bridge—and not catch their attention—we can make it to the shrine. Then if any of them see us while Meri is mending the shrine, we fight them and keep her safe."

"Understood." Haldrek squatted, pulling his sword fully out. As we made our way down to the edge of the bridge, I watched the ice drakes and the skies, hoping Rhaegos wasn't watching.

After a moment, the opening appeared, and Haldrek began running. The rest of us did our best to keep up with him. Once we got to the base of the shrine, the four of us hid behind a sizable chunk of rock and waited. Just like yesterday, it was quiet where we were, but the ice drakes still howled by the bridge.

I stared at the shrine base and noted the Lansiranikän man in the corner of my eye. Memories from the last few days flooded my mind, and I shuddered. I had been too busy trying to figure out my next steps—what offering to give, how to restore the shrine, how to get my armor back—to actually *listen*, but now... in my mind, I could hear and feel the overwhelming fear and sorrow of those who had been here when the avalanche hit. The ghosts and the ice drakes. My heart ached for them, but at the same time, it lit within me a burning desire to take action, to help them, to fix this.

I took a deep breath, and promised them I'd do whatever I needed to do to help. As I focused on the shrine, I readied my lackluster steel sword in my right hand and primed a fireball in my exposed left hand. Ready to defend Meri in case they attacked. Haldrek and Mattie did the same.

"You ready?" I glanced over at Meri in her dark green cloak. She nodded and turned to the base, the ice spirits still oblivious to her presence. After wiping off some snow on the ledge, she placed her hands on the stone and closed her eyes. The ice drakes howled as we closed in behind her, our backs to hers, and watched for any attacks.

*Restore us. Restore us. Before we consume you.*

I scanned our surroundings for where the voices were coming from, taking my eyes off of the ice drakes.

"Did you two hear that?" I twisted to see if Haldrek or Mattie had any reaction. They stood defensively and stared up at the sky above.

A screech echoed through the sky as something zoomed headfirst toward Haldrek and me. I dodged it, falling into the snow on my left as one of the ice serpents brushed past me, leaving ice on my eyebrows.

"Ina!"

A boom vibrated in the air above me and I glimpsed a fireball just as it hit the creatures. Pain seared through my chest, and I gasped. More screeching and the ice drakes zoomed back toward the bridge. Though they still writhed around and kept their distance for the moment, I knew they'd keep coming.

"You think they are talking to us, or Meri?" Haldrek asked as he pulled me up from the snow and readied himself again.

I shook my head, trying to catch my breath. "I don't know."

Haldrek looked up again as another screech ripped through the air above us.

The three of us shouted the spell for a fireball, aiming at the creature. Three fireballs emerged, causing the creature to pull up from its nosedive.

I glanced down at Meri as I heard her gasp and then some rumbling. It surprised me to see snow being shaken off of the surrounding stones. The brown dots in the stone turned bright green, as if coming to life. Her eyes were still closed, and she seemed serene despite the chaos.

*Why hurt us, Ottkatla heir? Why?*

"I'm trying to repair the statue! The shrine!" I said, without thinking.

Haldrek sent another fireball up to dissuade the third ice drake from coming down and shouted something that sounded nothing like anything I had ever heard. Something guttural and foreign. My chest squeezed tight with anger as the ice drake spun around to face Haldrek. An indignation not my own.

"These are...? They're part of the shrine, aren't they?" I gasped. Then it made sense. The shrine connected to them through the green veiny things in the stones. They had been protecting the shrine and felt pain as it had been wounded. Their rage came from their pain. Attacking them would only make things worse.

A screech pulled me from my thoughts as an ice drake zoomed toward Meri from my left.

"Watch out!" I ran to shield her, only to watch the creature dive into the slowly growing pile of rocks. It immediately disappeared as Meri shuddered and gripped the base of the altar. A chill flooded through me as I realized that whatever she was doing to heal the altar was hurting her.

"It's working! Keep going!" Haldrek said from behind me.

*Don't destroy us. Leave us be! Lead us home!*

I turned back to him. "Don't attack them! Just defend us!" Then to Mattie. "Ward magic!"

As I knelt at Meri's side, I sheathed my sword. It, all of a sudden, felt ridiculous to be wielding one so close to the shrine.

"Be careful, Ina!"

"Just make sure they don't attack Meri or me!" I shouted back at Haldrek and Mattie.

*Don't destroy us. Don't destroy Rhaegos' altar!*

I knelt down beside her and watched the skies above us. One spirit began weaving back and forth as if being pulled between where the other ice drakes were and where Meri and I knelt. I blinked, and it dive bombed the altar, crashing into the pile of rocks that was reforming into a dragon with its wings unfurled. With surprise, I noticed whitish gray vines wrap themselves around the stones, binding and blending in with the stones. Meri wobbled and gasped as another guardian spirit hit the altar. Despite the cold air around us, there was sweat dripping down her face.

Meri wasn't just healing the shrine. She was pouring her own life magic into it. In an instant, I knew what would happen. This would kill her.

Without thinking, I placed my hands on top of Meri's. In an instant, energy drained out of me as I dug my nails into the stone to keep steady. For a moment, I wondered if it'd be enough. It had to be, right? If it wasn't...

As my head swam and I focused all my energy on keeping Meri safe and healing the shrine, something screeched and brushed my head, sending shards of icy pain down my neck and spine.

Then the shrine shook, and a burst of energy and snow threw Meri and me away from the stone base and into a snowbank. The impact made my head snap back, and I gasped as Meri's head hit the top of my chain mail and gambeson. My vision faded out as I heard something or someone in the distance:

*Thank you, Ottkatla heir.*

When I opened my eyes, I found myself in a pale white place, much like waking up in a snowstorm and much like the vision I'd seen of my father when he'd come to Rhaegos' shrine. I sat up and surveyed the area. I was no longer cold, aching, or anything. Movement caught my eye, and I turned to see a familiar sight—Rhaegos in human form.

She was imposing in an earthy brown and green dress and *tall*. Her white hair was braided down her back and trailed behind her, almost like a tail. I stiffened up, wondering if I'd failed her this time and she'd brought me here to punish. She stopped a few feet from me, and cocked her head to the side, as if considering me. Then she smiled.

"Welcome home, little one."

A strange feeling came over me, as if wrapping around me like a blanket and making my heart swell until I thought it would break open my chest. There wasn't any fear associated with the feeling, though. Instead, there was a hunger. I couldn't name the feeling, but it was some I'd been missing for a long time. Something I'd wanted so much, and now that hunger was being fed.

"Where... where am I?"

"You aren't dead, if you are worried about that. And you are safe. Both body and spirit."

Unable to say anything, I nodded. I wondered what had happened to the shrine after Meri and I had been blown back. I wondered if Meri was okay, and if Haldrek and Mattie were safe as well.

"Do you know who I am, little one?"

"Rhaegos." I said, my voice soft as her voice pulled me out of my thoughts. "You look like... like you did when my father came to the shrine."

She smiled. "A human's lifetime is but an infinitesimal moment for dragons. But yes, I'm Rhaegos. Thank you for restoring my shrine."

"It worked then? I was afraid..."

"It worked. Between you and that Hethurin girl, you healed my shrine. Even though you risked much for it."

"Meri needed help." I shook my head. "I couldn't just watch her... Is she still alive? Please tell me—"

Rhaegos put her hand up, and I shut my mouth.

"Meri, as you call her, is fine. Though you risked your life, between the two of you, you had enough energy to restore my shrine and keep yourselves alive." She pointed to my pendant, and I looked down to see it glowing. "That would have helped you as well, should you have needed it."

I nodded again, thinking about what I needed to do to move forward. "Now that we've restored your shrine, I... I'll bring an offering. As soon as I can."

Rhaegos shook her head. "You have already given me an offering. When you restored my shrine, you offered your life. To aid one of those who you would lead. I've seen your heart and accept your offering." She paused. "Yours is strong. Stronger than many I've seen or aided. I know there are many voices in your head that fight for your allegiance. Heed only those that come from your heart."

"How will I know? Which voices... come from my heart?"

She laughed. "Listen."

I groaned, remembering what my dad had said.

"In time, you will know which voices come from your heart. You will sense the wisdom in their words and know when to follow them." She took a few steps toward me, reaching her hand out toward mine. Gently, making sure not to scratch me with her pristine, pointed nails, she helped me up.

"I'm going to send you back to the realm of Lohikärra now. I can sense Haldrek's anxiety growing." She smiled, more serenely this time. "Soon I will bind with you. I have been in this body—both human and dragon—for far longer than I wished. And one day, you will need my strength with yours. But not now. You still have much to learn and grow, little one, and if we were to bind now, you could not stand it."

I bobbed my head up and down, my mind swimming. As she released my hand, a thought popped into my head. "Wait!"

She cocked her head once again. "Yes?"

"Hardbein. I'll have to face him once this is all over. But I saw one of his men by the shrine. Did he...?"

Rhaegos shook her head. "It was not Hardbein's warrior who defiled my shrine. Though Hardbein's plans would have angered me had they succeeded. No, it was another man—or rather one who serves him—who created the avalanche. One who has come for you already and will likely seek you out again." She stopped, as if considering whether to continue. After a moment, she did. "The creature that tried to kill you outside of Ottkatla's Barrow was the one who destroyed my shrine. But the one who he has pledged himself to is the one you should stand guard against."

"Seirye?" I frowned, wondering who else would have something out for me.

She shook her head and laughed for a moment before turning somber. "Seirye... he is strong and persistent. A creature to be reckoned with, but not of whom I speak."

"Then who?"

"A haldraga. One who speaks as though he is close with the dragons and yet has rejected his dragon kin for darker magic and power. You will learn soon enough." She stepped to the side, revealing something that she had hidden in the folds of her dress. Something that now glinted.

"I think you have earned this." She gestured to the sword at her side. "Seek it by my shrine and use it to defend the title, which is rightfully yours."

I stared at the sword standing at her side, almost as if something were holding it up. The blade glistened, and I could see the runes on the hilt. It was the same weapon that my dad had received and yet... It looked brand new.

After a moment, I took a deep breath, trying to think of anything else I could ask. I got the impression it'd be awhile before I spoke with her again. "Thank you. And... what about the Isillas? And the Blodnar?" I knew I'd have to deal with them soon and if advice from Rhaegos could help me...

She shrugged. "You will face them. And they will fail. As always has been. For as highly as Ryluth's descendants consider themselves, they are of little consequence to the dragons. As for the Blodnar? Your time to fight them will soon come. Until then, do not worry." After a moment, she took my hand again and squeezed it. "Now it's time for you to return to Lohikärra."

Before I could say anything else, the whiteness of the room enveloped me like a snowstorm and Rhaegos faded from view. A blast of light and heat like what had sent me to Lohikärra blinded me, and everything went cold again.

"Ina... Are you alright?" The panic in Haldrek's voice brought me back to consciousness.

I groaned loudly as I opened my eyes. At my feet, Mattie tended to Meri, a golden glow emanating from her hands. Haldrek pulled me into a sitting position. I was still too disoriented to sit by myself, so I leaned on him, watching as Meri became more alert. The explosion had tossed us farther back than I'd expected. I grimaced as I realized that the dead Lansiranikän soldier had also been tossed back by the explosion and was now lying face down in the snow.

"Is it done?" Meri focused on me and Haldrek, and then on the statue as Mattie sat her up and let the golden glow wash over her. "By the dragons, it worked!" She scrambled up and then stumbled. Mattie steadied her as Haldrek pulled me up, letting me lean on him as my balance came back.

Meri turned to me and bowed deeply, reminding me again of her siblings Llamryl and Thandes. "My thegn. I thank you. I... I thought I could do it without harm to myself, but without your help, I think I would have died."

I smiled. Relief flooded through my body. "More than happy to help. What exactly did you do? To heal the shrine?"

"I used my healing powers to restore the statue. Just like your injury earlier." She laughed. "Mending and tending."

I laughed as well and caught a glance of something glimmering in front of the statue. Rhaegos's sword. As I walked past Meri and to the front of the shrine, I saw the shiny metal hilt of a sword and its scabbard embedded in the snow. And just as Rhaegos had said, *my* thegn armor sat next to it, unblemished. A weight lifted off my chest, and I beamed at the sight.

"The sword." I pulled the scabbard out of the snow and exposed the blade as Haldrek hurried over. He grinned as he glanced at my armor.

The crest of Svartån was engraved, where the hilt met the blade. Along the horizontal part of the hilt, there were runic letters.

"Haldrek, what does this say?"

He walked over and squinted at the sword. "Freya's Menace is on the left side. And Destroyer of Illusions on the right." He turned to me. "This was your father's sword. And his father's before him, I guess. The thegn blade. If this is here, then... Rhaegos accepted you."

My grin widened as he spoke the name. That weapon, I knew. It was one of my favorite weapons from the Lohikärra games. "Freya's Menace was a weapon used by Bjornulf's wife," I said. In the game lore, Freya had used this sword to fight off Ryluth.

"And she gave it to her daughter Ottkatla when she became a haldraga," Mattie said.

Neither the armor nor the weapon had been anywhere in sight when the altar was shattered, but now both gleamed in the winter sunlight, just as Rhaegos had said. I pulled the sword out to its full length. Much to my surprise, the handle fit my grip. The sword itself was longer than either of my previous swords, but about the same width. The blade narrowed to a point, and its edges were thinner than any of the others I had seen.

"It's a beautiful blade." Haldrek said, almost in reverence. He pulled his sword from his belt and compared it to mine. They seemed similar enough to me, but Haldrek pointed to the tips. Mine was sharper and narrower.

"I'm guessing your blade is more for piercing than slashing. Not that you couldn't do both well with it. How does it feel?"

"Good. Natural. It... it feels like it was made for me. Even though... I wonder if it's like the armor?"

"Reformed to fit each new thegn?" Haldrek shrugged. "It wouldn't surprise me."

With the ice drakes gone, the air was clear and silent up here at the shrine. Quiet enough to hear faint voices coming from beyond the bridge.

I frowned and tilted my head toward the sound, listening. Making sure I wasn't just hearing random noises from nature.

Haldrek put his hand on my shoulder. "I hear them too. Let's get your armor and sword on. Aldinnvollr needs to know who the true thegn is once and for all."

* * *

It wasn't too long before we saw a crowd approaching the bridge. Haldrek, Mattie, and Meri helped me get my armor on, so by the time the crowd arrived, I wore the thegn armor with Freya's Menace at my side.

Hardbein led the crowd. "The ice drakes are no more. They vanished as soon as I cut down the false thegn." His voice grated on my nerves as he walked toward us, oblivious to our presence. His head and attention were turned away from us, but a few of the people who followed him, including the gesith, stopped as soon as they noticed us.

It wasn't until Hardbein noticed people staring at something other than him that he turned around. He wore a large bandage over where I'd hit him with my shield, and his good eye widened as he saw us, his voice finally silent.

"What are you—" He paused for a second, "four doing here?"

I stiffened up, pushing my shoulders back. "I came to restore Rhaegos's shrine and receive her blessing. What are you doing here?"

Hardbein laughed and regarded the crowd behind him. When no one else laughed, he turned back to me, his expression darkening. "I highly doubt it was you who restored the shrine. Ottkatla *and* Rhaegos came to me in a dream—"

"I'm pretty sure they didn't." I snapped, interrupting him. "And it wasn't just me who restored the shrine. It was all of us." I gestured to Haldrek, Mattie, and Meri. "Especially Meri here. She used her Hethurin gifts to help restore the shrine."

Hardbein scowled. "So that's how *my* armor ended up here. You had one of your Hethurin thieves steal it for you." He gestured to one of the warriors by his side. "Kill the half-breed."

Meri stepped back as Haldrek and I unsheathed our swords. I took a step in front of Meri as the crowd gasped.

"Wait!" The gesith stepped forward as Hardbein's warrior ignored him.

Before I could think, I blocked his blade with my shield and raised my sword, slamming the edge into his helmet. He stumbled into the snow and dropped his sword as I pointed mine at him. I stayed still, ready to defend myself and Meri if needed.

"That's Ottkatla's blade!" The gesith gaped as he stepped in front Hardbein, eyes wide. "Where did you get that?"

"Here. Rhaegos gave it to me after I restored her shrine."

The gesith stared at the sword, focusing on the hilt, and then turned his attention to me. "Forgive me for my actions over the past few days. As the rightful thegn, you are welcome in Aldinnvollr at your leisure. If you would allow it, I will take my leave and return to Aldinnvollr." After a moment, he bowed and turned around to the crowd, gesturing for them to leave.

Hardbein spun on him. "What are you doing? Are you so easily deceived? She stole the thegn armor from Ottkatla's Barrow. How do you not know that she also stole Ottkatla's blade?"

The gesith turned to him. "The only people who may wield that weapon are true thegns of Svartån. When it is not in a thegn's possession, Rhaegos herself keeps the blade. If she," the gesith gestured to me, "is able to steal that weapon from a dragon as powerful as Rhaegos, I do not wish to be her enemy." The gesith then turned to face me. "That said, I don't believe you stole *your* weapon from Rhaegos. If you have it, then it was given to you."

I smiled and watched as he walked away, and Hardbein seethed with anger. "If you think…"

"Hardbein. Care to explain something?" Haldrek gestured to the frozen, mangled corpse behind us. I turned to the body as well, curious what the spirit's reaction would be to Hardbein's response.

"A warrior killed by the avalanche. What of it?" Hardbein tilted his head to look at the corpse with his good eye. "Ah, I know the man. One of the more reckless warriors. I don't know what he was doing up here, no doubt something stupid, but it wasn't on my account."

The spirit's eyes widened as he moved across the snow toward Hardbein. I watched as he raged in the gesith's face, swinging his arms around and gesturing in anger. Yet Hardbein was oblivious to it all.

"So, you admit he was one of yours?" I focused on Hardbein. "And do you not feel his presence?"

"The spirit of the man? Of course, I do. He… he stands by the shrine, ready to defend it from you." Hardbein turned back to Haldrek. "Yes, a few of my men wished to come up here to give offerings. I saw no harm in it. You should know well that Svartån isn't the only part of Lohikärra that worships Rhaegos."

"Then why did he have a note on him with orders to cut down the Hethurin as they gave offerings themselves?"

Hardbein's face paled for a second, then he scowled. "Perhaps… the note was forged. If so, then this man got his reward."

I watched as the spirit stepped back and tried to strike Hardbein. When his hand went right through him without a reaction, he stared for a moment and then shook his head before returning to the shrine.

Haldrek pulled the note from his glove. "Are you saying that one of your men forged your name? Either they are not warriors to be trusted. Or you're a weak gesith."

"I… I… my name is *not* on that note." Hardbein's face reddened as his lips pinched tight.

Haldrek looked back at the note. "I see your scrawled runes here at the bottom."

"Then I will deal with my warriors. I am *not* a weak gesith. Do you truly think—"

"Rhaegos told me your plan, Hardbein." I snapped, interrupting him once again. "She also told me that it would have greatly angered her if you'd been able to go through with it."

His eyes widened before he huffed at me. "You don't belong here, and you never will. Ottkatla and Rhaegos may have accepted you, but Svartån needs a *strong* thegn. Mark my words. When the Isillas attack with their full forces, you won't be able to do a damn thing."

Without another word, he marched off toward the bridge, leaving just the four of us at the shrine once again.

# Chapter Fifteen

As soon as we were alone again, I exhaled. Putting my new sword away, I viewed the shrine and the surrounding area. The spirits here began to hover, not around me, but the shrine. Even I sensed a pull toward it. I turned around and took a step toward the shrine. As I placed my hand on the base, I smiled.

"What do you want to do now?" Haldrek walked up to the shrine next to me.

"We need to go back to Aldinnvollr at some point. I feel like our business there isn't finished yet. Even with the gesith acknowledging me as the thegn here. But..." I watched the spirits standing at the shrine. "I wouldn't be a good thegn if I didn't help the people who died here pass on to Mirroth or elsewhere." I thought of the Lansiranikän soldier. He had been livid with Hardbein, and while I sensed a feeling of betrayal, I also sensed bitterness toward me from his spirit.

"How many spirits do you see?"

I tried to count them, but I didn't know if there were others who I hadn't seen. "A dozen or so. Does it matter if their body is nearby? Or buried?"

Haldrek shook his head. "It's better if the body is in view, but... not needed. Are you well enough to do twelve rites? That'd be a lot for even a well-trained priest of Tenelth."

"I feel better. And I have a weird sense of connection to the shrine now." I cocked my head, wondering if that was normal or something I should worry about.

"It's probably because you helped restore the shrine. You and Meri both gave a part of yourself to heal it."

I nodded. After a moment, I turned back to Haldrek and Mattie. "Would you two be willing to help me do the rites for these people? I might not be able to do twelve by myself, but with both of you help..."

"There is no need, little one."

All four of us spun around to see a woman in similar clothing to what the Priests of Tenelth wore walking toward us from the bridge. Haldrek dropped to his knees in reverence, and I bowed as well.

Looking back up at her, I asked, "What about the spirits here? Don't they need to have their rites done?"

Rhaegos smiled. "They do. And they will have their rites done. I am more than capable of sending these people to the afterlife where they will be most at peace. You, however, have other tasks set before you. You need to go back to Aldinnvollr to prepare, and then on to Katla. Your actions there will determine much of Svartån's near future."

I hesitated, trying to take the new information in, before nodding my head. "As you wish, Rhaegos."

She then turned to Haldrek with a small, entertained smile. "You can stand up, you know?"

He stumbled to his feet. "Mighty Rhaegos. I hope..."

She held her hand up. "You have done well, little one. Despite your own fears and sorrows."

"Have I succeeded?" Haldrek sounded breathless, even terrified, and I turned to him in surprise.

"You have. At least with the first vision the Vollr gave you. And chances of the second vision happening will grow dim—so long as you continue your course. Help Ina prepare, and both Svartån and Andrattür will benefit from your actions."

Haldrek nodded, but remained silent.

Rhaegos then turned to Meri and bowed herself, making Meri gasp. When she stood up, she said, "Honor to you, little one. You have given me an offering few of this realm are able to. For when my shrine was broken, it wounded me as much as fresh battle scars. But you were willing to give all of yourself to heal me. We dragons do not forget such things."

Meri's eyes began tearing up as she sank to her knees without a word.

Rhaegos turned her attention finally to Mattie, whose eyes were wide with surprise. "And you, little one, Sivath would have words with me if I didn't thank you." She laughed softly again. "You will bring much to the future of Lohikärra as well. Even if people are not aware of that and view you as only an outsider, your fate is just as much tied to Lohikärra as your friends' fates are."

Mattie gaped. "Thank you. That... that means a lot."

Rhaegos focused on the four of us as a group and then smiled again. "Go on. You all are needed at Aldinnvollr and Svangendom now. The Isillas have not yet advanced upon the ocean, but they will soon enough and the four of you need to be prepared." Without another word, she gestured toward the bridge, and we didn't question it.

As we crossed the bridge, I turned back to see snow swirling in the air like a silent tornado. Despite everything, there was a certain level of serenity to it. The shrine itself was restored and now Rhaegos was bringing everything back to normal.

"The dragons are certainly strange and magnificent creatures." Mattie murmured next to me.

I nodded. "They certainly are. More so than even I ever expected."

By the time we finally made our way back to Aldinnvollr, exhaustion began to creep into my bones, and I was glad that we were welcome again in the town, even if it was only to get a hot meal and a somewhat soft bed. Yet as we reached the gates, I noticed that Meri had lagged behind us and seemed hesitant to enter the town. Not that I blamed her.

I nudged Haldrek and then turned around, trotting back to where Meri had stopped.

As soon as I reached her, she said, "I'm sorry, my thegn. I... I know the gesith said you were welcome back in Aldinnvollr, but I doubt that was an invitation for *all* of us."

I grimaced, feeling anger for how Meri and the others had been treated. "You don't have to stay in Aldinnvollr if you don't want to. But if you're wanting to get a hot meal, I'll make sure no one will bother you."

She shook her head. "Thank you, my thegn. But that isn't it. If I return to Aldinnvollr... I know Thoreg won't want me to leave. I hated working at his tavern. I... I would prefer to go elsewhere. Even return to Svangendom."

"Then don't go back to Aldinnvollr. You can head back to Svangendom if you wish. You've helped me greatly here and I would appreciate your help in repairing the damage there. But it's your choice."

"Thank you. I can help repair it. Mend and tend. And I'm sure... whoever is left in my family will need my help—even if they still aren't happy with me."

"I think they'll be glad to see you. Llamryl seemed anxious about you being safe. As did Thandes."

Meri laughed softly. "Those two were the ones most ardently against me leaving."

There was a sudden desire to comfort her, and I gave her a quick hug. "Well, if they give you a hard time, tell them what you did at the shrine—and that I'm grateful for your help. I wouldn't have been able to restore the shrine by myself and that in turn helped to rebuff Hardbein. Hopefully, for the last time."

Meri nodded.

Someone touched my elbow, and I turned to see Mattie standing right behind me.

She turned to Meri. "Are you headed back to Svangendom?"

Meri smiled sadly. "I am. It's going to be a long time before any of the Hethurin feel welcome in Aldinnvollr, especially me. And with the village needing to be repaired and Svangendom having a new thegn," She glanced at me with a small grin. "There will be plenty that needs to be done there."

"Then if you'd like, I'll head down the mountain with you." Mattie turned her attention to me. "If you're okay with that, oh thegn of Svartån?" She grinned widely, reminding me of her excitement over the game back in Fargo. For a moment, it was like we *were* in the game, and we'd just finished a major quest. And a part of me wondered what exactly Lohikärra had in store for each of us.

"I'm fine with that. Svangendom needs help to be rebuilt and," I fiddled with my pendant, "I'll need someone to keep me up to date with what's going on while I'm in Katla."

Mattie nodded and turned back to Meri. "You ready? I think if we head out now, we can make it to Osvif's Refuge before nightfall. I remember someone mentioning there was a shorter path around Aldinnvollr that would help us save time."

Meri smiled, and they began walking down the hill. I waited until they were out of eyesight before making my way back to Haldrek.

"I guess it's just the two of us then? Unless you have business in Andrattür?"

Haldrek shook his head. "I left Mirratoft—and Andrattür—in solid, trustworthy hands. Plus, Rhaegos told me to help you prepare for Seirye's arrival. And she mentioned you needing to go to Katla?"

"That's what it sounds like."

He groaned, and I raised my eyebrows in surprise.

"What?"

"You'll see. The stubbornness of Gesith Aldinnvollr is nothing compared to Gesith Katla." He put his hand on my back as we started walking down the hill toward the town gates.

"Should I worry?" I was worn out from everything that had happened over the past few days, and part of me wanted a respite from that stress. At least for a few days.

He shook his head. "You'll do fine in Katla. You're already showing good leadership skills—with standing up to Hardbein and helping Meri—and those skills will come in handy when we get to Katla."

I smiled quickly, before my anxiety could hit again. "What about the gesith here? I know he acknowledged me as thegn at the shrine and there were a few people from Aldinnvollr there, but still..."

"If he wishes to stay in your good graces and keep his position as gesith, he needs to acknowledge you in front of all the people of Aldinnvollr. He knows this and you should expect him to do so." Haldrek pushed one of the city gates open slightly, letting us through.

"And if he doesn't?"

Haldrek's voice was firm and somber. "You would be within your rights to strip him of his title of gesith and even execute him. But I doubt that will happen. He seemed penitent enough at the shrine."

I hoped Haldrek was right. Ahead of us, I saw a crowd had gathered in the center of town. A few people walked toward it with us, watching us, but averting their eyes when I glanced at them. I hoped that the crowd was there because the gesith was going to announce that I was to be accepted as the new thegn.

"Looks like something's happening." Haldrek's voice jarred me out of my thoughts. "Let's go see if it's what I hope it is—the gesith announcing you as thegn and recanting what he did and said earlier."

As we stepped up to the crowd, I could see the gesith standing on something, making him head and shoulders above the crowd. A few of the people in the crowd stared at Haldrek and I in surprise when we stopped and stood there.

"My fellow townsfolk, I've asked you all here in order to let you all know what happened at the shrine today." He glanced up at me and Haldrek as I tried to keep my expression neutral. "And to correct an error I made. You all heard the thunderous noise come from the mountain this morning. That was the shrine being restored—"

The crowd began to murmur as the gesith held his hands up to quiet them.

"The shrine was restored when I arrived up there with... the Lansiranikän gesith—Hardbein. It seems... that the woman who arrived with Thegn Andrattür was truthful when she claimed the title of Thegn of Svartån."

He stopped, and the crowd parted to look at me. Anxiety made my nerves tingle with pain. I never liked people focusing on me, but I also knew that this needed to happen. That the people of Aldinnvollr needed to know that I was their thegn.

"Do you accept me as thegn then, gesith Aldinnvollr?" The words rolled out of my mouth as if someone else spoke them.

The gesith stiffened up in embarrassment, and after a moment, bowed his head. "I accept you as thegn-heir. And once your ceremony happens, I will accept you as thegn. I'm nothing if not loyal to Svartån."

"And?" Haldrek growled gently next to me.

The gesith sighed and bowed respectfully to me. "I am sorry for questioning you, my thegn and I ask your forgiveness."

I nodded, grateful that he didn't try to be more stubborn. "You are forgiven. However..."

He looked up in surprise.

"There is the matter of the Hethurin. Your cruelty toward them—casting them out because of who one of their parents or grandparents might be—concerns me. Should any of them desire to come back to Aldinnvollr, I expect you will treat them as equals to their non-Hethurin neighbors."

The crowd began to murmur, and I did my best to keep my nerve, focusing on the gesith. "*And* if you show any sign of wavering loyalty, if *anyone* questions me, or my right as thegn, here in Aldinnvollr, I have no problem stripping you of your title and casting you from Svartån. Understand?"

He stood back up. "I understand." Turning to the crowd, he said, "As we remember the late Thegn of Svartån and honor his might as a warrior and leader... let us now welcome and give honor to his daughter, the true thegn-heir of Svartån."

With that, the crowd gave a weak cheer. The mood of the crowd was still heavy as they dispersed, but there wasn't much more I could do. While I wished for a better situation—one where the Hethurin were here as well—I smiled and took this as a win.

# Chapter Sixteen

It was *much* later that night when Haldrek and I returned to the room we had had before in Thoreg's tavern. Aldinnvollr had taken the restoration of the shrine, at the very least, as a reason to celebrate. Many tankards, flagons and ale horns had been lifted to today's good news and downstairs I could still hear people singing along with the town skalds. I'd stayed away from the mead offered, but I was now drunk on exhaustion and when I had enough socializing, I bid the people we'd been talking to farewell and slipped away from the crowd. Haldrek followed me, his presence a comfort more than anything else.

I sat down on my bed and leaned against the wall, closing my eyes. "So how much time do you think I'll have before the next quest starts?"

Haldrek's silence made me open my eyes, and I saw that his head was cocked, brows knit in confusion.

I laughed. "I'm wondering how much time until our next adventure. Sorry."

He shook his head and sat down next to me, exuding a certain physical warmth that made me smile. "I suppose we could spend a few days here in Aldinnvollr. Resting. Training. With Hardbein's threat out of the way, we need to focus on your fighting skills. Wearing the thegn armor and wielding Freya's Menace may have been enough to stop Hardbein, but Seirye has never given heed to our tokens of authority."

"I figured as much." As I sat up, I turned to him. "Do you think I'll have enough time to train and practice before Seirye returns?"

Haldrek shrugged. "You'll have enough time to learn how to defend yourself. Just remember, you're going to be training until the day the Isillas arrive, and then every day afterwards. You will always be training and learning and becoming a better fighter. I was six, almost seven, when I wielded my first blade. And I remember playing around with other weapons when I was younger than that." He grinned. "Staves and the like. And even now I'm still learning. Such is life here. There will always be people trying to fight you. So, you'll never stop learning or practicing."

I grimaced, my head swimming. I had defeated Hardbein and restored the shrine, but now I had to face Seirye and...

"Rhaegos told me something interesting about the avalanche that destroyed the shrine." I whispered, "She said a person caused it. The man or creature that attacked me outside of Ottkatla's Barrow. She also said it was someone who serves a haldraga."

Haldrek frowned and shook his head. "It might've still been Hardbein. Many, if not all, gesiths are haldragas too, remember?"

"I don't think so. She said that whoever attacked me would likely come for me again. If he worked for Hardbein and I just squashed any chances of him becoming thegn... She also said something about the haldraga speaking as though he was close to the dragons, but who had forsaken them for darker things. Hardbein is an awful person, but I never got the vibe that he... he never seemed ominous, just bullying." I groaned. "I don't know if I'm making any sense, but my heart tells me that the assassin isn't tied to Hardbein."

"No, I understand. And knowing Rhaegos, she would have told you if the two were connected." Haldrek squeezed me tighter, and I took comfort in his closeness. After everything, I felt safe when he was nearby.

Our conversation lulled, and the realization hit me of how grateful I was for Haldrek's friendship—and companionship—ever since I'd arrived in Lohikärra. Despite everything, and even though he could have easily ditched me at any point claiming a need to go back to Andrattür, he was still here. My thoughts flashed back to the evening in Eldingheimr and how enjoyable it had been. That had been the last time I'd been relaxed. Though, how much of that and the enjoyment I had that night was because of the mead I'd never know.

I'd probably also never know if Haldrek and I would have kissed that night if we hadn't been interrupted. As much as I enjoyed being around him and *wanted* to kiss him, I guessed that he didn't feel the same, and his flirting that night had just been from the mead. With that thought in mind, I leaned my head on his shoulder and sighed.

He squeezed me tight again in a comforting side hug. Before I could react, his lips pressed down against my hair and the top of my head. I froze, and nerves all over my body started tingling. I shuddered without thinking.

"Sorry, I didn't mean—"

"No, I..." I sat up, nervous energy waking me up. A thought—desire—popped into my head, and I wanted to gauge his reaction. "I... liked it. You can kiss me other places too. Not just my head." As soon as the words left my mouth, I froze again, realizing what those words actually sounded like. Heat rushed up my neck and into my face. Haldrek stared at me with raised eyebrows before turning his head and coughing a few times.

He turned back to me with a surprised grin. "What? I... You..."

My chest tightened, and I felt like I was in an awkward dream. I started backpedaling as fast as possible. "I mean... I... That sounded different in my head. I mean... I like kisses, but I'm..." I slapped my hands in front of my mouth and groaned as Haldrek started to laugh. The serious mood from our previous conversation was now gone.

After a moment, he stopped, and I looked up. He was still grinning. "Would you mind if I kissed you?"

The words popped out faster than I could think. "Yes. No. I mean... yes, I want you to kiss me. No, I wouldn't mind."

His smile widened as he pulled me close until our chests touched. I wrapped my arms around his neck and stared into his eyes. They were intensely blue. Deep and piercing. I had felt vulnerable the last time I focused on them. Back at Osvif's Refuge. That sensation rose up again, but this time I wasn't so uncomfortable with it. I lowered my gaze to his lips. They were moist and soft. His hands moved up to my shoulder blades as he gently pulled me forward until our lips touched. The warmth from his body wrapped itself around me. He smelled of wood smoke and honey, residue from the festivities downstairs, scents that relaxed me even more. His lips *were* soft, gentle even, as they moved across and around mine, his beard and mustache softer than I expected. His tongue brushed against my lips, sending a thrill down my spine. I wanted more. I wanted to stay like this, his lips on mine, for as long as possible.

After a moment, he pulled back and grinned. "I guess we're more than just friends now?"

I laughed. "I guess." A part of me didn't care what we were at this point, just whether we were going to kiss again.

"Here's to more adventures together. As more than just friends." He leaned in once more and I let myself relish the kiss, enjoying the present and leaving the adventures to the future.

That night, I dreamt I was back in Fargo. Back in the basement and back in a world that I had wanted to escape for so long. I knew it was a dream, but still... a sense of dread I couldn't escape overwhelmed me.

"So, you were able to defeat that pathetic oaf?" Seirye's voice made me jump, and I spun around to see him staring at me from the bottom of the stairs. "Not hard. Harpy or Harby or whatever his name was... he would have been a weak thegn. Focused more on the crude, brute violence that Lohikärrans seem to love so much."

He surveyed the basement as if searching for something. After a moment, he focused back on me. "So, this is your homeland? Very bleak and dreary. Even without my magic." He waved his hand, and the room lightened up a smidge, but the heavy weight of being trapped remained. "Hmm, I can see why a place like Lohikärra would appeal to one such as yourself. Why you'd be desperate to claim rulership over a small portion of it." His mouth flicked upwards. "Or all of it. If you and that annoying dragon-speaking whelp stay together."

I frowned. "What are you talking about?"

"You'll find out. Eventually. If I don't kill you first." He took a step toward me, and I backed up. "You won't be as easy to defeat as your cousin, but I doubt you'll be a challenge. You've got creatures haunting you still. They make you weak. No matter how much you practice. No matter how much you train. I've spent millennia figuring out your and your ancestors' weaknesses. You haven't got a chance against me."

He jumped, and I dodged as I saw a blade emerge from his hand. Still, a burning, searing pain pulled through my chest, and I glanced down to see dark blood covering my chest.

"Good night, *little one*."

A sharp pain exploded through my neck, and everything went dark.

And then I opened my eyes. The room was dim except for the moonlight streaming in from the window above my head. I could hear Haldrek's soft snores from the other bed. Though they did little to calm my racing heart. My chest still burned, but it wasn't from a knife wound. Instead, the pain faded away as I relaxed my hand. As did the sharp pain as I removed a piece of straw that poked into my neck from the mattress.

I was still in Lohikärra. I was still in Svartån and Haldrek was by my side. Slowly, I relaxed, knowing that at least for tonight, I was safe.

Seirye was out there. Planning. Plotting. Scheming to take Svartån back. But... there was little I could do about that tonight.

Instead, I would rest. And tomorrow I would start preparing for Seirye. And whatever else he had up his sleeve.

# About the Author

L. L. Nelson is a full-time librarian, part-time genealogist, history buff, and contributor to the first two volumes of the Organic Ink poetry anthology. In short, she is a word nerd with a passion for poetry, fantasy, historical fiction, and just a little bit of romance. She's been creating worlds and figuring out the 'what ifs' in her stories since she was old enough to read the words 'Egg Roll King' on a local Chinese restaurant sign in 1992.

In college, she took all the creative writing classes she could to feed her need to write. This gave her enough credits to graduate with a minor in English and the ability to second guess her work like a true writer. It also introduced her to a variety of genres and their tropes that she now uses in her stories and poetry.

As a librarian, L. L. Nelson has honed her research skills to a science. (A library science.) This has given her mad talent when it comes to finding obscure facts to use in her stories and poetry. (Like the fact that the Vikings used rap battles as a form of combat.)

When not dealing with her scripturient nature, L. L. Nelson is a mom, inventive cook, wannabe linguist, and dreams of being not only a 'word traveler' but a world traveler. Fortunately, she lives in Southern California with her husband and kids, so she can go to Disneyland once a year and pretend that she's actually traveling around the world, even when she isn't.

**Love it?**

*Leave a Review!*

Did you enjoy *Heir of Svartån*? If so, I would be delighted if you left a review. (If you already have, thank you so much!) As a new author, book reviews are golden. You can leave reviews on sites such as Goodreads as well as other places. Book recommendations on social media (Youtube, Instagram, Twitter, TikTok, etc) is also awesome.

**Want to Connect Online?**

**Website:**

https://www.llnelsonauthor.com/

**Newsletter:** https://www.llnelsonauthor.com/newsletter/

**Facebook:** https://www.facebook.com/llnelsonauthor

**Instagram:** https://www.instagram.com/llnelsonauthor

**TikTok:**

https://www.tiktok.com/@llnelsonauthor

# The Lohikärran Chronicles


### <u>Visions of Lohikärra (Prequel)</u>
*A mysterious young woman, an elven invasion, and the tokens of the High King*

Haldrek Rodreksson has known his entire life where his future lies and what is expected of him. But on the eve of battle, soothsayers show him three visions of a different future: a mysterious young woman, a new invasion, and theft of the High King's tokens. Visions which make him question his future and that of his homeland, Lohikärra.

When the capital of Lohikärra falls, Haldrek's world is thrown into disarray and he must scramble to keep the young woman from his visions safe.

Injured, weaponless, and with little support, will Haldrek be able to save the woman and change the visions he was given? Or will he, his homeland, and his loved ones fall to their enemies?

### <u>Heir of Svartån</u>
*Lohikärra was just a game. Until it wasn't.*

Ina Svanunge lives in North Dakota, avoiding attention and counting the days until she's free of her abusive mother. But when she and best friend, Mattie, sit down to play the newest release from their favorite video game series, they find themselves in the game's world, Lohikärra. Only it's not the game - Lohikärra is real.

Once there, Ina finds out her long-absent father was a powerful thegn - and she's his rightful heir. Unfortunately, she isn't the only one claiming his title, and the others are more than willing to kill her for it. On a journey across Svartån, Ina must fight for her birthright or risk rejection from the world she has long wished to be part of.

Will Ina be able to claim her rightful title with help from Mattie and their handsome new friend, Haldrek? Or will she end up dying in a foreign, unforgiving land?

### <u>Thegn of Svartån</u>
***She will be Thegn of Svartån. If Svartån still exists.***

Ina Svanunge is the rightful thegn-heir of Svartån, but she must fight to lead and protect her new homeland's people, even as she's still learning how to do both. Can she learn to lead and bring her people together before they are brutally conquered?

An invasion from the Isillas elves - Svartån's most ancient enemy - looms imminent and Ina's first priority is to prepare her new homeland's defenses. Which would be easier if not for the deep hatred held by many of her subjects against their half-elven neighbors. With the Isillas at their doorstep, Svartån is fractured and in need of a leader to unite it once and for all. Racing to improve not only her fighting and leadership skills, she finds herself out of time when the Isillas attack and endanger not only Svartån, but those closest to her.

Weakened and alone, will Ina be able to protect Svartån from the Isillas? Or will she both lose her hard fought title and risk the destruction of Svartån?

## Queen of Drattüjert
### *Old enemies. New challenges. Ina is thegn, but can she be queen?*

It's been almost two months since Ina Svanunge officially became the Thegn of Svartån. With the Isillas conflict behind her, she must now aid her fellow thegns against an even bigger threat: the Blodnar Empire from the south.

Lohikärra will never be whole without its heart: the capital city of Drattüjert still under Bloodnar control.  Ina and her fellow thegns have a plan to take it back, but there are traitors amongst their ranks bent on obtaining their own power and glory.  The last thing Ina's beloved country needs is the emergence of a necromancer bent on destroying both Lohikärra and its dragons entirely.

When traitorous calamity strikes, Ina and Haldrek are forced into a race against time to save their loved ones, Lohikarra, and even Ina's hometown Fargo. But the cost could be Ina's life.

## Lady of Lohikärra
### *With great power comes great responsibility. And greater enemies.*

Fully embracing Lohikärra as her new home, Ina has taken her place alongside Haldrek as High King and Queen. But Lohikärra is a broken country on the verge of civil war. Respected by some, despised by others, Ina must rebuild the capital city of Drattüjert while Haldrek rebuilds Lohikärra.

When Henry, an old friend from Fargo, arrives in Drattüjert offering a solution to all her problems, it'll either be her saving grace or too good to be true.

Will Ina figure out which before it's too late? Or will fractured loyalties cause her to lose everything she holds dear?
*Coming December 2022!*

## **<u>Heart of Lohikärra</u>**
Coming Soon!